To The Lover,

January, 2021,

James A. Misino

The World Beyond Us

by James A. Misino

D1616894

This book is dedicated to the Reverend Sun Myung Moon whose spiritual teachings inspired much of this book.

Acknowledgements:

I gratefully thank Dr. Michael Hentrich, who helped make this book possible. I warmly thank my loving wife, Anne Marie, for her support. I thank everyone involved with the making of this book. Finally, I thank with heart my dog, Rocky, who made a section of this book possible.

CONTENTS

1. The Pick Five

A quiet, pre-dusk rural street lays deserted except for two figures running about thirty feet apart from one another. The man in front is an ordinary, average fellow – one you would meet almost anywhere. The form behind him is a demonic evil spirit of hideous features. It is in hot pursuit of its prey.

Panting from exhaustion, the man mumbles to himself, "Must keep running. I must get home, but it's gaining on me… Oh my gosh, there's my house. Just a little bit further. Come on Mike. You can make this. Just another fifty yards!"

He gives it all he's got and lunges at the door. Fumbling to find his key, he snags it and desperately turns the lock and opens the door. He rushes inside and slams the door behind him, thinking he is safe. Standing back from the locked barrier, he hears rustling outside. And with a giant gust the door begins to open, despite the lock. In walks the demon. Shocked and horrified, Mike runs to a desk in the foyer, opens the drawer and pulls out a large cross. Pointing it at the demon, he cries out!

"In the name of Jesus Christ I command you to leave and go back to the hell from which you came." With a smirk on its face, the demon retorts: "This is the 21st century, guy. That no longer works."

The demon moves closer and closer to Mike, who falls down in disbelief and horror. The demon's face gets ever so close now as Mike screams out in terror.

Mike awakes, covered in sweat. "When is this going to end?" Another night where I can't go back to sleep!

At 8:30 a.m. Mike drives down the scenic route of Highway 1 from Oxnard to Los Angeles. He has a 10:00 appointment with his therapist, Dr. Joy Bender. His main concern at the moment is the 4 weeks he took off from work at the Ad Agency. Two weeks down; two weeks left to resolve his dilemma. His nightmares started three weeks before. They have brought him to a state of high anxiety. His only relief is watching his favorite baseball team, the L.A. Dodgers, play in the playoffs against the Atlanta Braves. The Braves lead the 4-out-of-7 series two games to one. The Dodgers just beat the Cincinnati Reds to advance to the championship series.

Now pulling into the parking lot, he parks the car and proceeds to the third floor of a small office building. Entering suite 302, he checks in at the front desk and waits.... After five minutes the receptionist announces that Dr. Bender is ready to see him. "You know the way, so please just go in," she says to Mike. So, he enters the room and sits down on a comfortable chair. Dr. Joy Bender is in her mid-sixties with attractive features. She and Mike know each other quite well. They have been seeing each other on a professional basis for four to five years; ever since Mike started working for the Ad Agency.

"So, are you still having that same nightmare every night?" she asks. "Yes! I'm just about at my limit, Joy. I need immediate help. Is there anything else you can do for me? Please, you're like a sister to me," answers Mike.

"And you're like a brother to me, Mike. But we've discussed this over and over again. I think the time has come for you to

2

decide to act on the resolution we've decided. I'm sorry to see you suffering like this, she said.

"Do you still think the demon is my boss trying to force me to work harder?" asked Mike. "You know, to get those new accounts?"

"Yes," she replied, "and the deserted streets symbolize that you can count on no one except yourself. Then, you finally reach home where you think you are safe, but he follows you in, regardless of the locked door, showing the power he has over you. Even in your home his spirit is with you."

"How about the cross? What does that mean?" asked Mike.

"Your boss is an atheist. He has no belief in any religious artifacts."

"So, what do I do to stop this?" pleaded Mike.

"You're going to have to stand up to your boss. Lay down the law. Tell him what you want. When he gives in, and he will, I can guarantee it because he *really* needs you, then your nightmares will end."

"I don't know," responded Mike. "There's something not right about all this. I think there's a much more deeper meaning to this whole thing. I just feel it."

"Don't put too much into this, Mike. It's a simple problem with a simple solution. Don't make more out of it."

"I hope you're right," said Mike, "because I'll try anything at this point."

"Great! Let's get on to other matters now." So, Mike and Joy discuss other things for the rest of the hour. At the conclusion, Mike raises his hand and bends his pinky finger to Joy and she returns the gesture. This was a sign they developed years ago in order to let each other know "I love you my dear friend," without

3

anyone else knowing what's going on. They smiled at each other as Mike left the room while getting to his next appointment. He strolls down to his car, gets in and drives back home, stopping shortly for lunch.

In Chicago, a man by the name of Billy Pace and his wife Cindy will have their wedding anniversary tomorrow. They're ashamed because the apartment they live in is a small two-bedroom dump. They have an eight-year-old boy named Calley. Billy has not been able to provide Calley with much more than basics. In this, he finds a peaceful dignity that enables him to respect himself and to expand this to his friends, believe in people in general, and to especially love his family. There are other black families in the neighborhood seemingly in the same circumstances, but there are many better-off white families which somehow doesn't seem fair. Billy has resentment in his heart, which he desperately tries to overcome.

Cindy gently asked, "Can we afford to do anything for our anniversary tomorrow, Bill?"

The car wash couldn't afford to advance me anything right now, wo we'll have to settle for a small celebration at home. I'm sorry, hon. Maybe next year," he said.

"I keep hoping, Bill. If only we could get $200,000 then we could open up a Second-Hand Store here. In this neighborhood it would go over great! But, so much for dreams," she replied.

Calley jumped in, "What about Halloween, Thanksgiving, Christmas and New Years, daddy?"

"Well, you'll be able to go trick-or-treating, and we'll have a small turkey and side dishes, but don't expect too much for Christmas and New Years. I'm so sorry, Calley. I know other kids will have a lot more than you. Unfortunately, we can only have modest celebrations. Please understand," said Billy.

"I do, daddy. I do understand."

"I wish you were able to get a job too, Cindy, but I know you're raising Calley and taking care of even this small place is a full-time job."

She echoed, "You know I wish I could, but all this *is* a full-time job. If only you could get together with my father. He could get you started training in his auto shop. He makes pretty good money. You could eventually own the shop," she told Billy.

"Sure, but you know your father never approved of you marrying me."

"But, after ten years he might have had a change-of-heart," she said optimistically.

"Maybe so. I'll go pay him a visit Sunday and see if he could do something for me. I mean, if not for me, then maybe for his daughter and grandson."

"I know it won't be easy," Cindy said, "but thank you for trying. I'll go make supper for us now." But Cindy breaks down in tears.

Calley reaches out to her, "Mommy, why are you crying?"

"I'm just worried about you, daddy and myself, dear. But mommy will be okay in a minute. You don't worry, sweetheart. I have faith that everything will turn out fine."

Billy added, "Daddy will do his best to make it better for all of us," as he hugs his wife and Calley. After what seems like quite a while, there is a sudden knock at the door.

5

"Who could that be?" asked Cindy.

"Let's find out," answered Billy. He opens the door and faces a sharply-dressed man standing there. "Can I help you?" he asks the stranger.

"Are you Mr. Billy Pace?"

"Yes! Why?"

"This envelope is for you," he replied.

"What's in it?" asked Billy.

"It's a gift from someone you don't know, but who knows you," the man responded.

"I don't understand," said Billy. "Who...."

The man interrupts Billy with, "The contents will explain most of it. The rest you will find out later. Good bye and good luck," he said.

"But wait! Come back," yelled Billy. The strange man continued down the hallway until he disappeared.

"What was *that* all about?" asked Cindy.

"I don't know. I never saw the man before. Anyway, I'm excited to see what's in this envelope," Billy said. So, he anxiously opens the envelope and finds several papers, an airplane ticket, a hotel reservation, and $12,000 in cash inside.

"Wow! How much money is it?" Cindy asks in amazement.

Billy then counts out the money in $100 bills. "Twelve-thousand dollars, and this is a First-Class plane ticket to Denver and back. But there's only one ticket. The hotel is also a First-Class hotel. The plane ticket has my name on it and it leaves Chicago this month, from October 15th and returns October 22nd. That's this Sunday!"

"What do the papers say?" asks Cindy.

Billy reads... "Hello! My name is George Braxton. I'm a self-made billionaire. You are one of five people chosen to attend a conference with me to discuss a very important subject on each of your futures. I've painstakingly selected the five of you from over 10,000 candidates to choose from. How I have come to these decisions is not important now. What *is* important is that the five of you have a golden chance to have a full and eventful future. As you can see, the flight is First-Class, the hotel is First-Class, and you've been given $12,000 cash to pay for your week in Denver and money to leave your family so that they can live comfortably while you're away. If you accept my invitation, I guarantee you, you will be completely enlightened with physical and spiritual rewards beyond your wildest dreams. If you should decide not to come, then simply discard the airplane ticket and hotel reservation in any manner you wish. The $12,000 though, is yours to keep. Consider it a thank-you gift from me to you, simply because I believe you deserve it. Don't be too surprised. $12,000 to me is like a penny to you, so don't give me too much praise. I will then focus on those that do come. Remember, all your other questions will be answered if and when you do come. Whatever your decision, I wish you the greatest success and happiness. As you can see, if you do come, the other page has directions and instructions of what to do once you get to Denver International Airport. Finally, I have sent only one ticket and reservation because I need to focus on you, and you alone. You cannot have any distractions whatsoever. I'm sure your wife can appreciate the situation. So now I bid you farewell, and may the power of the universe be with you." – Sincerely, George Braxton

"This is incredible. What do you think I should do, Cindy?" Billy asked in amazement.

"I don't think you have anything to lose by accepting his offer. $12,000 is a lot of money for us, and if he really has more to offer, then I say let's go for it. That money is a year's salary at the car wash. So, take the time off, and if they won't give it to you, then quit! This money will carry us for awhile and give us the chance for a better future. Let's go for it!" she said with excitement.

"I agree," said Billy. "I just feel somewhat uncomfortable about it. I know so little about this guy."

"True," said Cindy, "but he's obviously not a phony. I wish I could go with you, but I have confidence that you will make the right choices when they come up. I love you, and nothing will ever change that. So, take this shot, and when you come back, I know you'll have great news for us."

"Okay! It's settled. I'll leave this Sunday. I thinks it's best, though, if I just quit my job at the car wash. This way my mind can be completely relaxed for the possible life-changing chance. As you said, the $12,000 will cover a year's wage."

"Agreed!" said Cindy. "This being Tuesday, it gives us plenty of time to work things out."

So, Billy and Cindy work out the specifics, especially having to leave Calley and Cindy alone for a week.

A middle-aged woman, about 45, is driving home to Manhattan from La Guardia Airport. She's in a rush because she has a 9:00 p.m. appointment with a dear friend. The roads are icy and slick. Doreen is somewhat spiritually sensitive, yet thoroughly confused. Questions such as, "Do we always have to be at arms-length with God, at best?" or "Can we have a closer relationship?" and "People think God is found within us!" Is that true or not? So many questions, but no answers. While in deep thought, Doreen doesn't notice all the black tar and ice on the road. She's driving too fast. She tries to slow down, but it's too late. The car starts to spin. "Oh, why didn't I go with the shuttle that would have taken me home in safety?" her mind races. With the speed of the vehicle, it crashes through the side rail and plunges twenty feet down a crevice to rocks and trees at the bottom. She's now trapped in the car as both doors are jammed. Agonizing pain shoots through her legs, chest and arms. After about 20 minutes of what seems like an eternity, the police, ambulance and fire truck are on the scene, helping her get out. Carefully wedging the car door open, they get Doreen out and onto a stretcher. They whisk her away to the nearest hospital as she loses consciousness. Then, her spirit seemed to lift out of her body. She floated through dark, dense fog. As she felt herself rising, the fog grew lighter and less dense. It seemed to go on for ages. Then, the fog started to clear. She could now begin to see a beautiful green pasture with a snow-capped mountain in the distance. It became brighter and warmer. She noticed what appeared to be bright figures of people far away. She tried to get closer to them. Then, all of a sudden, she was shocked back into her physical body. Doreen is in the emergency room being resuscitated. When she became alert, the doctor told her that she had been clinically dead for 15 minutes, but then came back to life. After a short while, Doreen is brought up to a private room and put in bed.

"Now you get plenty of rest, sweetie. Your mom will be here in the morning," said her nurse. Exhausted, Doreen had no trouble getting to sleep.

The next morning, she woke up to the pleasant sight of her mother by her bedside. "Hi! How are you sweetheart?" her mother said.

"A lot better, mom."

"I heard you had a close one, but the doctor says you'll be okay to leave the hospital by tomorrow morning."

"It's great to see you, mom. After everything that has happened, I wasn't quite sure I'd make it. It really is good to be with you!" said Doreen. They embraced each other tightly.

"For a while there, I thought you were going to leave us, too," said her mom.

"But that's just it, mom. For a while, I DID leave you, somewhere outside of my body."

"Hush now. We all have strange illusions while under such circumstances."

Doreen realized it was no use trying to explain her story, for no one would believe her. It would be better for her to just drop it.

"When you get home," her mother said, "you should take a couple of weeks off until you recuperate from your reception job."

"Probably so; I agree. You look exhausted, mom. Have you been here all night?"

"Most of it, and I am a little bushed. If you feel good enough now, maybe I'll go home and get a little rest."

"That sounds fine, mom. Give me a little kiss and I'll see you later."

"Bye, dear!" Mom kisses Doreen and leaves. After an hour, Doreen rings for the nurse.

"Can I help you?" asks the nurse.

"Yes. Does this hospital have a library?"

"Yes, it does. Can I get you something?" she asked.

"Do you know if they have any books on life after death?"

"Actually, I believe we have two. Would you like me to bring them to you?"

Doreen perked up, "Would you please! I'd be very grateful."

"Sure thing, hon. Be back in 10 minutes." The nurse left and came back with the two books. Doreen thanked her and feverishly began devouring the books. The books weren't long and she finished them both by early evening.

"Interesting concepts," Doreen whispered to herself, "but not quite my experience. Maybe it was all in my mind after all. Yet, it seemed so real. Whatever... I'm exhausted. Better get some sleep." Just then there was a firm knock on her door.

"Come in," said Doreen. A sharply dressed man comes in. "May I help you?"

"Actually," said the mystery man, "I'm here to help you." He then hands Doreen an envelope. "This is for you. Please don't ask me many questions. I cannot answer them. The contents of that envelope you hold in your hand will explain many of them. Good bye and good luck."

Doreen yells at him, "BUT HOW DID YOU KNOW I WAS IN THE HOSPITAL?"

The man disappears but Doreen's mom walks back into her room.

"Who was that?" she asked.

"I don't know," answered Doreen. "He just came in, handed me this envelope, said a few words, and then left. I never saw him before."

"What's in the envelope, then?" asked her mom.

"Let's find out!" So, Doreen opened the envelope and found the same items as Billy's. The letter was the same, except for her it says, "This should be a well-deserved vacation for you, and I'm sure you can use the $12,000."

"You're not considering going, are you?" asked her mom.

"I'm not sure. It's obvious this man Braxton is pretty serious by all that he's offering. If this is a scam, it's a very expensive one. And, as you said earlier, I could use a vacation at this time, and it's a perfect time to take one. And, with all expenses paid, I can't lose. Besides, I'm very interested in what he has to offer."

"Well, when you put it that way, I guess it's worth the trip. I just hope nothing happens where you'll regret your decision."

"As they say, mom, nothing ventured, nothing gained. I'll be out of here tomorrow morning. I can make all my plans then."

"Remember," cautioned her mom, "if you change your mind, no one will blame you."

"I know, but I'm now dead set on going. Nothing will change my mind."

"All right. I guess I should leave you alone now so you can get some rest. I shouldn't have come this late anyway, but I got detained."

That's okay, mom. With everything that's gone on, I'm really wiped out. So please excuse me now. Thank you for coming by. I really hope you can come again in the morning and help me get out of here and back home."

"Certainly. I'll see you around 10:00."

"Thanks," said Doreen. "Oh, by the way, I was supposed to meet Karen at 9:00 last night at my place. Did you get a chance to let her know what happened?"

"Yes, I explained it all to her. She'll catch you when you get home."

"Great! I'll see you tomorrow, mom. Have a good night."

"You too, dear. Good night," her mother said as she walked out the door to let Doreen get her much-needed rest. Doreen peacefully slept through the night.

The next morning, Mr. John Ralph was the guest speaker at a seminary in Denver, Colorado. John was highly respected for his knowledge on the subject of angels and the angelic world.

"The angelic world is the highest realm there is, and next to God the most holy and closest to him," John summarized. "In conclusion, since I've never actually seen an angel, I can't tell you the size of their wing span," he jokes. "So, if any of you see one, please take a picture. I'm sure it would be monumental." When the laughter dies down, he adds, "Now it's time for questions and answers, so who's first?"

"How come there are only male angels mentioned in the Bible?" asks one participant.

"The male angels took the main brunt of responsibility, while the females were supporting in the background. And, since they are spirits, they are unable to have sex and have children," John answered.

"Where does it say all this in the Bible?" asked another participant.

"Not everything I tell you is in the Bible. Some of it has been revelations given to certain individuals. I have interviewed many of them, and although all of their stories don't coincide exactly, the main gist of it explains everything I have told you. One must search for the answers in every possible outlet. I have thoroughly tracked down every possible answer," said John.

"Then you admit that much of your information comes from sources that may have nothing to do with the Bible?" added the second participant.

"Not true," replied John. "Just the fact that they believe in angels points to a Biblical connection. They all may not believe in the story of Noah and the ark, but they do believe in a higher entity. Call it God, Allah or Yahweh, or whatever you want, it makes no difference, but it's all related to some kind of story, and in this case, many of us are calling it the Bible. So, you see, all my sources refer to the Bible or some other book. I hope this clarifies at least most of your questions or comments."

"It does, Mr. Ralph. Thank you."

"I have time for one more question. The person with her hand raised next to the South exit sign…"

"How long would you say angels have been around," the girl asked.

"That's a very good question," said John. "I wish I had a very good answer. But, unfortunately, there's no indication in the Bible, and I've never spoken to anyone that even had a guess. In the Bible, even though there's no time mentioned, it states that God said, "Let us make man in our image," so that tells us two things. One, angels were around before man, and two, angels obviously looked at least similar to man. There are several mentions in the Bible that angels looked like man. One such example is in Sodom and Gomorrah when Lot was visited by two angels, and the people in the city begged Lot to 'let them get to know them' which meant have sex with them. Again, the angels looked just like human beings. In conclusion, angels look like man, but as to how old they are, we're really not sure. I'm sorry I could only answer three questions, but I'm pressured for time for I have another appointment elsewhere and unfortunately it immediately follows this one. Do please excuse me as I have to leave now. It's been a pleasure lecturing all of you and I wish you the best. I have signed books of mine in the lobby for anyone wishing to purchase one." John then gathers his belongings and rushes out the door. Outside the ballroom, he is approached by the same smartly-dressed man.

"I'm sorry, but I don't have time to answer any more questions," John said to him.

"I don't have a question, Mr. Ralph; just an envelope for you," said the mystery man.

"What's in it, and who are you?" replied John.

"The contents will answer many of your questions. Thank you. Good luck and good bye," he said, as he disappeared into the crowd.

John is left dumbfounded. He leaves the building and gets into a limousine he uses from time to time to get around whatever town he happens to be in. He lives in Colorado Springs, which is where he is headed right now. While driving there, he opens the envelope, sees the contents, and reads the letter. Once again, it's similar to the others but has a personal paragraph just for him which reads: "I know this is a strange proposal, Mr. Ralph, but I have information that will give you new insight and answers into your own topic of interest, which is angels and the angelic world. I guarantee you won't be disappointed. Think about it; answers to some of the most puzzling questions even *you* have. Now is your chance. Don't lose it," the letter said.

John said to himself, "Strange! But it does grab my curiosity. I'd have to cancel some appointments, but I *must* know. Does he really have new information, or is he a kook? If he's a kook, he's certainly spending a lot of money for a prank. No, it's my responsibility to find out everything I can about angels and so forth. What the hell. It's not that much of a gamble. Yes! I will go." So, John informs the driver of the limousine: "Bob, get me home as quickly as possible without breaking any laws."

"Always, sir," he replies.

In Port Richey, Florida a twenty-five-year-old woman is in her pajamas, relaxing before going to bed. She lives on the eighth floor of a ten-story high rise. She closes the refrigerator door after getting a glass of orange juice when all of a sudden all of her lights go out. Sharon Grace checks out her window and then in the hallway through her peep hole, but all the lights are on everywhere else.

"Oh no. It's starting to happen again, she murmurs. It's been two weeks since this last happened; almost a record. Why? What does it want from me? And it seems to be getting worse each time!" She runs to the closet door, opens it and pulls out a flashlight. She shines it on the telephone and begins to dial out.

But, the line is dead. Sharon freezes as she hears slushing sounds coming from the hall outside, approaching her door. The air in her apartment begins to turn icy cold. The slushing sound now turns to thumping, which stops right outside her apartment door. There's a darkening on the outside at the bottom of her door, as if something waits for her to open it.

"DEAR GOD! IT'S RIGHT OUTSIDE MY DOOR!" She runs to the door, making sure the lock and chain are secure. As her left hand rests on the doorknob, she begins to feel it turn ever so slowly. Her eyes widen and her heart begins to race. She takes her hand off the doorknob; her palm is extremely sweaty. "IT'S TRYING TO GET IN NOW!" she sobs. Then she hears whispering. Someone or something is calling her name... "Sharon, Sharon... let us in." Then, all of a sudden there's loud screeching and banging at her door.

"DOESN'T ANYONE ELSE IN THE BUILDING HEAR ALL THIS?" she screams. "MY GOD IT SOUNDS LIKE ITS GOING TO BUST THE DOOR IN! SOMEBODY HELP ME! PLEASE!

Sharon holds her ears as all the noise stops. She debates whether or not to look into the peep hole. As she draws closer to it, very heavy breathing comes from the other side in the hallway. Should she look or not? Can she bear what her eyes might behold? Closer and closer she gets to the device that could give her a glimpse of the thing that is terrifying her. She presses her eye up against the peep hole. She brushes the sweat away that blocks her vision. She looks out, and in the distance she sees a black, deformed shape immediately come up against the peep hole. Sharon screams and turns away as all of the screeching and banging starts up again. She runs awkwardly into her bedroom and slams the door shut. Jumping into her bed, she grasps her pillow and holds it against her chest. All is silent now as she notices the doorknob of her bedroom door begin to slowly turn.

"GOOD LORD, IT'S IN MY LIVING ROOM! GOD HELP ME! IT'S IN MY LIVING ROOM! STOP IT! STOP IT! STOP IT!"

She screams once more and then faints. The next morning, she awakens at about 8:20. Now, everything seems different in the daylight. Sharon gets out of bed and opens her bedroom door. Everything seems normal. She walks to her front door as it's still locked and chained. She unlocks it and looks in the hallway, which also seems normal. She turns and goes back inside and begins to wonder. Did last night's incident, just like all the others, really happen, or is all this just in her mind? She could never share any of this with any of her friends for fear they would think she was unstable or, worse yet, haunted by spiritual or other strange phenomena. So, Sharon gains her composure, takes a shower and gets dressed. After preparing breakfast and sitting down to eat, her doorbell rings. She gets up and answers the door. Once again, that smartly-dressed man stands outside.

"Can I help you?" Sharon asks.

"Actually, Ms. Grace, I'm here to help *you*. Please take this envelope; it will explain many questions."

"What's in…."

"Just open it. You'll be happy you did." And the mysterious man walks briskly down the hall and gets into the elevator. Then, he's gone.

"My goodness. That was quick. Better check out this envelope," Sharon said to herself as she slowly opens it. She is shocked to see the First-Class plane ticket, hotel reservation and the $12,000 in cash inside. The basis of the letter is the same except for the personal section made for her circumstances. It reads: "It might be of interest to you that I can help you find out what all these strange occurrences have been about in your life. And, I DO have the answers. Plus, the money could be helpful to you since you are between jobs right now. Of course, the money, as mentioned, is yours to keep no matter what you decide. I do hope you'll take me up on my offer."

"How does he know so much about me?" Sharon wondered. "Even though he's a complete stranger, he must be serious. Otherwise, why would he offer so much just to listen to what he has to say, unless of course he's a complete eccentric. But, then even though it's a risk, it's a risk well-taken if he really does have answers to what's been happening to me. I'd better ask my best friend, Jan, to come over. I need a second opinion."

So, Sharon calls Jan and asks her to come over ASAP. Jan's there within the hour as Sharon explains about the mysterious man and the envelope, and everything else.

"Oh Sharon," Jan confronts Sharon, "why haven't you told me about what's been happening to you for the past three months?"

"I was afraid I'd lose your friendship if I were totally honest," said Sharon.

"Look, girl. You couldn't lose my friendship no matter what happens. And, to have the burden of all these terrifying experiences on your shoulders is just too much for one person to bear."

"I feel better to have told you," said Sharon, "but what do you think I should do about this Braxton and going all the way to Denver for a week?"

"Well, you know I'm not the type to jump willy-nilly into things, but under these circumstances I feel you should take a chance. I mean if he wants you to be alone with him in a small room, that would raise flags, but if you get to know these other four people and all of you are in a good-sized room that is *unlocked*, then what do you have to lose? Besides that, from what he says in the letter, you just might come back smelling like roses."

"That settles it," said Sharon. "I'm going. But I don't have much time left til Sunday, today is Friday."

"Also, the fact that you are in-between jobs makes it perfect, though the one thing that *does* bother me is how the hell does he know so much about you?" exclaimed Jan.

"That bothers me, too," said Sharon, "but I guess we'll find out all that next week. For now, I should start packing and organizing. Do you want to help me?"

"Sure. Better too early than too late," answered Jan. The two girls start getting everything ready for the upcoming week.

Back in Oxnard, California Mike Wakings is in his house just finishing lunch. The doorbell rings and he rushes to answer the door. Yes, it's the same smartly-dressed man that visited the other four people.

"What can I do for you this afternoon?" He checks his watch and sees that it's 12:18.

The man hands Mike the envelope. "This is for you, Mr. Wakings. Please don't ask me any questions for I cannot answer any. The contents of that envelope will answer many of your questions. Have a good day."

Mike slowly closes the door, but then remembers one question he needed answered. He jerks the door open and yells out, "BUT WHAT IF…" Mike is then shocked to see that the man is already gone. How could he have disappeared that fast, he wonders? "Strange. Very strange," he whispers to himself. "Oh well, better check out the envelope."

Mike opens the envelope, which is the same as all the others, and so is the letter except for his personal message. It reads, "I know about your nightmares and I can help you find the answers which, by the way, are not the same as your therapist Ms, Bender says. Also, you are going to be the key for the other four. You are the main person, in general, for the whole situation. So, even if you come just out of curiosity, it will be well worth your time and effort."

"What the heck does this guy think I'm gonna do?" said Mike to himself. "And I'm sure I'm not the only one asking this question, provided of course he's treated the other four this way. But, how in heaven does he know all this about me? And who is he really, besides being a billionaire? I think I need to speak with Joy about this. Maybe she can help."

So Mike calls up Joy's secretary to find out if she has any time available to see him for an emergency visit, especially since he would have to leave on Sunday. Mike is in luck. Joy has an opening at 3:00. Mike gets into his car and drives back to L.A. He arrives in Joy's office at 2:45, anxiously waiting for his turn to see her.

"You may go into Dr. Bender's office now," the receptionist announces.

"Thank you," Mike replies, as he walks down the hallway to Joy's room, goes in, shuts the door behind him and takes a seat.

"So, what's the emergency all about, Mike?" Dr. Bender asks with a puzzled stare. Mike explains everything to Joy and then shows her the letter.

"You're right," she says. "It's a first-class airplane ticket, and what's the name of that hotel again?"

"La Costa Plenty!" Mike replies. Joy looks at Mike with that puzzled stare again. "Sorry, that's a joke. I saw it once on an old Three Stooges episode," he said.

"What is it with all you guys? It seems like you're all into the Three Stooges. Us women can't see the attraction they have on all of you."

"I guess it's in our genes," he said. "But, all jokes aside, what do you think?"

"I'll tell you. I think you should go to it, even though he's knocking my interpretation of your dreams. Everything is totally paid for and you still have two weeks left of your vacation time. This might be a chance for you to find out the answers to many of your questions. Also, a chance for me to satisfy my own curiosity."

"What do you mean?" he shot back.

"With your permission, I would like to accompany you to this excursion. I think I could get valuable insight into human behavior; information I might not be able to get elsewhere."

"That's fantastic, Joy!" Mike shot back. "The only glitch is that when I'm in the room with the other four, you'll have to wait either in your room or the lobby because, as you read, he only wants the five of us in there for private reasons; No one else allowed. As a matter of fact, if he knew you were coming, he might have objections to that."

"First of all, I'd have no problem waiting in my room for you. Secondly, I get the impression that he would object to family members, but not to a friend, especially your therapist."

"You're probably right," said Mike, "and I really would like you along. But, do you think you could get a ticket on the same flight as mine?"

"First things first. I have to reschedule all my appointments next week which my secretary can do." Joy tells her secretary to begin the process before the weekend. Then, she calls her travel agent to book a seat in First Class on the same flight as Mike's.

"Well, as you may have heard, there were two seats left in First Class. I won't be in the seat next to yours, but I'll only be some ten feet away. Not bad for such short notice. It helps that the flight is on a non-holiday Sunday," said Joy.

"That's great, Joy." Even though, I can understand why you think this trip is important to me, but is it that important to you to go through all this for some information that might or might not be helpful to you?"

"I guarantee this meeting and all concerned will be invaluable to me. That reminds me, I have to make a week's reservation at… what hotel did you say it was? And, don't give me that La Costa Plenty stuff. I know it's one of several…"

"It's the Hotel Stanwick," said Mike.

"Of course, that was it. Let me make the reservation and we'll get together after my last appointment at 6:00. Let's meet at the coffee shop across the street."

"Sounds good. I'll see you then, so we can make plans. I have a feeling this is going to be a very interesting trip."

23

"Me too, Mike. Me too"

So, at 6:15, Mike and Joy meet at the coffee shop and make plans to meet on Sunday at the LAX, while in Chicago. Billy Pace prepares to leave on Sunday, Doreen Perry in New York, John Ralph, already in Denver, and Sharon Grace from Port Richey. It's now October the 15th, a big day for all six of them. The five travelers arrive at their prospective airports, and as for John Ralph, he will get his instructions at the Hotel Stanwick. The flights to Denver, which should be landing without a single problem, are disturbed a bit by an early snowfall and heavy fog. With just a short delay, the planes land at DIA. The four flights land within an hour and a half of each other. The first one to land is Doreen's. Coming off the plane, she heads to the luggage area by taking a shuttle train which goes from one side of the huge airport to the other. As she gets to the luggage ramps, Doreen notices a line of men and women holding up name cards in front of them. She knows that they are the chauffeurs ready to drive their customers to their prospective destinations. Doreen locates the one with her name on the sign, held by a young man in his twenties.

"I guess you're waiting for me," Doreen said to him.

"If you're Doreen Perry, then yes I am," he replied.

"Great! Just let me get my luggage and we'll be on our way. Are you allowed to give me a hand?

"Yes, Mam! It's my privilege to help."

"Great! My luggage is right here. These few pieces, and my carry-on." The driver loads Doreen's luggage into the limousine and then escorts her inside. He drives to the Hotel Stanwick, just as Billy Pace and Sharon Grace also load up and head to the hotel. Mike Wakings and Joy Bender are at the terminal, waiting for their luggage to come down the ramp.

"Do you see that, Joy?" asked Mike. "That limousine driver has _both_ our names on his card."

"Now that you mention it, yes! That's very odd, to say the least." Their luggage now comes down the conveyer belt. "I'll get our stuff, Mike. Why don't you go talk to the driver?"

"Hi. I'm Mike Wakings. But how did you know about Joy Bender?" he asked.

"I'm just paid to pick up the two of you. I'm sorry, but how or why, I have no idea. Let me give both of you a hand with that."

After they load up, they head to the hotel. John Ralph is also brought to the Hotel Stanwick by limousine from Colorado Springs. Once there, they are all instructed to meet in Conference Room 3. When all have arrived, they begin to get acquainted with one another.

"How come you were able to bring someone else along with you, Mike?" asked Billy. "My understanding was that we were to be alone."

"That's what we thought too," said Joy. "We figured we would have to explain my coming here, but to our surprise, our host somehow already knew about my arrival with Mike. Just another mystery of how he knows so much about us all."

"This, though, is more than a mystery; it's downright weird. I mean, he's like a fortune teller or something," said Mike.

"If you ask me, he knows too much," added John.

"Well, I guess we'll learn more tomorrow when we meet him," said Sharon.

All of a sudden, Mike collapses to the floor. Joy immediately bends down over him.

"WHAT HAPPENED?" Doreen frantically shouts. "Is he all right? He just dropped to the floor!"

"Damn. I can't feel a pulse or a heartbeat," said Joy.

"Well, DO something for him!" said Doreen.

"I'm a therapist; not an M.D.," said Joy. "We'd better call an ambulance before we waste any more time. He might only have minutes."

As they speak, Mike's spirit rises up out of his body to the ceiling. As he looks down, he notices everyone frozen as if they have become statues. Now he starts floating higher and higher into a warm bluish cloud. As he drifts, the cloud becomes less dense. Now he can start to see a field with green grass and full trees. He's completely out of the cloud now as he steps foot onto the warm grass. Even though the sun is high, the temperature is very pleasant. It's a warm coolness to be understood. No one is around, until a woman appears before him. She is dressed in a beautiful elegant dress. Mike just stares a few moments at her, and then begins to talk.

"Where am I? I was in a conference room in Hotel Stanwick with friends when I blacked out. I saw my body as I floated upward, saw everything freeze, and then after drifting through some kind of cloud, I found myself here, wherever this is." As Mike looks at the woman, her appearance is actually not that of a beautiful woman of earth standards, but there is a glow about her. It makes her the most beautiful woman he's ever seen. It's an inner beauty that magnifies as she moves. Mike can't quite make out what nationality she seems to be.

"Hello! My name is Genia. I've been waiting for you. What happened to you was that your organs stopped working and you died," she said.

"YOU MEAN I'M DEAD?" shouted Mike.

"Yes. But, it's only temporary. When you return, you'll be in perfect shape again. As for everything being frozen, that's because once your spirit left your body, time almost stopped. But, it did continue at a very slow rate because time here is not measured as it is on earth. What is hours here is just a few minutes on earth. Also, you had to die in order for you to come here to the spirit world."

"You make it all sound so simple," said Mike.

"Actually, it's not simple at all. It's all a very sophisticated process. Everything God created was done with great care and effort, and also with very precise creativity. The Bible states that God created all things in six days, when actually it wasn't six days at all, but six periods of time. It could have been six months, six years, six hundred years or even thousands or millions or billions of your earth years for each period."

"This is all amazing," Mike said. "But, before we go on, where am I now?"

"You're in Paradise."

"You mean Heaven?"

"No," said Genia. "I mean Paradise. Paradise is one level before Heaven. For example, Jesus talked about Heaven often. But, when he was on the cross, he told the thief on his right that he would be with him in Paradise, not Heaven. But, don't make a mistake about it; as you can see, Paradise is highly beautiful and has God's love and warmth in it. It's just that in Heaven, everything is totally alive with great sensitivity and the very air you breathe is God's love. It's almost like 3-D with having a euphoric experience 100% of the time. If you think Paradise is Heaven, then Heaven itself will really blow your mind."

"Then why didn't Jesus qualify for Heaven?" asked Mike. "I mean wasn't he even perfect as well as being a sinless man?"

"It's not that he wasn't qualified, but it was because the gates of Heaven were closed until recently. Now he *is* in Heaven, along with many of the people who had earned that right in their lifetime."

"Why was Heaven closed until just recently? I thought it was always open."

"I'll explain that in time," said Genia, "along with great revelations of so many other mysterious questions, and God's plans."

"You make it sound like I'll be coming back here many more times."

"You will be, Mike. Let me explain just a little to you in more detail."

"Please do. Right now I'm so confused about everything that's happening to me," said Mike.

"We, meaning all mankind, are at a time in history when all things will be revealed. These are the Last Days we're living in; the time spoken about by Jesus and *The Book of Revelation* are upon us. The prelude to all this has been history being set up for two thousand years to prepare the world for our time. I'm speaking, of course, of the 20th and 21st centuries. The promise of Jesus' return must be fulfilled now. All the technological inventions since the end of the 19th century and 20th have been for one reason: to make it easier for the Lord of the Second Advent to spread his words by news, radio and travel, faster than at any other time in history. The human race has been prepared for his return. One such preparation as you may well know is the story of "The Lady of Fatima". Millions of people have been given signs and revelations. You are one such person. But, in your case, more of Heaven's secrets are going to be revealed which only a very few people have received."

"I know my next two-word question is probably going to be boring to you, but... Why ME?"

"Mostly because of ancestral merit. Things your ancestors have suffered over hundreds of years. They, and even yourself have laid the conditions for you to be prepared to be able to receive all of this information, right down to the very nightmares you've been having. You're in a very central position to help other people become informed, in particular the four other people with you on your trip to Denver; even your therapist. Each of them is in a central position to many other people. The next seven days you will all go through several occurrences that will bring you closer to one another. *You* will be visiting us here five to ten more times, in which you'll receive the truth about the spirit world - including the angelic world - the fate of mankind, your four friends' answers to their own questions, and untold other secrets. Each time you come back, you'll learn a great deal more."

"You mean when I drop dead some more?" asked Mike.

"Crudely speaking," Genia laughed, "yes."

"So, can I see Heaven, or am I not allowed?"

"You'll see Heaven, hell and everything in between. That is your destiny. But, for now you must go back," she said.

"But why do people have different experiences and stories when they taste life-after-death and come back to tell about it? And how about…"

"Next time, Mike. In turn you will find out almost everything."

"ALMOST everything? What do you mean?"

"Next time, Mike. Now, go back. Go back to your earthly body. Go back. Go back."

Mike is once again engulfed by the bluish cloud, and everything he experienced going to paradise he went through in reverse until he found himself back in his body, lying on the floor in the conference room. At this point, Billy was just about to go get help as he is stopped by Joy.

"Wait a minute, Billy," cries Joy. "Mike seems to be coming out of it. He has a strong heartbeat and pulse. He's even starting to regain consciousness. He is having a miraculous recovery!"

"How could that be?" asked John. For all intents and purposes, he was dead. Now you're saying that Mike is as good as he was before collapsing to the floor."

"As I said a minute ago, I'm a therapist, not an M.D.," said Joy. "He seems like he's as good as new, but I'm not 100% sure." As Mike starts to get up, Joy grabs him and cautions him, saying "Hold it there, Mike. You just put a big scare into all of us."

"I'm sorry for the scare, guys, but I'm fine now; really," said Mike.

"I mean, you *were* dead," said Sharon. "How could you come out of it so quickly and be in such good health as you apparently are?"

"I'll explain everything to you, that is, if you believe me. All I can say right now is, we're going to have one hell of a week, and each of you is going to have his or her own private week."

"What do you mean?" asked Doreen. "What happened to you while you were dead and scared us half to death?"

"Everyone, grab a chair and have a seat," said Mike. "This is going to take a lot of explaining, and I hope none of you will think I'm nuts. Let's begin." They all encircled their seats around him.

2. And One Makes Six

After everyone sat down and relaxed as much as possible, Mike began explaining everything that had happened to him while he was unconscious. Listening intently, the five of them had different emotions towards Mike's story. But, the general feeling was that Mike had a hallucination because of his condition; everyone, that is, except for Doreen who had had a near-death experience of her own, and for Joy who had an open mind about almost everything.

"I know most of you think I imagined all of this. I don't know what to tell you except if you give me some time, I'll be able to prove all this to you. Once, that is, when I've got a lot more information about things, and in particular about each of you. I'll know things no one else could know unless one has been informed by psychic or spiritual phenomena; personal things."

"I'm willing to take a lot of what you say," said Doreen, "because I…"

"Please don't tell me anything," Mike interrupted. "Let me tell *you* and everyone else here their story. All I know now are a few generic things we've shared with each other."

"Good idea Mike," said Joy. "I think it would be much more effective if we wait for you to talk to us about ourselves, although I'm not too crazy about the idea of you having near-death experiences over and over again. That could be very dangerous for you, while who knows what effect it will have on the rest of us."

"That's all taking into consideration that Mike isn't imagining all of this in the first place," said John.

"Well, that's why we have to give him a chance to prove himself to us," said Joy. "It's just that each time we've got to be ready in case Mike has a problem coming out of it. Do you ever know where these experiences are going to take you? It would help us if we even knew that much."

"Sorry, Joy, and to the rest of you," answered Mike, "but I only know as much as the rest of you."

"Maybe our host tomorrow morning will be able to shed a little light in our direction," said Billy. "I'll bet he knows something about our situation."

"I'll bet he knows a lot more than that," said Sharon. "I'm quite anxious to meet him."

"Maybe it would be best if we all just got a good night's sleep," said Doreen.

"I think you're right," said Mike. "We'll be able to figure all this out with a clear mind in the morning. Heck, nothing like a good night's sleep after you just died. But, putting all jokes aside, I guess I'll head up to my room now."

"I think that's a good idea for the rest of us too," said Joy. But, as the rest of them head to their rooms, Mike and Joy share a few additional words.

"Mike, I already regret our coming here. We just might be getting more than we bargained for. I mean, with you dying, and this guy knowing as much as he does, *even* my arrival here with, I might say, his approval! Something's just not right about this. I don't like it."

"Relax Joy. It'll all work out in the end."

"But, the end to what?"

"I guess we'll have to find that out by the end of the week. You have a good night. I'll see you around 8:45. We don't want to be late for our first meeting with Mr. Braxton now, do we?"

"I imagine not," answered Joy. "Have a good night yourself." They raise their hands and bend their pinkies to each other, then head to their respective rooms.

At 3:15 a.m., Mike wakes up in another cold sweat from the same nightmare. He whispers to himself, "This is ridiculous. When and how will this end? All I know is, Braxton better have an answer for me. It might be old fashioned, but a glass of warm milk might be the answer to me getting back to sleep."

So, Mike finally does get back to sleep, only to awaken at 7:30. He showers and heads to the lobby for a quick breakfast. He finishes up with a cup of coffee as John comes over to join him.

"Would you like a cup?" asks Mike.

"No thanks. I already had two, and that's my limit. Too much caffeine isn't very good for one's system," he said.

"Neither is the polluted air we breathe," replied Mike.

"But, we have no choice about breathing. We do have a choice about how much caffeine we ingest. It's like smoking," said John.

"I'm sure there's more on your mind this morning than our general health," said Mike.

"You're right. But, health *is* on my mind; your health. Are you really planning to die, shall we say, several more times?"

"Whatever it takes to find out everything we can about as much as we can. I have a feeling each of us is going to have to

34

take some sort of chance. Maybe not as grave as mine, but some kind of chance, nonetheless."

"What makes you say that?" asked John, as Joy walks in and interrupts the conversation.

"Good morning, gentlemen."

"Good morning, Joy."

"Sleep well?" John asks.

"Yes, quite. We should go into Conference Room 3 now. We don't want to be late for our first appointment with Braxton."

"You're right," said Mike. "It's ten-to-nine now." The three of them go into the conference room and meet Billy, Doreen and Sharon who are already there.

"Good morning, everyone," says Mike. "I see we're all ready for our first meeting."

"Not only that, but as you all might have noticed, there are six and only six chairs in this room. I guess Braxton isn't expecting any other company besides the six of us."

"He's already giving me the creeps, if nothing else he has done hasn't already," said Billy.

In a few minutes, the big grandfather clock chimes 9:00. In through the door enters two men; one about six feet tall in a gray suit and tie. He has a strong, yet friendly face. The other man is about 5'10" and is smartly dressed. They make their way to the podium at the front of the room. The first man adjusts himself to the podium as the second man stands close by. Everyone is talking to one another, realizing the second man is the same one who gave each of them their envelopes and quickly disappeared. The first man begins to speak…

"May I have your attention, please. My name is George Braxton, and this is my associate, Mr. Grea Silver."

"How colorful," whispers Sharon.

"I'm sorry for all the mystery," begins George, "but it's quite necessary. Also, if you would please hold your questions until I've finished speaking, for not only will it be simpler, but you might find out that a lot of your questions will be answered as I speak. To begin with, I was born and raised in Fairbanks, Alaska while my associate is from Anchorage. I started out on a fishing boat, diving for kelp, while my real interest lay in the stock market. I worked on the boats until I was 28, saved enough money so I could buy shares in what I studied to be a solid investment. By the time I was 31, I had made my first million and was able to work the market full time. Also at that time, I became good friends with Mr. Silver, and I asked him if he would invest with me. Because of my previous success, he agreed. Grea was just a year younger than I. Unlike myself, though, he did not invest as heavily. By the age of 45, I became a billionaire and multiplied that until my present age of 63. Grea was satisfied with earning several million and we grew to become as brothers. A short, but accurate, description of my rise to fortune…

For the present, you'll just have to take my word that at my disposal I had every resource available to enable me to find out everything about each of you right up to the present moment. You'll find out in detail exactly how I knew about you by the end of the week, provided of course that you stay the whole week. And, I do hope you'll stay because you'll find the things you'll learn to be invaluable not only to me, but to each one of you. You have no idea what waits for all of you. You will be receiving the keys to doors that will open up your imagination to the truth and secrets of the here-and-beyond; things that only a handful of people know. It will stagger your mind. You will stretch out beyond the ordinary and reach to new levels of information. Your lives will not only be richer in knowledge, but also in wealth. For, if you stay the whole week and follow not only mine, but your own heart's direction, I will give each of you $10 million."

"WHAT!" shouts Billy. "Ten million dollars. For what? I mean, are you on the level about this?"

"Yes!" added Joy. "And why in the world would even a multi-billionaire give five strangers ten million dollars each for sticking around here for a week and following some directions, unless of course what you'll be asking them to do is illegal, and I mean like murder or something even worse, if one understands that there *are* things worse than murder?

"For heavens sake," said George, "I would NEVER ask you or anyone else to do something illegal. I may be foolish at times, but I'm no fool. One could not dream of getting away with paying people a fortune to commit a crime so horrific in our day and age. Besides, before you get paid next Sunday, you will all be informed thoroughly what's being asked of you, and you'll plainly see that there is nothing illegal or immoral about what I'll be asking you to do. You'll have the time and provisions to check out my requests. If you feel uneasy about any of it, you'll be free to go; without the money, of course. This is the reason I permitted you to come along and attend the meetings, Ms. Bender; so that you can give the others advice."

"I'm not an M.D. or a lawyer, Mr. Braxton," responded Joy.

"True! But, given your profession, I do believe the others will respect your opinion. You *are* a professional whom everyone here feels is becoming their friend, as well," said George.

"But that still doesn't explain how you know even the personal facts about each one of us," said Mike. "That goes beyond the usual information one can find out even with *your* kind of money. There are things here that are just plain uncanny."

"I promise you," said George, "everything will be explained before the week's up. For ten million dollars, one thing I require from all of you is patience. You must have trust, and all will be revealed. Besides, what other alternative do you have except to leave before the week is up, in which case you'll forfeit the money and all the astounding truths that will change your lives forever?"

"You must have some pretty stern qualifications for that kind of money," said John.

"Enough! Make your choices by noon today. Of course, if you change your minds anytime between now and Sunday, your decision will be respected," said George.

"What does your associate have to say about all this?" asked Doreen.

"I go with whatever George decides to do," said Grea. "You might say I'm a silent partner."

"How are we to make a choice without knowing what you want from us?" asked Billy.

"It's merely to decide if you're going to stay the week or not," George said. "Getting the money will be decided by your option to follow my instruction at the end of the week. You'll have 'til then."

"Then you want us back by noon?" echoed Mike.

"Yes! We'll go on from there," said George.

"Fine! We'll see you then, replied Mike, at which everyone got up and proceeded into the lobby. Mike realized he forgot one important question, so he went back into the conference room to ask George. But, he was shocked to see that the room was empty;

no one was there. He turned around and went out to join the others.

"What's the matter now, Mike?" asked Billy.

"I went back inside, but neither George nor Grea were in there. It's as if they just disappeared into thin air." Billy rushes in and then comes back out again.

"There's an exit door in the room; maybe they went out there," he said.

"That quickly?" said Mike. "I don't think so."

"So, what do you think? They really disappeared? Come on, Mike!"

"I don't know, Billy. I just don't know. But, it's strange. That's all I know; very strange indeed."

"Well, let's not mention anything to anyone else. We don't need paranoia, even though I'm beginning to get a little paranoid."

"Sure. Whatever you say, Billy. Whatever you say."

Everyone goes to one corner of the lobby and seats themselves. Then, in conversation, one-by-one they all go over the decision to stay or go back home. Logic, curiosity, and a little greed convince each of them to stay; all that is except for Billy, who wants to talk to his wife about it on the phone. Needing to hurry, he goes up to his room and calls her. He explains the situation, she contemplates everything for a while, and then gives him her opinion.

"I've thought about it, Billy, and my response is: Are you kidding? said Cindy. "For a possible ten million dollars? You're not committing to anything except a week out of your life. Then, you can listen to what he wants and make your decision. I trust you, honey. I know you'll make the right choices. Just think what we can do with that kind of money. All our financial problems would be solved for the rest of our lives. So, stay the week. Then, see what he wants you or us to do for the money."

"You're right, Cindy. So I'll accept his invitation. How's Calley doing?"

"He's doing fine. He just misses his daddy."

"Please give him my love and a kiss."

"I will. Listen, Billy. Even though I'm anxious about the money, you be careful. If anything gets dangerous, you pull out and come home. Money or not, you're more important to us than any amount of money."

"I will, sweetheart. Remember, I love you very much and I'll call you when I know a lot more. But, bye for now."

"Good bye and God bless you."

Down in the lobby… "How's everything at home?" asks Sharon.

"Fine. My wife and son aren't used to me being gone overnight, not to mention for a week.

"Then you decided to join us and stay?" she asked.

"Yes, and thank all of you for your concern for my family. I'm really touched."

"No problem Billy," said Joy. "I guess we'll have to become a family now in order to get through the upcoming week."

"Well, we have an hour and a half 'til noon. Why don't we explain to one another what moved each of us to come out here," suggested Mike.

"That's a good idea," said Joy. "But are you sure you want to learn about each other before you find out from your near-death experiences?"

"Yes, I do. I guess I'll just have to make all of you believe in some other way," said Mike.

"Great," said Joy. "Why don't we begin with you, Doreen? And, I suggest we keep it to approximately fifteen minutes so we aren't late for the afternoon get together."

So, Doreen explains about *her* near-death experience and her quest to find answers to many deep questions about God and the universe. Billy discusses his desire to get out of the slums and give a better life to his family. John tells of his yearning to find deeper answers about angels and the angelic world. And, Mike discusses his nightmares and his hope of ending them while finding their meaning, as well as coping with his near-death experiences. Disturbing is Sharon's brushes with the spirit world and her terrified desire to end them. Finally, Joy explains her hopes of gaining great insights by everyone's stories of searching, plus Braxton's and Silver's own stories and their purpose for all six of them. After everyone shared, the time was 11:55 a.m.

"Well, I guess it's time we go talk to Braxton and Silver," said John.

The six of them again gather in Conference Room 3. A few minutes later, George and Grea enter. Once reaching the front, George immediately begins speaking.

"So, what have each of you decided?" he asks.

Joy stands and happily announces: "Everyone has asked me to speak on their behalf. And, each of them has decided to take advantage of your hospitality and stay the week."

"Excellent!" replied George. "None of you will regret your choice to stay. We'll begin at six this evening. Each of you have a rented car leased in your name, so you can go about as you wish. The only thing I ask is that you're all on time for each of our meetings. Tardiness will not be accepted and you'll be asked to leave. So again, I plead... don't be late. Have a good day and I'll see all of you tonight," after which they all get up and go back into the lobby.

"That was short, but to the point," commented Doreen.

"You're telling me! Braxton is a man of few words, and Silver is a man of no words," said Billy.

Just then, Mike quickly goes back into the conference room to check on Braxton and Silver, but again, they're gone.

"Were they in there," asked Billy, "assuming of course that's what you were checking on?"

"No!" replied Mike. "Disappointed again. But, tonight I'll be ready for them. If they go through that exit door, I'll know."

"Now you have me curious as hell," said Billy. "Whatever you're planning, please let me in on it. I must know myself; I must."

"Don't worry. I'll inform you tonight."

Everyone gathers in the lobby and all decide to have some fun and entertainment by going to the gambling towns of Black Hawk and Central City nearby in the mountains. It's a slick ride because of the snow that has just fallen, and even more so in the higher elevations. Once there, they rent a room, even for the few hours they'll be there, as a private place they can talk with one another. While discussing Braxton and Silver, Mike kneels over and falls on the floor again. Everyone gathers around him and frantically discusses what to do.

"Oh no, not again!" exclaimed Sharon. "Does he have a pulse and heartbeat, or is he...?"

"Dead?" asks Joy. "I'm afraid so, but according to Mike, this is the second of many episodes."

"I know he said not to worry, but we can't help it," said John. "It's not natural. I mean, alive one minute, then dead, and then alive again, providing of course he does come out of it this time."

At this point, Mike's spirit floats out of his body again. He sees everyone below him, frozen. He then drifts through the cloud and once again finds himself in the field, coming out of the cloud. He remains motionless there as Genia stands before him.

"Hello, Mike. It's good to see you again."

"It's so warm and pleasant here. I have to say the same to you. It's beautiful here. So pleasant, as I said. And the love I feel is extraordinary, like I never want to leave again," said Mike.

"One day you won't have to, but for now we just talk. Are you ready?"

"As ready as I'll ever be, I guess. But tell me, this is the second time I'm in this area. Aren't there other areas?" asked Mike.

"For goodness sakes, yes! The spirit world here is as vast as the galaxy. And, speaking of galaxies, one would be able to travel to all the universe, the entire universe, whenever one wants to. Also, one would be able to study even a pebble for a thousand years before going on to something else. You would never be bored in the spirit world. Not even for eternity."

"It's amazing," replied Mike. "The love is so strong here, I don't want to leave."

"I understand, but you must go back after each visit here this week. Live your earthly life to the fullest that you're able to, and one day you will be in Heaven."

"If Heaven is truly as wonderful as you say it is, then why can't we be there instead of here?" Mike asked. "I'm anxious to see it."

"In time you will, but for now I have much to explain to you. We will start with the levels of the spirit world."

"Well, once I thought there was just Heaven and hell. But, being here in Paradise tells me there's more to this realm than I ever imagined."

"Yes!" answered Genia. "First, there are three stages. They are called Formation, Growth and Completion. For each stage there are also three stages, called Formation, Growth and Completion, and then each of those sub-stages also has a Formation, Growth and Completion stage, which total up to be 27 stages, or levels. Above and beyond the top of the Completion Stage is Perfection; the realm of Heaven. There is only one level of Heaven. Once there, you are engulfed in God's love and domain. You can have anything your heart desires."

"Previously you told me the gates to Heaven were closed until recently. As I asked before, why was that?" Mike asked.

"I cannot tell you right now, but I promise you, I will when the right time comes. For now, you'll just have to be patient. As the old saying goes, 'All good things come to those who wait.'"

"Then I guess I have no choice but to wait," replied Mike.

"So, let me go on. I said above Completion is Heaven, but below Formation is the realm of hell. There are five levels of hell, making a total of 33 levels. That is where the term 'rock bottom of hell' comes from. And, unlike much belief that hell is fire and brimstone, it is actually a very cold place because it is so far away from the warmth of God's love. The bottom of hell is reserved for suicides and people who have committed horrendous crimes. Very importantly, one must understand that each person is born with a physical body *and* a spirit man. The spirit man grows by the person doing benevolent things or good actions. But, the most

44

important thing is how much love you can grow for God and for your fellow man. When your physical body dies, depending on how much your spirit man has grown determines where you will go in the spirit world; i.e., to what level of the spirit world you will go. That is why there are so many different levels, each for the level your spirit man has grown to. Is everyone condemned to the levels below Heaven for eternity? The answer is no. Each spirit person in the spirit world can continue to grow their spirit man. This is done by a spirit person in a level of the spirit world descending down to someone in the earthly world, preferably a relative, and tempting them to commit the same sins they had done while alive on earth. If the person in the physical world can overcome that temptation, then not only will the earthly person grow spiritually, but the spirit person that tempted them will also grow. This is why so many people on earth and in the same family have the temptation to commit a crime such as robbery, murder, rape, incest, suicide and so much more. Overcome the temptations and everyone benefits from it. Praying for a spirit is also beneficial. God's intention and desire is that, one day in the future, all souls will be in Heaven. God being our Father could never be happy if even one soul was lost. One can also grow by an earthy person reading and studying the Word of God, such as the Holy Bible, and something else."

"What is that 'something else'? asked Mike. "I only know of the Bible. What else is there?"

"In time you will learn."

"That's the second thing you told me 'in time'," said Mike. "Why not now?"

"Because you're not ready for such information right now. You must learn more."

"So, with all these different levels, where is Paradise?"

"At the top of the Completion Stage," Genia replied.

"And what about God. Where is He, and what is our relationship to Him, if any?" Mike asked.

"God cannot be measured by our idea of an individual. He's transcendent of time and space. In other words, God doesn't have a physical body. He is pure energy. God is a being of emotion, intellect and will. Most of all, God is a God of love. We are his children. And, when we are hurt physically or emotionally, He feels the same, but intensify it ten-fold. When we are happy, He also experiences joy. God is not just 'out there' somewhere, but He is within us. People think they have to do something to satisfy, please or appease God, but His intention is for us to just be our true selves, and for us to be as holy and good as He is. To 'be perfect as our heavenly Father is perfect,' as Jesus said. We relate to God by obedience to rules, laws and so forth, but we should relate to Him through love in our hearts as his children, even as his family. We have no concept that God needs our love. Man doesn't feel the relationship with God as His parent and we as His children, but more as a servant. Also, many people think we should live alone to get closer to Him when God actually wants us to have a family. This is called the Four Position Foundation, which is composed of God, man and woman, and then children. God is the center when many people think they can do it without Him. That was also Lucifer's idea, as well. We think we can only be arms-length from God, when we should be 'one with Him' or be His 'temple', as Jesus said. Humans worship God more like servants or angels, instead of being His sons and daughters. We believe that we are only in an objective position to Him, when we can also be in the subjective position so that *we* can comfort God and take care of *His* needs. Our relationship to God is far more profound than we think or realize."

"Wow! This is some heavy stuff you're laying on me. I don't know if I can get the full concept of everything you have said," responded Mike.

"You will. Another reason you were picked is because you have a photographic mind. You can retain everything told to you so it can be shared with your friends on earth. Also, in your trips here, you'll be able to visit the other realms or levels of the spirit world," Genia added.

"You mean I can freely move back and forth from one level to another?" he asked.

"Yes!" replied Genia. "A spirit person can go to levels below the one they come to be in, but cannot go to levels above the one they're in. The exception is when a soul comes here upon their death, many times they will go to a higher level. This is because when they start at a higher level, they eventually become uncomfortable there, and go down to a level where they are more comfortable. Let me explain something to you. Human life has three major phases. The first phase is in a mother's womb. You live in a liquid world and breathe that way. Second, you come out after nine months and breathe air for some eighty or ninety years. Then third and finally, you die and you come to the spirit world, where in the highest realms you breathe God's love. So, if you didn't have enough love inside of you, it would be difficult to breathe love in the higher realms or levels and you would go back down to a level where you can 1) breathe easily and to fully develop your love-lungs, so to speak; and 2) be with people that are similar to the kind of person you were on earth. For example, thieves with thieves, murderers with murderers, church-goers with church-goers, and so on. Not only can you go down to lower levels, but in your case you will be required to visit all the levels so you can not only tell your friends, but the whole world what you've seen and experienced."

"When can I see Heaven?" asked Mike.

"Before the week is up," promised Genia.

"Please. Can't I see it now? Just a glimpse and I'll be happy, or even ecstatic. I so much want to experience it."

"Soon, Mike. Soon. I promise you."

"If Paradise is this great, I have got to see and feel Heaven... By the way, why do people who have near-death experiences have similar but different stories?"

"Because they go to different levels and each level has different parts with different spirits and entities; similar, yet not the same, based on level."

"So, how do I travel from level to level, and place to place?" asked Mike.

"Just really concentrate and imagine yourself from one place to another. Go to whatever level or area you want. But remember, you must visit at least one spot in each realm so you will have visited all 33 levels."

"Please. Won't you let me visit Heaven just for a few minutes. It will give me great enthusiasm to go on."

"Oh Mike, I feel your heart and desire. But, just for a short time."

"Thank you, Genia. I'm ready whenever you are. Can we go now?"

"Yes! Take my hand and concentrate on a higher level than ever before. Think of heaven, even though you've never been there before. Imagine something so beautiful it staggers your mind. Now, let me take you up and up 'til we reach another place." Mike and Genia drift through another cloud, this time goldish in color. The cloud has the most delightful scent. It becomes more and more dense until finally it begins to dissipate. They are now in a flush valley with flowers of every kind abounding. The fragrance is glorious, as well as the land. The air is full of God's love, in all his glories. The sun shines bright, but as in Paradise, it brings in little heat but a cool breeze. The sky is bustling with gorgeous colors. There are illuminating rays of bursting sunshine. It this isn't Heaven, then nothing else is.

"I'm filled with joy, happiness and contentment as love abounds in me. There's no way I can explain this in words. It's truly exhilarating. A treasure among treasures. Just a few moments here and I never want to leave again. Look! A waterfall. It's gorgeous."

"You'll see billions of things here that will give you millions of years of enjoyment," said Genia. "It's never-ending. God's love abounds limitlessly. The end never comes."

As they reach the top of the valley, Mike is astounded to see a bright, bright city in the distance. After generating thoughts of the city, they appear at the entrance of a marble building that begins the start of a glorious new world. The buildings are all made of stone, marble and even petrified sand. They have a brilliant shine and glow about them. As the two of them walk the streets paved with silver and gold, they come to an extra-bright glowing building with 80 steps leading up to four thrones. Each one is so bright you can't see if anyone is sitting on them or not.

"My God!" said Mike. "Who sits in those four thrones? I'll bet one is for Jesus Christ."

"You're right, Mike. But, can you guess who occupies the other three? If you can guess right, then you can stay here in Heaven."

"That's not fair, Genia. How can I guess who sits in those three thrones. It's not right that I can only stay here in Heaven if I guess right."

"But you will have chances all week long to figure out what three people sit there. When you do, your whole world will change for a God-centered purpose. Then you will qualify to live in Heaven when you die for good."

"Then I will find out who sits in all three thrones!" Mike defiantly determined.

"Yes, Mike. You will if you persevere."

Then, the light around the first throne clears away enough so Mike can see who it is. And Mike falls on his knees as he realizes it is the Lord Jesus Christ. "Dear Lord," he says with all humility, "I am humbled before you. Please accept me into your grace."

It then becomes a brilliant light again, as Mike and Genia are transported back to the place he first met Genia, in Paradise.

"Genia! Why are we back here again?" Mike asks.

"Your time in Heaven has ended for now. Hopefully, you will return one day again forever. You have a mission, and it starts with helping your five friends back on earth. So, go back now and you will return to find out about angels and the angelic world. Also, you must begin your journeys through the different levels of the spirit world. Return now; return back to your physical body back on earth! Return!"

Mike then finds himself back in the hotel room with Joy and everyone else frantically watching him.

"He's coming to, again," exclaimed Joy. "He seems to be all right. Mike. Mike. How are you? You've been out again."

As he slowly sat up, Mike reassured his friends, "I'm fine, everyone. I have a lot to tell you. Please have a seat and we'll begin."

So, Mike explains everything that happened to him while he was in a state of physical death. When he finishes, everyone looks at each other as they start firing questions at him.

"So, you're telling us that there are 33 levels to the spirit world?" asks Sharon.

"Yes, but each level has a million miles of different parts where people have their own personalities, mistakes, evil and goodness unique to them. No two places are exactly alike, even on the same level. Spirits stick to those other spirits with which they share commonalities."

"You say there are a million miles to each level?" asks Billy.

"Figuratively speaking," responds Mike. "It could be thousands or it could be billions; remember, Genia said the spirit world is as large as our galaxy. There is no real measure as to time and space in the spirit world. It's boundless."

"Christ? What did he look like?" asked Doreen.

"Unlike the descriptions of him throughout the centuries where he's tall, slender, blond hair and blue eyes. He's actually shorter, around 5'8" to 5'10", quite stocky, brown hair and best I could tell from a distance, he had dark eyes. He *did* have a beard and long hair."

"You say this woman, Genia, was going to tell you about angels and the angelic world. *This* I would love to hear about, providing of course that all this happened the way you say it did," said John.

51

"Well, you all admit that I *was* dead, and then miraculously came back to life. *Something* happened to me during that time."

"That's just it, Mike," responded Joy. "I believe you, as does Doreen. But, just to us, only seconds elapsed during your down time. We all heard your explanation for this, but still it's skeptical for John, Billy and Sharon. If only you had more proof."

"It's 2:40 right now. Why don't we all go down and relax and enjoy ourselves for a couple of hours before returning to the Hotel to meet Braxton and Silver at 6:00. Maybe in the meantime, I can think of something," suggested Mike.

"That sounds like a winner. We can start at the Roulette Wheel and then go on to another place someone else would like to go to. That should help us clear our minds," said John.

They all agree and proceed to the nearest Roulette Wheel. John takes the first shot at the Wheel.

"I think I'll put ten dollars on 23 Black. That's one of my favorite numbers," declares John.

Mike pauses a few seconds, then turns to John and advises him… "Put your money on 8 Red!"

"Why? Do you know something I don't know? I mean are you psychic now?" challenges John.

"Just do it, John! What do you have to lose, except for the ten bucks?" shoots back Mike.

"All right, Mike." He looks for the caller and tells him: "Ten on 8 Red!"

"All bets are in. And around she goes." The wheel turns as John anxiously waits for it to stop. The wheel slows down and the tiny ball finds its mark. "8 Red, and the gentleman wins!" the caller announces.

"Mike! How did you know?" excitedly asks John. "Was it a coincidence, or did you *really* know?"

"Let's find out. Put all your winnings on 18 Black. Hurry!" Mike tells him.

John nervously puts his winnings on 18 Black. The other four wait patiently as the wheel spins around and around until finally it stops. "18 Black!" yells the caller. "The lucky man wins again."

"This is fabulous, Mike. Do it again!" said John.

"No! No more. This isn't a game," answered Mike.

"But it *is* a game. A game of chance," said John.

"It's not chance; it's cheating. I just wanted to prove a point," said Mike.

"Which is?"

"That I'm becoming spiritually open and sensitive to everything around me. I can foresee certain futures. This includes people around me, and it's unnerving. Besides, why be interested in winning several thousand when we're talking about ten million each. I want to go back upstairs to our room now."

"Okay, Mike," said Joy. "Come on, guys. Mike needs our support. Let's go back to the room."

Everyone agrees and proceeds upstairs. When they get there, they talk to Mike. "What do you mean when you say you can foretell the future of people around you?" asked Doreen.

"It doesn't happen all the time, but when I touch someone, sometimes I can see into their future or even past. And, as for gambling, I can see the results before they occur," said Mike.

"How does this happen to you?" asked Billy.

"I'm sure it has to do with me visiting the spirit world. Because of the time difference there seems to be, I think I've brought this back with me."

"Is it that bad, knowing the results of gambling chances or knowing someone's past or present or even future?" asked John.

"In terms of gambling, as I said earlier, it's cheating," said Mike. "To make money this way, a price would have to be paid spiritually by all concerned. What price that is, I do not know. And, as of knowing one's past, present or future, it's not fun, nor is it rewarding in any way. You don't know what you'll find out. It could be extremely disturbing." Mike then collapses on the floor.

"Is he having another episode again?" asked Sharon in surprise.

Mike responds from the floor, saying "No! I'm not. I'm just dizzy. Please help me up."

The other five all help Mike to his feet. Mike then sees flashes of everyone.

"What's the matter, Mike? You look as though you've seen a ghost, if you pardon my saying," said Billy.

"When all of you touched me, I had a vision of you and myself," said Mike.

"What did you see?" asked Joy.

"We were all in some kind of basement, running in terror from something," said Mike.

"Is that all you can tell us?" said John.

"I'm just a man having a vision. I'm not a swami!" said Mike.

"Then maybe the next time you visit the other side, you could find out more," replied John.

"Does that mean you believe me when I tell you of my out-of-body experiences?"

"Right now, I think we're all ready to believe anything," John said.

"SHHHHHH!"

"What's the matter, Mike?" whispered John.

"Someone is listening outside our door," Mike said as John quickly goes to the door and opens it up. He finds a thinly balding man in his thirties, standing outside.

"WHAT DO YOU WANT" shouted John angrily, "and why were you listening at our door?"

"I made a mistake. I was at the wrong room," replied the man.

"You're telling us you made a mistake, alright. Come into our room right now; you have some explaining to do," demanded John. The man suddenly starts running down the hall as John yells to him… "COME BACK HERE YOU LITTLE WORM. COME BACK! We know what you look like."

"Leave him be, John. This wasn't the last we'll see and hear from him again," said Mike.

Everyone looks at Mike puzzled… "Do you know this man?" asked Joy.

"Not yet, but we all will in the coming days. Right now, I suggest we go back to the Stanwick Hotel and get ready for Braxton and Silver," said Mike.

"Was this another demonstration of your, shall we say… power," asked Sharon.

"I was just in tune to him. He means no harm now that I've picked up from his spirit. He's in great distress."

"I think we're all in distress right now. With everything you've told us, and/or confided in us, I'm worried and frightened," said Sharon.

"A better reason we should do what Mike suggests and go back to the Stanwick," added Joy.

"On the way to town, I think we would all want to hear what you think of all this, Joy. I mean, you have been chosen to give us all advice," reminded Sharon.

"Sure, Sharon. While driving back." So, the six check out and head back down to town while Joy gives her opinion about everything.

"First of all, I *do* believe Mike's story about where he went while unconscious; all except for his actually visiting Heaven," said Joy. "I believe he went somewhere, but not to Heaven. It's a fact that while he was out, he *was* clinically dead. The rest of his story I believe."

"Then why not Heaven?" asked Doreen.

"Because I don't believe anyone can see Heaven until they're dead for good, permanently, never to come back. It's reserved for these people," answered Joy.

"Then, you don't believe he saw Jesus, either, or even the four thrones."

"That's right, Doreen. I *do* believe he could visit the other realms, but Heaven is reserved for all the souls that are going there for eternity. As for his 'powers' as you call them, I do believe they were bestowed upon him by the spirit elements that he encountered. He possesses a remarkable sense of grandeur, if you want to call it that. He does have extraordinary powers; something we can't understand, but nonetheless he has them."

"Then you also believe his vision of all of us running in terror from something," said Billy.

"I'm afraid so. I just wish we knew more," replied Joy.

"You're not the only one," said Billy, as everyone shows their agreement. "What do you think about Braxton and Silver? Are they really going to give us ten million dollars each of we stay the week?"

"Yes! But, staying the week isn't what they really want from us. It's the other stuff that bothers me. You can be sure it's not going to be a walk in the park for the money, but something much more challenging than we can fathom."

"And you have no guess as to what?" asks Billy.

"That department is reserved for Mike. He's the one of us that might be able to figure out what they want from all of you. As far as myself, I believe there's more to it than just giving out advice. It just not that simple."

"Well, what do you have to say about this, Mike?" asked Sharon. "Can you tell us their intentions for us, or are you at a loss, too?"

"I'm glad to be included in the conversation. I was beginning to think you forgot I was here since you were speaking about me as if I weren't," said Mike.

"Sorry, Mike. We didn't mean to omit you," said Joy.

"That's all right since I'm doing the driving, I guess. But, in reference to their ulterior motives, I have to at least be around them to pick up anything that would help us. That's the way it works, guys. If I can't touch someone, I at least have to be near them."

"I guess everyone will have to give Mike some time. Then maybe he can inform us of something pertinent," advised Joy.

"I forgot my watch at the Stanwick this morning. Who has the time, please?" asked John. Doreen informs him that it's now 4:10. "Good. We'll be arriving around 5; time enough for

57

freshening up before 6." Just then, Mike swerves the car to the shoulder of the mountain road.

"What the hell happened?" shouts Billy.

"Didn't you see that?" said Mike. "Across the road. It ran across the road."

"But, we weren't looking out the front," said Joy as everyone shakes their heads. "We were all in conversation. What *did* you see?"

"Someone or something ran across the road right in front of us. It was so fast. I didn't get a good look at it," said Mike.

"It was probably a dear or some other related animal," said Joy. "What gave you the idea that it might have been a person?"

"Because this deer, or whatever it was, ran on two legs, not four. But from the quick glance I caught, it didn't look human."

"Oh great! Now we have monsters in our picture," said John. "This is going too far, Mike. What do you say we keep on driving?"

"No! I saw it go into the woods over there. I'm going in there to see if I can find someone or something," as he starts to get out of the vehicle. "Is anybody going to come with me? I need someone to confirm anything I see."

"John, why don't you go with Mike?" Joy asks.

"Are you kidding? I'm not looking for a close encounter of *any* kind."

"But, it's still daylight out there," she adds.

"Forget him, Joy. I'll go with Mike," says Billy.

"Thanks, Billy. You should be ashamed of yourself, John," blasts Joy.

"You save your analyzing for your patients, Joy."

As Sharon and Doreen whisper to each other that they now know who has the guts in the vehicle, Billy jumps out. "Mike! Wait up. I'm coming with you," as the two men run off into the woods together.

"I think I saw it come this way," says Mike.

"Please don't refer to him or her as 'it'," pleads Billy. "It gives me the creeps."

"Sorry! How about you go that way and I'll go this way. If it *is* someone, they could be hurt."

"All right. How about if we meet back here in, in 15 minutes?"

"Fine, but if you find someone, yell out," said Mike.

"Oh, don't worry! I will," assured a nervous Billy. The two men split up and go in opposite directions. The woods are eerily quiet now as Mike makes his way deeper into them. He whispers to himself, "It's really dead out here."

"Hello! Is somebody out there?" he shouts.

"There's no sound out here; not animals or birds or even the sound of insects. But, most of all, no people," he mumbles to himself. "I wonder if Billy has found something? Whoa! What's that? I hear rustling."

"BILLY! IS THAT YOU?" He shouts... "IS ANYBODY OUT THERE!"

Mike walks deeper and deeper into the woods. He then realizes he should start heading back to meet Billy. Mike suddenly feels a presence nearby. He starts to freak out and starts walking faster and faster. He calls out to Billy, but there is no reply. "I think this was a bad idea, coming out here like this," he tells himself. "I'd better find Billy and get back to the minivan.

But, I know there's something right on my tail. But, damn it, I can't see anything. What's out there? I hope Billy's okay."

As Mike moves along, he trips over a log and falls down. As he gets up, he senses something behind him. His heart starts pounding as if it were going to throb right out of his chest. His hands get clammy, his legs go weak, his vision blurs. Out of his mind with fear, he realizes that it must be Billy. One hand goes on his shoulder and squeezes on the shoulder blade. His anxiousness and fright now elude him as he speaks out… "Billy, I've been looking for you."

As Mike turns around, he is horrified to see the figure of the demon from his nightmares, standing just a foot away from him. All of a sudden, his terrified heartbeats accompany his cloud of fear as he crumbles and calls out in utter frightfulness; a cry that makes him feel like an ultra-scared eight-year-old facing his ultimate fears. The wind and leaves blow in his face as he cries out.

"MY GOD! HOW COULD *YOU* BE HERE? YOU WERE ONLY IN MY…"

"Nightmares. Is that it? That was just the beginning. You'll find I'll be with you in both your dreams and every waking moment of your life."

"How could that me?" Mike says in desperation. "Who are you? What are you?" Then, Mike hears Billy's voice behind him.

"Mike! I… WHAT THE HELL IS THAT?" yells Billy as the apparition disappears. "Mike! Are you all right?"

"Yes! Let's get back to the others and get back to town. I'll explain everything on our way back. Let's get out of here!"

The two of them get back to the minivan and drive back to the Hotel in town. At 5:30, all six of them are in Mike's room, discussing all that has happened.

"It's only Monday, early evening, and already we've had a week of thrills and action," said Joy. "When I gave you therapy, Mike, I never dreamed of all that could happen, especially your nightmare demon coming to actual reality. I would still be questioning you if it weren't for the fact that Billy witnessed it too."

"That was absolutely terrifying for me," said Mike. "It's my nightmare come into reality."

"Well, it wasn't thrills for me, either," said Billy. "If I hadn't seen it myself, I'd have to admit, I probably wouldn't have believed it any more than you guys."

"What's the matter, Sharon?" asked Joy.

"It makes me think of the things that have happened to me."

"If we stick together most of the time, we should at least be able to comfort one another. It helps to know you're not alone. We all have a stake in this."

"So, what do we do from here?" asked John.

"We should probably freshen up, then go meet in the Conference Room," answered Joy.

"Sound advice. Let's do it," said Mike.

The six of them get ready, and then go to meet in the Conference Room at 5:55. As they sit and wait, at precisely 6:00 p.m. George Braxton and Grea Silver walk in and go to the front.

Billy whispers to Mike... "Where did you go before? You just disappeared."

"Speaking of disappearing, you'll find out after the meeting," answered Mike.

"Just see if you can pick anything up from these guys with whatever it is you have," he said.

"I trust you all had a pleasant day," said George.

"No, we didn't. But, the two of you know more than you're saying, isn't that true?" asked Mike.

"I'll admit, we do know more about your circumstances than one may assume," said George. "But, that just brings me to the next order of business. What and how we know is not important at this time. You will all learn in good time. What *is* important is that today and the rest of the week, you will all have to help one another as well as others. You must learn to unite together and tend to each other's needs and problems. It's crucial that - you might say - become a family. And yes, Ms. Bender, this includes yourself, as well. You may not be the recipient of ten million dollars, but the information, techniques and experiences you learn will become invaluable to you in your work. But, for your time and effort helping everyone else, you *will* receive a check for three million dollars.

"Not too shabby for a week's work," John whispers to Joy.

"You'll receive the three million dollars regardless of what everyone else decides. So, you can say you are the sixth person to join our family," proclaimed George.

"Is there going to be anyone else joining us during our week-long excursion?" asked Joy.

"There will be other people the six of you will help, but no, there will be no further additions to the six of you. After tonight's meeting, we will not meet again until Thursday at noon. Trust me. There will be things to do until then. The minivan will be at your disposal until Sunday. Which brings me to my next point of business. I have a house located in Idaho Springs in the mountains. I realize you're all reserved here in the Stanwick all week, but I would like each of you to go up there Wednesday and spend the night there. This will be especially significant to one of you in which the rest of you can assist with their problem," said George.

"Why do we have to be secluded away?" asked Doreen.

"We need to see how you can handle yourselves just by yourselves with no outside help. And, since the house is a mile from any other, that makes it perfect. On Thursday noon, we will discuss what has transpired from now 'til then. Remember, help each other and help those around you in desperate need. You must have Faith and Hope."

"It seems to me that we're proving it every day that we stay," said Mike.

"And that you have," said George. "You will especially need it at the end of the week when you make your final decision. Nothing worthwhile in life comes easily, but the six of you have the capability to accomplish almost anything. Now unless there are any questions, I'll leave you with the instructions to the house along with the keys." After a few moments… "Fine. We'll see you at noon on Thursday. Good luck!"

Everyone gets up and walks out of the Conference Room, closing the door behind them. After a few minutes, Mike goes over to Billy. "Billy! Are you ready?" he asks.

"Ready for what?"

"To see if Braxton and Silver are in the room." So, the two of them go over and open the door, seeing no sign of either man. "See, I knew they would be gone again."

"And again, they probably left through the exit door," said Billy.

63

"We'll see. Come with me," said Mike.

"Where are we going?" asked Billy.

"Earlier you wanted to know where I had disappeared to. I'm going to show you." They leave the Conference Room, go out another exit door, and wind around until they come to the back of still another exit door.

"Just as I thought. You see, this is the back of the exit door inside Conference Room Three. As you can see, I put a chair up against it so that anyone in the room couldn't get out this way. I know because I tried it myself. I couldn't budge it," said Mike.

"But suppose you just loosened it, and then Braxton and Silver were able to get the door opened, leave through it, and then they simply placed the chair back against the door. Isn't that possible?" asked Billy.

"In the remote chance that happened, I took a fool proof precaution. Take a look at the floor under the chair."

"Why, it's powder. A very thin layer of powder. One could hardly see it, but it's there," said Billy.

"Just in case they *did* open the exit door, they would have disturbed the powder, and even if they saw it, unless one of them just happened to be carrying a container of powder, the powder on the floor would have been disturbed if they came this way. As you can plainly see, it's undisturbed. So, there's no way they could have gone through this door," concluded Mike.

"Then how the heck did they get out of that room without any of us seeing them?" asked Billy.

"Well, that's the million-dollar, or should I say the ten-million-dollar question."

"Right now, I'll settle for a thousand-dollar answer," said Billy.

"Come on. Let's get back to the others before they wonder where *we* have gone," said Mike.

"Do you think we should say something about this whole thing now to them?"

"Still, not quite yet. I will tell Joy though for two reasons: One, she has her laptop with her and I can use her help with it, especially since no one else thought to bring one along with them. And two, Braxton and Silver seem to trust her a little more than the rest of us. Something we might be able to use to our advantage. As for Doreen, Sharon and John, we can tell them Wednesday at the house in Idaho Springs when we know a little more. As for myself, I picked up some very strange vibes from the two of them which I will also share with them all Wednesday. In the meantime, I'll just have to hold off their curiosity about what I've learned 'til then."

"You know they'll be looking to you and Joy for answers," Billy reminded him. "How are you going to stall 'til Wednesday? Besides, I'm curious myself. What *did* you pick up?"

"All in good time, Billy. All in good time. Now, let's get back to the others."

After removing the chair and cleaning up the powder, Mike and Billy join the other four and then promptly go up to Joy's room. Once there, they do ask Mike what, if anything, he picked up on Braxton and Silver. Mike casually tells them he got a blank on them, but he'll try again on Thursday when they meet. Accepting his excuse, being tired from the day, they all turned in, except for Mike who stayed in Joy's room. He explains what has transpired and begins to tell Joy just what he did really pick up from Braxton and Silver.

"It's strange, Joy. Actually, some of what I told the others was true, in the sense that I picked up nothing. But, that's the point," said Mike. "When I say 'nothing', I mean absolutely nothing, like they didn't even exist; no past, no present, and no thoughts about a future. I don't know. Maybe I couldn't pick up anything because I just wasn't open enough."

"Can't you tell the difference as to which is which?"

"I'm new to this, Joy. What I think I'm picking up in this instance could merely be my ineptness to read other people," said Mike. "But, I do know one thing, and that is, I'm not giving up. I want another crack at them, and by Thursday I'll have my reading under full control. So, there won't be any questions about what I do or don't read. All I need is a couple of more days of practice in order to fine tune my abilities."

"Then keep practicing until you're sure of yourself. You said there was something I could do to help."

"Yes! You know I'm not good at computer work since I acquired this new talent, and I need to find something out about Braxton and Silver. I need you to do it for me. Besides, I trust you most right now. Also, I don't want any of the others to catch on to my reservations. I did tell Billy a lot, but not everything. As for John, Sharon or Doreen, they're completely in the dark about any of this."

"What exactly do you want me to look up?" asked Joy.

"Braxton said he was born in Fairbanks, Alaska while Silver was born in Anchorage. I would like you to check out the census bureau of both places and see if they told us the truth. We can narrow the year to within one since Braxton said he was 63 and Silver one year younger than he. How long will that take you on your laptop?"

"Well, knowing their names, first *and* last, and their exact age, it won't take me very long at all."

"Good! Then you wouldn't mind me waiting here while you do it?"

"No, not at all," said Joy. "Just be patient."

"Oh, I will. You can count on it," replied Mike.

A short time lapses and Joy announces that she has one more thing to check out. After another fairly long wait, Joy tells Mike she's finished.

"What did you find out?"

"Well, this is more interesting than even I thought. Not only weren't they born in those cities, but there's no record of either of them being born in Alaska."

"I knew it," said Mike. "They lied. We know that much. But, why did it take you so long to find that out? I thought you said it was pretty simple to find out?"

"That's the reason why this became extra-interesting and mysterious. Not that there's no legitimate reason for it, but neither of them were born *anywhere* in the United States, and I'm sure of it," said Joy.

"My God! Where the hell were they born, then? They also have no accent of where they could have come from. I mean, do you think they could be spies? And maybe they never left the conference room, but were hiding there for some reason."

"I don't know. It doesn't make sense. Why would they be hiding there. For what logical purpose? And, not just once, but three times. There's no reason for it."

"None that I know of," replied Mike, "but for them it could have been for a very purposeful reason. Is there any way we can find out where they come or came from?"

"Yes, but it will take a much more powerful computer than what I have. I'm into this thing now; I have to find out for all our sakes where they're from. I'm willing to invest in a far better computer. I've been thinking about it for some time now, and this time is as good as any to buy one. So, tomorrow I'll find an appropriate outlet and go there, wherever that may be. Then can you excuse me to the others for not being with them for however long that may be?"

"Sure, Joy. I'll do that. And when you get back, find out exactly where they were born. Once you find out, please get ahold of me so I can come back to your room because I'm dying to find out."

"Sure. But, speaking of you dying, I hope you don't have an episode while I'm away. I should be there when you have one."

"I hope not, too. But, as you know, I don't have any control over that; when, or where, I have no idea."

"I know, Mike. It may just take me a couple of hours or all day long. I don't know, either. At least until I find out where, then I'll have some idea. If you give me another 20 minutes, then I can find out where the computer outlet is and approximately how long I'll be."

"Fine. It'll be worth the short wait. But, I thought you were going to do that in the morning?"

"Changed my mind," said Joy. "I thought it better that you know approximately when I'll return. Also, it'll give me a chance to leave early in the morning before any of the others come down. This way, it will avoid the possibility of someone asking to go along with me. I won't have to explain anything until we both have found out first. I really hate having to be so sneaky about all this, but before we say anything outrageous about Braxton and Silver, we need more concrete proof."

"I agree. Guess it's time for me to sit back down and wait again," sighed Mike.

"As I said, it'll be about 20 minutes."

After about an hour passes, Mike finally blurts out, "Joy! I don't mean to be impatient, but you did say 20 minutes, and it's been over an hour. Is there a problem of some kind?"

"No! As a matter of fact, I'll be finished in just a few more minutes. So, please hold on... There, all finished. It took me a lot longer because I decided to get a laptop with fingerprint identification since we can't be sure they're even using their real names, which if they're not, would make our efforts a total waste of time."

"Heck, I didn't think of that, in which case the info we already found could be totally deceiving. But, identification through fingerprints would be foolproof."

"That's right," said Joy, "but to check worldwide would take a little more than 24 hours. Unless, of course, we lucked out and ID'd them from their birthplace pretty quickly."

"That's great. We'll know one way or another, in no more than 24 hours. Wow. I didn't think of this, but that kind of laptop must cost you a fortune."

"As you just said, it *is* an investment. I felt for a while I needed one. And now, with my plans for the future, it'll come in very handy. Which reminds me, I'll need *your* hand for some help."

"Anything!" said Mike. "Just name it."

"Since I'll have the capability to search for their birthplace with their fingerprints, I'll naturally *need* their fingerprints. That's going to be *your* job, Mike."

"I was really afraid you were going to say that. How long do I have?"

"Well, the outlet is down south in Colorado Springs. I wish John could direct me since that's where he's from. But, since this is without his knowledge, I'll have to find it on my own. So, give me two hours to get there, two hours in the outlet, and another two hours to return. I'm leaving at 6 a.m. so I'll be back sometime around noon. If we stall our departure on Wednesday 'til 1:00 or 2:00, then we'll have their real names and location of birth. Knowing their room numbers as we do, do you think you could get their prints by the time I get back?"

"I think I can, with a plan I already formulated in my mind. I will need the help of the other four. I can do it giving them minimal information. Yes! I know I can do it by the time you return. I just have to catch everyone early in the morning. Since I don't know when Braxton and Silver leave, I have to put some letters on their doors tonight."

"Good!" replied Joy. "I trust your abilities. I guess then I'll see you in your room around noon tomorrow. Have a good night, Mike."

"You too, Joy." The two wink their pinkies at each other and then leave for the night. In Mike's room, Mike writes a letter, then copies it and puts them on Braxton's and Silver's doors. The letter is short, but to the point. It goes as follows:

Dear Gentlemen,

This is Mike Wakings. Something of the utmost urgent matter has arisen and I need to speak to the two of you this morning. So, please meet me in Conference Room 3. This concerns all six of us and yourselves. So, please meet me there at 10:00 a.m. sharp. Unless we meet, the six of us will not be able to stay the rest of the week. You both know that would be a shame. See you at 10:00 a.m.

Sincerely Yours,
Mike Wakings

Mike then goes to his room and to sleep. The next morning he awakes at 6 a.m., cleans up, and then goes to everybody's room and tells them – even though most are half asleep – to meet in his room at 8:00. Groggily, they agree. The time passes, and by 8:10, all five of them are in Mike's room.

"Where's Joy?" asks Sharon. "Isn't she coming?"

"No. Joy won't be back 'til noon, or sometime near to that. You see, she went to Colorado Springs to get a special laptop that will give us important information pertaining to Braxton and Silver."

"She should have told me," said John. "I'm from there and I could have helped. Besides, what kind of information on them is she getting, and when will we have it?"

"Do all of you trust Joy and myself?" asked Mike.

Everyone agrees with a 'yes', especially since they've only been together for a couple of days, they show amazing trust for them. It is trust you don't develop in a normal relationship.

"Why do you ask at this time?" says Billy.

"Because we're asking all of you to have that trust now. And regarding when, the latest would be right before we're supposed to leave for Idaho Springs. It could, though, be as soon as this afternoon if what we're looking for comes sooner, if we're lucky.

I'm telling you more than Joy or I had planned at this point. That's because we don't want to make a mountain out of a molehill and feel like complete idiots for something that might be explained away simply. Let me tell you what I have planned for Braxton and Silver. I wrote a short letter to each of them explaining it's an emergency that they meet me in Conference Room 3 at 10:00 a.m., otherwise all six of us would leave before the seven days are up. Unknowing to them, all five of us will be waiting there for both of them. We'll say we were meeting in order to thank them and have a toast to seal the commitment."

"But Mike, don't you think they're going to be pretty pissed off at you and maybe the rest of us as well," said John.

"I'm sure they will be. That's where you two ladies come in and soften them up. I'll calm things down from my end. Once they are calmed down, we'll then have a toast. At the end, which will probably be quite soon, they'll leave. At this point, I'll take the glasses they used very carefully and get their fingerprints off of them in my room. When Joy gets back, everything will be ready for her."

"Is that what all this is for?" asks Doreen. "Their prints? And, by the way, what are they for?"

"Again, I ask you to just trust us. We *will* explain everything to all of you very soon. Just make sure you don't grab their glasses. I'll get them as soon as we're sure they're gone. Let's make this as quick and short as possible. Any questions?"

The four of them ask Mike several questions as he answers them one-by-one. At the end, Mike starts talking to the group when suddenly he falls to the floor. Everyone gathers around him.

"Oh my gosh," says Sharon. "It's happening again. Joy isn't here, so what should we do?"

"Let me feel for his heart beat," said John... "There is none. I'm afraid he's gone back to wherever it is he goes to."

Mike travels back to the place he's becoming very familiar with as he sees Genia appearing again. Meanwhile, back in the Hotel room, everyone is quite upset when all of a sudden Doreen collapses to the floor, as well.

"Good heavens!" shouts Billy. "What's happened to Doreen, now? She was fine a minute ago."

"I'd better check her heart... My God, her heart has stopped, too."

Billy, John and Sharon go into a frenzy. After Mike and Doreen see everyone frozen, Doreen goes through the same phase as she did after her accident. Mike goes through his phase.

"Welcome back, Mike," greets Genia. "I see you're a little more at ease with your surroundings this time."

"I am. Tell me, is there anything more I can do to convince the others that my visits here and elsewhere are true?"

"That's coming right now," says Genia. Tilting her head, Doreen appears to the right of Mike.

"Doreen!" shouts Mike. "What are *you* doing here?"

"I don't know. One moment I was with the others, leaning over your body, then the next moment I saw everyone like you, frozen in time. Then, I went through what I told all of you and then expected to be in the pasture, when instead I came here with you. And, let me guess, this is Genia?"

"Yes! But why, Genia? Why Doreen?"

"Because of her previous spiritual visit, it was simpler to bring her back. And you asked for some more proof. Well, Doreen is it. She'll go back in a while and confirm everything that you had told them. It will be easier to believe both of your stories instead of just yours, Mike. And, when you return to your body, a short time will have elapsed due to Doreen returning, but nothing compared to the time you would have spent here. You see, Doreen, Mike is about to journey to other realms of the spirit world."

"I am? When and where?" asked Mike.

"Now Mike, you're going to start traveling in just a moment. You're in Paradise, or in other words, the top of the Completion stage. Think of a place lower than this; one of the other 31 levels below us. I suggest you don't travel to one too low, for you may not be ready for it yet. Just imagine it in your mind and you will be there... Now think; think of another realm and imagine being there."

Once again, Mike is engulfed in the bluish cloud and then disappears. Genia turns to Doreen, discusses a few things with her, and then sends her back into her body in Mike's Hotel room. As Doreen wakes, she informs the others of what has transpired. Shocked and amazed, they are now past the point of not believing Mike. They are ready to believe.

Back in Paradise, Genia herself disappears and then reappears with Mike. "Genia! You followed me. Is that good or bad? And, where are we? It's very grayish and cool here. As you can see, there are many houses and even apartments. But, they look run down."

"I followed you because you need guidance as you travel. It's neither good nor bad. As for where we are, you brought us to level six, which is the first level of Formation. As you may remember, there are Formation, Growth and Completion realms. And, to each realm there are nine levels above the five lower levels of hell. This is one area of level six. Let's walk down the street with the houses."

As they do, Mike notices what seems to be boarded up houses, but yet people occupy them. Coming down the street is a man pushing a grocery cart filled with food and even electronics. As he begins to pass them, he steps over to talk with them.

"Stay away from my stuff!" shouted the man. "If either of you try to take something, I'll have to hit you. Stay away I say!"

"Relax," responded Mike. "We're not trying to take any of your stuff. We…"

"Don't lie to me! I know you're thieves. Keep away! keep away!" The man quickly pushes the cart past them.

Then, a man and a woman come out of one of the houses that seems to be boarded up. The woman starts screaming! "Who stole our stereo? Come back here with it, you thief!"

"Come back inside, sweetheart," her friend said. "We'll just have to steal another one ourselves."

"What's going on here, Genia?" asked Mike. "Everyone is so paranoid about stealing."

"You brought us to an area where all the people here were thieves themselves when they lived on earth. Now they're bound to an area where everyone steals from each other. There's no peace here until the day they can all be liberated to a higher realm."

A car comes down the street and stops by Mike and Genia while the man inside yells out to them, "Did you see him come by this way?"

"Who?" Mike responds. "What are you talking about?"

"The guy who took my son's minibike."

"Neither one of us saw anything like that," answers Mike.

"You're a liar; both of you. You're probably in on it. I should run both of you over. Now get out of my way or I will."

The man speeds away, leaving Mike all tense and Genia with an attitude of "Well, what do you expect?"

"My God!" said Mike. "This is like hell itself."

"I warned you," said Genia. "I warned you about going to a level too low. This is just one level above hell."

"Good Lord. Then what is hell really like?" he wondered.

"It depends on which level of hell you're referring to. Level one, remember, is the rock bottom of hell. Don't go there until you're completely ready. It's going to take a little time to be prepared for such a place," answered Genia."

"How horrible to always be in fear of being robbed while, on the other hand, having the pressure of knowing you have to steal, yourself, to live. You said this is just one area of this level. What are the other areas like?"

"Oh, they are filled with people with other fixations and addictions to different things," she replied.

"Can we check out just one more such place?" asked Mike.

"If you really want to, but why?"

"Because if I'm going to deal with people from all walks of life on earth, then I need to learn about what they're really going through. Also, I need to learn what kind of thinking commits people to be here in the spirit world by their life on earth. I must learn as much as I can in order to help these people; not just on earth but here as well. If time is really almost suspended on earth while I'm here, then I can spend a lot of time learning about all different levels *and* areas while very little time has passed on earth."

"I'm happy to hear the sincere reason you want to check places out. You *will* be able to help a lot of people here in the spirit world as well as back on earth. Also, time is almost frozen on earth in special circumstances, but as of most times one visits the spirit world, time will run as normal on earth as it does here. It's now running at an extremely slow pace while you're here because your time on earth is very valuable this week, more so than others. We don't do it too often… Now, as you wish," said Genia. "We'll go to one more area in this level; then I'll allow you to visit levels and areas all by yourself. After about a week here, then I'll return you back to your body on earth where only minutes have elapsed. Are you ready?"

Mike nods.

"Then, imagine yourself in another area of this same level. Think; think hard."

Then Mike disappears into the cloud as Genia follows him. They now appear in a small town with a population of about 7,000. It's hazy and seems like dusk, even though the time is 1:00 p.m. by the City clock. There are very few people on the streets and sidewalks. A shabbily-dressed man in his mid-thirties comes up to Mike and Genia.

"You two look out-of-place here. Have you come from somewhere else to get some of what we've got?" asked the man.

"We definitely come from somewhere else, but we don't even know what it is you people have here." said Mike.

"Just about everything," answered the man. "We have heroine, cocaine, speed, weed, as well as prescription drugs. Vicaden, Percoset, Morphine, Oxicotton, all strengths as well as Valium, pep pills, sleeping pills, you name it, we've got it."

"Who are 'we' you keep talking about?" asked Mike.

"Why, we're the traders, of course. We offer the most for the least amount of vitality from your spirit man. Hey, wait a minute. You guys are much higher spirits from higher parts of the spirit world. We've got nothing for either of you here, so get lost! Unless, of course, you *do* want something of what we've got, then you're both welcome. For you, of course, we require a higher payment." Then, another man quickly comes down the street to the dealer.

"Hey jack. Have any special deals today?" asked the man.

"We do," he replied. "But, you're tapped out this month. Come back next cycle and then we can do something for you. As for now, Frank, we can't help."

"Come on!" responds Frank, very shaky and sweaty. "You know I'm good for it!"

"Yes, I know that. But rules prohibit me from taking vitality from anyone's spirit man more than a month at a time. How many times have you people been told to ration your supply out? You're one of the worst. Most people that use their supply up before the end of the month usually are two or three days early. In your case, you're always five or six days to a week early. How many times have we gone through this, Frank? And the answer is always the same. You first have to wait until time is up. It's too bad, but that's that."

"Hey guys!" Frank turns and says to Mike and Genia. "Can either of you help me. Can you get me some stuff and I'll pay you back double vitality when my time is up in six more days."

"I'm sorry," said Mike. "We can't help you. We're really sorry."

"Why don't you let the lady speak for herself?" objected Frank. "What do you say, mam? Can *you* help?"

"I'm sorry too," answered Genia, "but my friend does speak for both of us. Hold on a little longer. All of you will be helped soon."

"I DON'T NEED SOON! I NEED NOW! *PLEASE*!"

"Leave them alone, Frank," said Jack. "Go home and I'll come by right after I talk to my friends here. Then maybe, just maybe I'll be able to help you out. So, go home… NOW!"

"Really? All right, Jack. I'll go home. But, please hurry as fast as you can." So Frank slinks back to his home and waits for what seems like an eternity.

"I thought you said rules prohibit you from helping anyone that has used up their so-called spirit man vitality?" asked Mike.

"These rules are meant to be guidelines. We can go past these guidelines whenever we deem fit. So, how about the two of you? Do you want anything, or not? There's only a handful of us and we got hundreds of people to take care of. I can't afford to waste any more time with you if you're not interested in anything I have."

"I'm afraid not. Or maybe I should say we're happy we don't want *or* need anything," answered Mike.

"Fine!" said Jack. "As I said before, get lost! You two don't belong here, anyway. Good bye!"

As Jack walks away, people from all walks of life start to come to him; people with desperation in their bodies; people who will do anything for just one more dose of their favorite choice of drug.

"I truly feel sorry for all these folks," said Mike. "Tell me, Genia, what do they mean by getting vitality from people's spirit man?"

"Everything is made up of energy. It's the same for earthly beings. Every person has a physical body and a spirit which is called a spirit man. This spirit man grows either with good or bad vitality elements depending on what one does while on earth, or should I say *back* on earth. When your physical body is worn out and one dies on earth, they go to the realm and level in the spirit world where their spirit man has grown to, according to their actions on earth. Since one's spirit man has vitality elements, either good or bad, it has energy either way. That energy, or vitality, is what allows even a spirit to exist. Actions you do in the spirit world use some of your vitality elements, in which case you become weaker. Some spirits have the ability to draw elements from another spirit. In this case, Jack and people like him have that ability and use it to trade for people's vitality elements. They then store this vitality to make themselves more powerful. In other cases, they in-turn trade the vitality elements to other spirits, all low or evil ones since no good spirit would take someone else's vitality. This is what gives evil spirits power and they become more powerful to attack people on the earthly plane. Also, once an evil spirit is powerful enough, then they can even steal vitality from weak spirits. It becomes a horrible, endless cycle until something powerful enough can change this whole dilemma. The evil spirits that gain enough vitality from the lowest levels are known as demons," explained Genia.

"What can be done to stop them, or even to help these low spirits go up to higher levels, even those in hell?" asked Mike. "I know you mentioned some spirits working with earthly people can grow, but what about those that are so far gone, or are in such low levels that they are trapped there? How can they grow?"

"For those answers, you'll have to wait awhile. Be patient. Everything must be revealed to you in its proper time," said Genia.

"Why is it that everyone, including myself, tells someone they have to wait and be patient for an answer to questions?"

"Because, as you know by keeping answers from *your own* friends 'til they could accept them, people have to be ready or matured to the point where they can understand the answers in their proper order. So again, I say, be patient and it will come to you; answers to all the questions you ask."

"Okay, Genia. As I ask my friends to be patient for answers, so will I," said Mike.

"Very good! Now, do you want to continue to check out more areas of this level?"

"Yes, I would. Will you still come along?"

"If you prefer, then yes I will," said Genia. "Just be prepared for even more disturbing areas, such as people who can't stop eating or smoking or dozens of other habits they brought to their realm and level of the spirit world. Also, one of the worst is the sexual hang-up area. They are people who committed unprincipled sex acts; pedophiles, incest, rape, and other related areas. There's more than you might want to see. Your course requires you to be very strong. If you really want to help people, you must understand where they're coming from. So, are you ready to go on, because if you are, then we will spend one week in this level while but 10 minutes would have passed by on earth. As you travel from one level to another, you will just have to check out each for one day. Including this week, you would have to spend 40 days here, not counting time I spend with you personally, giving you information. All-in-all, you would spend one actual hour of earth time."

"Well, I guess I'm as ready as I'll ever be to go through the spirit world. Let's begin…"

So, the week of learning starts for Mike. They go from one area to another, another and still another. He's amazed at all the intense hang-ups and habits that people have. Mike grows to understand them. It becomes part of his very soul. The depths that people have sunk to in order to achieve their desires. And, it's seems that they are 'desires' not to attain purposeful accomplishments, but rather just pure selfishness; an endless cycle of wanting, looking for and searching for raw, black enjoyment; every minute, every day, month, year, decade, century, millennium, until it can finally be broken by something, someone. This is just one of the answers that Mike must find. For until he does, he'll never be satisfied… The 40 days comes to a close, and Mike and Genia gather this time at a beautiful log cabin in the woods with a clear, cool stream nearby.

"A change of scenery, I see," says Mike. "It's about time."

"I thought you would like it," says Genia. "It's time now, Mike, for you to go back. You have much to do. Next time, we'll discuss angels and the angelic world."

"Tell me, Genia, what can you tell me about George Braxton and Grea Silver?"

"You must find those answers yourself. Go back now. Go back to your earthly body. Go back! Go back! Go…."

Mike starts to regain consciousness now, back in his room with the others. The time is 9:30 a.m., just a half-hour before they're supposed to be in the Conference Room to meet Braxton and Silver. The four of them rush over to greet Mike.

"Hey, buddy! How you doing?"

"Fine, guys" as he gets up slowly. "It's been a long time."

"It's only been an hour, Mike" says Doreen.

"Oh, I keep forgetting the time difference. But, I've been gone for 40 days this time."

"I can't wait to hear this one," said Sharon.

"Well, you'll have to until Joy gets back. I can tell you all then. For now, we have to get ready for Braxton and Silver. Let's go over what we're going to do one more time."

The five of them talk and then go down to the Conference Room. It's 9:55 now.

"Everyone ready?" Mike asks. They all affirm, and in a few minutes it's 10:00. The door opens and in walks Braxton and Silver. Everyone then yells, "Surprise!"

"What's this all about?" asks George.

"Don't ask me, George," responds Grea. "I'm in the dark just as much as you are."

"Now I'm sorry for all the mystery. We just wanted to get together to thank the two of you for everything and have a toast," says Mike.

"Well, this is a pleasant surprise," said George. "Thank you guys."

"We hope neither of you are too upset, but we had to be sneaky in order not to give it away," said Sharon.

"Not at all, are we George?"

"As I said, thanks. It's been a long hard day and we could use a drink right now," replied George.

"Great! I know what everyone except the two of you will have to drink," said Mike.

"I'll have a gin and tonic," said George. "How about you, Grea?"

"I'll have a whiskey and coke," said Grea.

"Coming right up," says Mike as he pours their drinks. After everyone has their drink in-hand, then a toast is offered. They all chat for maybe 15 minutes while Mike keeps a sharp eye out for where Braxton's and Grea's glasses are put down. Shortly thereafter, the two give their thanks once again and then bid farewell to all. Mike then talks to everyone. "This was too easy."

"What do you mean?" asks John.

"I mean they weren't even a little bit upset, not to mention irate. And what was this about a long, hard day? It's only 10:00 a.m., not p.m." answered Mike.

"That *was* strange, now that you mention it. But, at least we got what we came for," said Doreen.

"You're right," said Mike. "Let's worry about the rest some other time," as Mike grabs two napkins and the two glasses from the bottoms. They check to make sure the coast is clear and then all go back to Mike's room.

"Let's chat for a while as we wait for Joy to get back," suggests Mike.

Just before noon, Joy knocks on Mike's door and then comes in.

"Joy, it's good to see you," says Mike. "How did everything go?"

"I was about to ask you guys the same thing. Did you get the prints?" she asked.

"Yes, we did," said Mike. "Do you have everything else needed to get the information? (Yes!) Then how about we meet at your room in about an hour. Is that enough time for you to get the ball rolling?"

"Yes," answers Joy. "Meet me in my room at 1:00," she says.

"Good, 'cause I've got a lot to tell. And, I picked up a little info from Braxton and Silver when I shook their hands," said Mike.

"Okay, see you at 1:00," says Joy as she leaves the room and the remaining four wait patiently for Mike's report on his latest visit to the spirit world and what little he has sensed from their two hosts. The time ticks to 1:00 and the five of them head up to Joy's room. Once there, Joy invites them in and they all sit down and wait for Mike to inform them of all the latest news.

"Joy, before I say anything, I think it's actually a better time to tell everyone everything we know about our hosts. That includes what you and I know, Billy," said Mike.

"You have been keeping secrets from us?" asked Doreen.

"Yes, and some from you too, Billy," said Mike. "But, that's because we didn't want to alarm you about Braxton and Silver until we were certain about them. But, what I picked up earlier from them I think it best to confide in all of you now."

Everyone listens intently as Mike tells them about how Braxton and Silver got out of the conference room mysteriously and everything he and Joy know.

"And what I picked up was, first, they know a lot more about us than even we thought," said Mike.

"That's hard to believe," said Sharon.

"Well, it's uncanny," said Mike, "but true. Secondly, that's not their real names. I don't know what is, but not George Braxton and Grea Silver. Thirdly, not only aren't they from the United States, but they're not from anywhere in North America."

"You could have told me that earlier," said Joy, a little upset. "It would have saved some time. But knowing that now will still save us a lot of time. Please excuse me everyone while I go and adjust my laptop."

She goes to the den of her suite for a short time and then returns. "We'll know where they're from by about 8:00 tomorrow morning. Now Mike, do you want to let me and everyone else know what has been going on?"

Mike then explains to Joy about his most recent near-death experience as well as all his experiences going through all the areas of level six of the spirit world. He now tells them that Genia told him of one incident in the five lives that only he or she knew with just one other person. With everything that Mike has already known, plus the confirmation from Doreen's visit, only confirm Mike's stories. If there were any doubts at all, they all have been put aside now. It's obvious Mike has truly been visiting the other side. But is it done just to pass the information from there to here, or is there perhaps a deeper reason?

"Well, it definitely looks like you haven't imagined most of it. It's truly a miracle," said Joy.

"Most of it, Joy?" asks Mike. "Then what part do you believe was just my imagination?"

"Yes, Joy. We believe everything Mike said has happened to him in the spiritual world. What do you have a problem with?" asked Billy.

"This is regarding an event in an earlier visit. And that is your visiting Heaven, Mike," said Joy. "My strict belief is that no one can see Heaven unless they die for good, permanently. Then and only then can one even have the chance to enter through the gates of Heaven and not before. That part had to have been your imagination. I'm not saying you're lying, but that you made some sort of mistake."

"Come on, Joy. You're a therapist. Does it make sense that everything I said is true except for that one part?" asked Mike.

"In the state you were in, anything is possible," said Joy. "You simply couldn't have seen Heaven. It's not possible."

"I think we all believe in what Mike has told us. Especially since he told us of things that we said no one else could possibly have known. I also think we're all surprised at you for your disbelief in that one experience," said John.

"Well, I'm sorry. As I said, I believe in everything except his visit to Heaven. I simply can't accept it to be true," said Joy.

"Well guys, at least Joy believes in everything else and that's a start. It's 5:15 now and I, for one, would like to get some supper, then take a ride around town. I need a break. Anyone want to come along?" asked Mike.

"Yes! I'll come along with you, Mike. I think a little relaxation would do us all some good. How about the rest of you? Can we convince you to come along with us for three or four hours?" asked Billy.

"No!" shot back Doreen. "And I really feel that something terrible will happen to the two of you and anyone else going with you."

"Terrible like how?" asked Mike. "Please explain!"

"I can't," answered Doreen. "All I know is something really bad will happen if any of us go with you, Mike. As for yourself, I have a strong spiritual sense of doom if you go out, even by yourself. Please stay in."

"Do you sense anything, Mike?" asked Billy.

"No, but I could be being blocked."

"Then what are you going to do?"

"I refuse to be intimidated by feelings that are unsure," said Mike. "Someone or something could be trying to control my actions and very life. I appreciate your warning, Doreen, but I must go on with my life. But, I promise all of you that if I sense something myself, then I'll turn around and come back. How about you, Billy?"

"I'm very hesitant about this, but I'm not going to let you go by yourself."

"And I think I should go along, too," said Joy. "The other three of you should stay here. Have any idea where you want to go, Mike?"

"Yes. To the Rocky Mountain Mall. It closes at 10:00, so we'll be back between 10:30 and 11:00. Please try to stay awake so the six of us can go over anything that might have happened to the three of you, or the three of us."

"Okay," said Sharon. "We'll do our best. Just be careful, you three. Doreen may not be as open as you, Mike, but she *is* open to a certain degree."

"Agreed. Doreen is no phony," said Mike. "Joy, Billy, are you ready to go now?

They leave for the Mall and arrive at 6:20. "Anyplace in particular you two had in mind?" asks Mike.

"I was thinking it would be interesting to go through a big electronics store," replied Joy.

"I'll join you, Joy. I would find that interesting, too," said Billy. "How about you, Mike?"

"I still want to get something to eat. Then I'll hit that CD store over there," he said.

"Actually, something to eat sounds pretty good right now," said Billy.

"Myself as well," said Joy. "When we finish eating, we can go our own way to the stores. Then, if it's okay with the two of you, we can meet back here at 8:30."

"That's fine with me," said Billy. "Is it with you?"

"Sure," said Mike. "We'll meet at the water fountain at 8:30."

"Great!" said Joy. "According to this wall map, the Food Court is down the hall and to the left. Shall we go?"

"Why not!" as they all take off together down the hall. They order their meals and then sit down. Mike excuses himself as he forgot the ketchup. On his way back, he bumps into a man dressed in an expensive suit, heading toward his booth. Nervously, Mike talks… "Please excuse me, I should have been looking where I was going better."

"Yes!" said the man. "You should have. Just let me get back to my booth." When Mike gets back to Joy and Billy, they can't help but notice something very wrong with Mike.

"What's wrong?" asked Joy. "You look like you're having a nervous breakdown or something."

"That man," said Mike, very distressed. "the one in booth number six; he, he had a very powerful bomb."

"WHAT! HOW DO YOU KNOW?" cried Billy.

"I bumped into him accidentally and picked it all up. I'm still getting information even now. I can't shut it off," said Mike.

"You said he *had* a bomb," said Joy. "Where is it now?"

"He put it in a trash can up on the third floor. He put it there 15 minutes ago."

"How powerful?" asked Billy.

"I'm not quite sure. But I know it's one of those new bombs called NI.CON."

"NI-CON!" screamed Joy. "A bomb like that is powerful enough to take out this whole Mall."

"Good Lord! I didn't know there was such a bomb that small that could do that much damage," said Billy. "We have to do something. We have no idea how much time we have!"

"Mike. Can you tell if he's suicidal?"

"If you mean is he planning to be blown up with the bomb, NO! He's not that sick. So, we have enough time 'til he's way out from the Mall."

"Still," said Joy, just the fact that he would plant a bomb like that upstairs, then come down to the Food Court to eat says he's either cool as a cucumber or crazy as a loon. But putting all that aside, we better get some help ASAP. Who knows when he'll leave. Do you know which trash can he left it in? If so, then we can get the Mall Police on it right away. The only problem is, how do we explain how we know about this without being accused ourselves?"

"You let me handle that," said Mike. "Billy, your job is to stay here with that guy and… Wait a second, I've got a name."

"What is it, Mike?" asked Joy.

"Lack. Robert Lack. As I was saying, Billy, when he leaves, you follow him. Follow him to his vehicle when he exits the Mall and get his license plate number. With the Lord's help, the Police will be able to disarm the bomb."

"And if they can't, what happens then?" asked Billy.

"Then we'll be going to the spirit world permanently. So why don't you and I, Joy, go find the Mall Police, and I mean FAST!" said Mike.

Joy and Mike find the Mall Police on the second floor. The detective in charge is Captain Joe Haney. Mike tells that they have been watching their neighbor, Robert Lack, for a month now as he threatened to blow the Mall up with a NI-CON bomb that he and his friends had built. Captain Haney had dozens of questions to ask, but he knew that if this was a real story, they may only have minutes left. The three of them, plus two Police officers, follow Mike to the trash can on the third floor as Captain Haney searches the trash can thoroughly.

"Nothing. Nothing but trash," said the Captain.

"What happened?" exclaimed Joy. "Mike, where's the bomb?"

"I don't understand it," said Mike. "I know he put it in here. I swear to you, he put it here."

"I don't take kindly to pranks," the Captain growled at Mike. "Especially ones of this magnitude. The two of you come with us. You're under arrest," he said.

Just then, Mike sees three teenagers quickly go up the escalator with a big box of some kind in their hands.

"Captain! There, those kids on the escalator, they have it. Quick! Before they get away!" shouted Mike.

The Captain and two Policemen run down the escalator and catch up to the kids.

"Leave us alone! We didn't do anything wrong. We found this in the trash up there," said one of the kids.

"You crazy kids. You have no idea what you have in your hands. Now give it to me or I'll arrest all three of you," said the Captain.

"We're sorry. We just thought…"

"I know what the three of you thought. Now give it to me and go home. NOW!"

The kids give Haney the box and leave, happy to do so. Haney, the Policemen, Joy and Mike head back to the Mall

Police's office. Meanwhile, Billy starts to follow Robert Lack as he seems to be heading out of the Mall. Being very careful, Billy is lead out to the parking lot where Lack is headed to a new Cadillac. He pulls out his keys, opens the door and as Billy is hiding behind an adjacent car, Billy's cell phone starts to play music. He quickly turns it off, but it's too late.

"Who's there?" yells Lack, as he pulls out a 38-caliber special. "I don't see you behind that car, but I know you're there. Come out! I won't hurt you. I promise."

As Lack heads towards the car Billy is hiding behind, Lack's alarm on his watch goes off. Lack says to himself, "Damn. I gotta get out of here. There's no more time to get clear enough away. It's now or never."

So, Lack gets in his car and drives away while Billy gets his license plate number and then heads back into the Mall. Back in the Mall Police office, Joy, Mike, Captain Haney and the two Policemen are all inside. After Haney takes what appears to be the bomb out of the box…

"Well, is it a real NI-CON bomb or not? Need I ask?" said Mike.

"I need to take the casing off first. Then I can tell you," said Haney. "GOD HELP US! IT'S REAL!"

"Can you disarm it? And how much time do we have?" pleaded Joy.

"Ten minutes and thirty-two seconds," said Haney. "And I don't think I can disarm it. You see it's a random wire NI-CON bomb. It's the simplest to disarm, but yet the most difficult at the same time. And that's because THIS bomb has three different colored wires that can be any different color combination on any bomb. To worsen things, wires are also changed in position every time, as well. To disarm it, you have to cut the main wire to the detonator, which can be any color in any position in any one bomb. Cut the wrong one and boom; it blows. Try to disarm it any other way by moving any other part and boom; it blows. In its own right, it's a perfect bomb. Very simple, but very complicated at the same time. I just don't know which wire to cut. So I really can't disarm it. There's not enough time to get a bomb squad in here or to get it safely away from the Mall. In other words, we're screwed."

"So what can we do?" asked Mike.

"Just one thing. I'm going to have to take a big chance and cut one of the wires. If not, we're all dead anyway. So this way, we have a one-in-three chance of making it… There's a black, red and white wire. We have just under nine minutes left." Haney grabs some wire cutters. "If anyone has any prayers they want to say, now's the time to say them."

Just then, one of the Policemen interrupts to say something.

"Excuse me, Captain, but I would greatly appreciate you allowing me to cut the wire. I've got a hunch."

"Why not let him, Captain?" said Joy. "If he makes a mistake, we'll never be around to know it anyway. But, if he does pick the right one, we'll all be in his debt. So, what do you say?"

"Well, he couldn't do any worse than myself. Besides, we don't have much time to make the decision. So, go ahead, Harold. A lot of lives lay in your hand now. Here – take the wire cutter and stand over the bomb."

He contemplates what he is about to do. A snip of the wrong wire and boom, it's all over. But, the right one would make him a hero. His whole life could change in the right direction. He would be on the television, radio, and in the newspapers. He starts to

93

sweat heavily now as he attempts to make sense of it all. For if he makes the wrong decision, no one would ever know it was *his* mistake, *his* error that caused total destruction of the Mall and everyone in it and even nearby. What should he do? Which wire should he cut? Black? Red? White?

"Take your time, Harold. There's no need to rush, now. Not as long as you have at least five or ten seconds left. It makes no difference when, nor or as time just about runs out. Feel your inner self and try to sense which wire it is to cut. We still have five minutes and twenty seconds left.

Just then, there's a knock at the door. Haney goes over to open it to see Billy standing outside. Mike explains to the Captain that Billy is okay. Haney lets Billy enter.

"Good Lord! Is that the bomb?" cries Billy.

"Yes!" replies Mike. "Let me quickly explain to you what's happened in a nutshell." When he finishes, they see that there's just over a minute left. Harold is a wreck by now. He can barely hold the wire cutter. He senses time is almost up. He *must* make a decision right about now.

"Yes! I've got it! I'll cut the black wire," says Harold.

Then, as times before, Mike falls down unconscious, and again, time almost freezes. After the usual trip through the cloud, he appears before Genia. This time, though, they are both in a cold, dark place.

"Where are we?" asks Mike.

"We're in a corner of the first level of hell," says Genia. "In other words, rock bottom."

"With all my curiosity, Genia, I have no time for this, even if time is just about frozen on earth... Wait a minute. You brought me here to help us, right?"

"That's correct," said Genia. "And, I brought you down here because this is where the answer lies. Also, with as much as we care for all the people in and around the Mall, our main objective is to save you and your two friends, for your safety is paramount to saving millions of lives later on in *your* lifetimes. But, you must listen carefully or even your three lives will be ended. Now listen: The white Light saves all, while Red Blood brings ultimate darkness."

"Then it's the white wire that has to be cut!" said Mike. "Quick. Send me back."

"Just do as the phrase tells you. It's so simple, but still I can't just come out with the answer plainly."

"Thank you, Genia. Now please send me back right away even though only a second might have elapsed. Harold was just about to cut the black wire."

"Just understand that transferring you back to your body too quickly can leave you confused. So, remember what I told you!"

Mike's spirit returns to his earthly body just as Harold is about to cut the wire. Mike abruptly gets up and rushes towards Harold.

"Stop! Don't cut the black wire. Cut the white one."

"Are you crazy? We're almost out of time. Just fifty seconds left," said Haney.

"Please trust me. It's the white wire, not the black. Please cut the white!"

"Don't ask how he knows. He just does," pleaded Joy.

"I can't take that chance. Over a thousand lives depend on it. Go ahead, Harold!" said Haney.

Just then, Mike punches Harold to the floor as he grabs the wire cutter from his hand and is about to cut the white wire.

"Stop right there, Wakings!" warns Haney as he points his gun at Mike. "Cut the black wire or I'll shoot. I'm not kidding."

"Okay you win, Captain. Watch!"

Mike leans toward the black wire, but in an instant pushes the wire cutter to the white wire and cuts.

"YOU FOOL!" shouts Haney. "What did you do?"

"Save all of your lives as you can see. We're still alive. No explosion," said Mike.

"Excuse me, Mike, but why is the countdown at thirty seconds and still counting down?"

"What the heck! What's going on?" shouted Mike.

"Good God! That's a multi-wire trip. You have to cut the wires in a certain order. Quick, Wakings. The next wire: black or red?" said Haney.

"I'm confused. What did Genia tell me?"

"Twenty-one seconds, Mike," said Joy. "Don't you remember what Genia told you?"

"I'm not sure. Damn it! Come on, Mike. What did she say?" Mike shouted at himself.

"Come on, guy. Whoever this Genia is, she must have told you the last two wires. Eighteen seconds left," said Haney.

"What are the last two wires in order, Wakings?" shouted Harold.

"I just need the next one. The last one is obvious, you idiot!" said Mike.

"Leave him alone! Let him think!" said Joy.

"Go ahead, Mike. Ten seconds left," said Billy.

"THINK, MIKE! THINK! I GOT IT. RED BLOOD BRINGS ULTIMATE DARKNESS. NEXT THE RED, THEN THE BLACK."

"ARE YOU SURE?" shouts Harold.

"WHAT DIFFERENCE DOES IT MAKE? WE'RE OUT OF TIME! IT'S NOW OR NEVER. CUT, WAKINGS! CUT!" shouts Haney.

Mike cuts the red wire. And now, knowing he was right, he cuts the black wire last.

"You did it, Mike! shouts Joy. "You disabled the bomb with five seconds left."

"Atta boy, Mike. You saved us all!" added Billy.

"Yes, you did! You saved the Mall and over a thousand people," Haney admitted. "I don't know how to thank the three of you. You said this guy Lack is a neighbor of yours. We'll need all the info on him before the City Police and F.B.I. get here."

"Well, we weren't totally honest about that. And, if you're really grateful to us, then the best way of showing it would be to let the three of us go before the city Police or F.B.I. get here. You know they'll never let us go. I think you know we had nothing to do with this guy," said Mike.

"Then, do you have any more info for me?" asked Haney.

"Please tell me you got his license plate number," Mike says as he turns to Billy.

"You bet I did. He almost caught me there for a moment, but Lady Luck was on my side."

"I don't know why you don't want the recognition due to the three of you, but if it means that much to you, I guess I could say you took off while we weren't watching," said Haney.

"One more thing," said Mike. "Our description."

"It would mean my badge and job if they found out, but I can cover for you and your friends. As for my men, they're loyal to me, so they'll follow my lead."

"Thank you, Captain," chorused Joy, Mike and Billy.

"Now get lost, you three. With Lack's name and plates, we'll have no trouble locating him. Now I said, get lost while you can!"

Joy, Mike and Billy head back to the Hotel and arrive there at 8:10. They find Doreen, John and Sharon in John's room.

"Well," said Doreen. "Was there anything to my premonitions?"

"You can say that," said Mike. "We just foiled a bomber from blowing up the Rocky Mountain Mall with over a thousand people. That's all."

"WHAT! What are you talking about?" she asked.

"Now sit back and we'll explain everything," says Mike, trying to calm Doreen, John and Sharon who are literally on the edge of their chairs. Their explanation lasts until about 9:00 p.m.

"Well, we're glad to see Doreen's premonitions were for the better of you three, and not for the worse," said John.

"I'm sure you three are wiped out and want to get some shut eye right about now," said Sharon.

"You're right," said Joy. "A nice cozy bed sounds fabulous right now. Also, I'm sorry to say that the info on Braxton's and Silver's prints won't come in 'til around 1:00 p.m. So, why don't we all meet in my room at noon? Then we can talk before their information comes in. Is that okay?

Everyone is happy with that, except Mike. He has other plans now.

"This works out perfectly for me. You see, I have to go visit someone at the Home for the soon-departed."

"Where did *this* come from?" asked Joy.

"All I know is I got the direction while we were driving back. Who it is, I have no idea or when they are going to die. But, it's located in Littleton and I should be there around 9:00 in the morning," explained Mike.

"Direction from whom?" asked John.

"Where I get a lot of information; from Genia and from the spirit world."

"It seems like you're becoming a very important man to them," said Doreen. "Do you know when you'll be back? In time for our meeting, I hope."

"Yes! I should be back by noon or 12:30. I have to help this person in their transition from this world to the next," reiterated Mike.

"That's so tender and sweet," said Sharon. "I wish you the best as I'm sure everybody else does, as well."

"Thank you. I think I'll turn in now, too."

"Let me walk with you to your room, Mike" said Joy. "I have a few things I want to say."

"Okay, Joy. The rest of you, have a good night and I'll see you in the afternoon," said Mike.

"And I'll be going straight to my room after talking to Mike. Good night, everyone."

After everyone bids good night, Joy and Mike go to his room. "I just want to say," shared Joy, "a great deal of things have happened to all of us in two-plus days, especially you. I mean, with all this dying and clairvoyance, visiting different realms of the spirit world, plus too many other things to speak of. What happened to that Ad agent whose only problem was a repeating nightmare? The three of us could have been killed along with eleven- or twelve-hundred people tonight. Even though we have a close relationship as friends, I'm still your therapist and I have a professional concern for your welfare. Remember, I had a hand in your coming here, and if anything would happen to you, mentally or physically, then I wouldn't forgive myself. Also, to a lesser degree, I would lose my license as well as be banned from the profession permanently, and especially because I went along with you in this."

"You mean they don't know you came along?" asked Mike.

"No!" said Joy. "I didn't record it or tell anyone in our meeting. My only saving grace is I came because the main purpose was to get valuable insights into my journals for future therapists as well as psychiatrists. It would be invaluable as I once mentioned to you. If they knew of our close relationship, they would strongly disapprove. So, you see, a lot is at stake here for everyone here, especially you and me."

"I see. But, for both our sakes, it's even more important now than ever before that we keep going. There are many questions which need answers, and we have five more days to find out. Don't worry. If it really gets too tough, I *will* bow out," said Mike.

"Well, I can't say that this comment didn't make me feel a lot more assured of your well-being," said Joy. "It's been a long day and it's getting past our bed time. Besides, I have a lot to put down in my log. So, have a good night and we'll see you around noon tomorrow. You might want to pack a few things to stay at Braxton's house tomorrow. Sleep well!" said Joy.

"Good night, Joy." They then give their sign to each other by bending their pinkies. Mike gets into his pajamas, thinks a little about everything, and then falls asleep on his bed. The next morning, Mike gets up, has a small breakfast, and then leaves for the 'Home of the Soon Departed'. Mike introduces himself, and to avoid questions that have awkward answers, asks the nurse if there is anybody there that's going to pass away within the next couple of days. The nurse says, "Yes. There's one man by the name of Jack Perro who has cancer of the lungs. He was expected to die a week ago, but definitely will be dead by tomorrow."

Mike explains that he has a gift of soothing people's fear of dying and that he would be happy to ease Mr. Perro's transition from this world to the next. Also, a lot of people would like to tell someone who really cares for them something they feel inclined to do before they die. Mike said he would like to be that person due to the fact that he has had near-death experiences. The nurse was amazed and agreed with him. She gets Mike's personal info and leads him down the hall to room twenty-one. She checks on Mr. Perro to make sure he's awake. He is. Then, she proceeds to tell him about Mike. The man, after deep consideration, agrees to talk to Mike. So, the nurse goes out of the room and leaves the two of them alone.

"So, you've been to the other side, I hear," said Mr. Perro.

"Yes I have," said Mike. "And between you and me, several times. Now, why don't you tell me a little more about yourself?"

"Well," Mr. Perro began, "I'm eighty-two and I lived a long and happy life. My wonderful wife I met when I was nineteen and she was twenty, a year older than I. I loved everything about her, even her scent. Some people would call it an odor, but I thought it was the fragrance of her personality. My only regret was that we never had any children. Don't ask me why; we just didn't. I was a successful real estate agent. She was in sales, and also very successful. We saved every penny until I was sixty and she was sixty-one. We then traveled the world together. We had such a good time. When she was sixty-six, she developed a brain tumor. She died a year later. We were married forty-six years by then. I wrote a poem for her when I was fifty. I always kept a copy of it. Would you like to hear it?" asked Mr. Perro.

"Certainly," replied Mike. "Please read it to me."

"As I walk the streets of Denver
I dream of a long time ago.
When sad and lonely times engulfed me
And I cried in the streets covered with snow

With eyes of long lost angels
Sent to me straight from above
Could end the sadness that imprisons me
That wears like a tightly fit glove.

I know she'll make me happy
And maybe end her loneliness, too
For this wonderful world we live in
Has somebody meant just for you.

She'll be sweet, gentle with kindness
And her eyes would see visions so bright
That the world she now lives in
Would be opened in heart with light.

The birds in the sky will ponder
What wondrous woman she be
That the sky they're in becomes wider
Cause she's definitely meant to be free.

The path that she travels gets shorter

In a direction that's leading to me
I'll go halfway to meet her
'til we greet each other by the sea.

We finally get there together
And talk about each other's life
Before the years could escape us
She consents to become my wife.

Although I am always with her
I find I am never bored
For I found a Heavenly angel
her name is Anne Marie Ward.

"That was beautiful," said Mike. "A real tribute to your wife. Does it have a title?"

"Yes! It's called 'And Her Name.' I sure hope she reads it with me when I read it. I miss her terribly. I hope she'll be waiting for me in Heaven."

Holding Perro's hands with his eyes closed, Mike says to him, "I can tell you that Anne *is* in Heaven and is waiting for you. Your destination is to be with her. Be happy, for your loneliness will soon be over."

"Are you sure? Can you be sure?"

"Yes, I'm sure," said Mike. "For I've been given a gift to tell you so. Please continue your story. I'm truly listening to you."

"When Anne died, my heart was broken and I was so lonely. A friend talked me into getting a puppy. Well, there was a dog that was four months old and he went from one home to another before coming to me. At first, I did not want him, but I gave him a one-month trial. By the end of the month, I was in love with him. I named him Rocky, because he had a black eye. He was half chihuahua and half rat terrier. He was white and black. He was the sweetest dog I ever had, and I had many. I bought him a bunch of toys and named each one. He could pick them out by name. One thing, though, was that he had several physical problems. One such problem was with his back legs. Even so, he was a real trooper. Even in pain, he would walk outside to do his business and run after his toys back and forth until the pain stopped him. With all of his problems, I loved him as if he were the son I never had. In time, my loneliness became bearable. I had an object to pour my love into, and that's just what I did. Funny thing was, he was born on Christmas Day… The years passed as Rocky was always by my side. He lived to a ripe old age of fifteen. Tears flowed down my face as I had to put him to sleep. That was last year. My days are filled with utter loneliness now, for I have no one left to love. I sure hope there's a dog Heaven, because I could not imagine being there with Anne but not Rocky." Perro looks up toward Heaven as he continues, "Please, God, let me be with my wife *and* Rocky." He turns now to Mike… "Mike, do you know if I'll ever see Rocky again?"

"Well, Jack, animals don't have spirits." Perro gets a dejected look on his face, "*but* a person can recreate any animal he or she would want to be with them for as long as they want; even eternity if they desire, and they'll have all their memories that they had back on earth. So you see, you will be with Rocky again by one side, and with Anne on the other," explained Mike. Perro brightens up again with a big smile.

"Thank you! Thank you very much. Please, let's talk some more."

Mike and Perro do talk, until it's 11:15. Realizing he must get back to Joy's room by noon, he hugs Perro and as he does, Perro whispers in Mike's ear: "I'm not afraid to die anymore, because of an angel… you."

The two men bid farewell to one another wondering if they might cross paths on the other side. Mike gets in his car and drives back to the Hotel. It's 12:05 now as he quickly rushes up to Joy's room, knocks and goes inside. Joy had yet to come out of her den, so Mike shares with everyone his meeting with Jack Perro. He sips on a cola as the clock reads 12:35. Joy then emerges with the information everybody has waited for.

"Well, what did you find out?" asked John. "Where are they from?"

"I still don't know. It looks like they're from nowhere. Their fingerprints don't match anyone's on the face of this earth," Joy reported.

"My God!" said Sharon. "What do we have here?"

"I'm not quite sure. But, I am sure of one thing. They're from an organization so big and powerful, to erase their existence, and we're smack in the middle of it and we don't even know what we're in the middle of… God help us all!" said Joy.

3. The Trials Grow in Numbers

Everyone is shocked when Joy reports to them about Braxton and Silver. They try to make heads or tails out of it, but come up empty each time.

"This is crazy," said Billy. "They have to be from somewhere, but how do we find out where?"

"We can't," said Mike. "So, we play along for now."

"What do you mean, play along?" asked Doreen.

"Look. Sooner or later they have to show their hand," said Mike. "With as powerful as they are, if we tried to leave now, it could prove to be disastrous for all of us. They obviously want something from us and as long as they don't ask us to do something illegal, I say stay out the week. On Sunday, they're bound to tell us what they want from us."

"Do you really think they'll let us go home on Sunday?" asked John.

"How are they going to keep us here?" answered Mike. "We're in a busy hotel in the middle of a large city and we come and go as we please."

"I agree with Mike," said Joy. "Let's play this thing out as long as no one gets hurt or does anything illegal. Let's play with them.

106

"So, I guess that means we're going to his house in Idaho Springs!" said Doreen.

"Yes, it does," replied Mike. "And I assume everyone is already packed and ready to go. (Yes!) All right, then. It's 1:10, so is it okay with all of you to meet in the lobby at 2:00? (another Yes!) Then, I guess I'll see you downstairs in fifty or so minutes."

Mike then motions to everyone to stay silent as he goes to Joy's outside door and quickly opens it, finding on the other side that same man who had been listening outside their Hotel room in Central City. Mike grabs him this time.

"WHO ARE YOU?" says Mike. "AND WHAT DO YOU WANT? Besides that, how did you know where to find us both times?"

"You can let go of me. I'm not going to run this time, considering my wife hasn't much time left. I have to be honest with you now," said the mysterious man.

"All right then," said Mike. "Come on in and have a seat… So, explain everything. We're listening and we don't bite."

"I nibble a little, but otherwise I'm harmless," added Billy.

"Hush, Billy! said Joy. "Can't you see he's nervous enough?"

"My name is Joe Taylor. I'm 32 and my wife Gloria is 28. She's been sick for several years, but just recently has been told that she needs a very delicate operation. Otherwise, she will have two months max before she dies."

"What's wrong with her?" asked Mike.

"She has a liver infection. A few years back, they found a way to save her, but it costs $125,000, which we don't have and our insurance won't cover it. We've been married six years now, but our lives have just begun. Our families live a simple life they don't have the money to help. You people are our last hope. I knew where to find you because I've been guided spiritually through dreams. I'm a religious person, but never had guidance like this before. I don't know why I've been helped like this, but I'm a very grateful man to God above and would be to all of you if you can help. I would do anything for you; work for you, serve you, anything if only you can help us get this operation."

"Just tell me that everything you said is the truth," said Mike as he holds Joe's hands.

"I swear to my death that everything I told you is true. Not a single lie," Joe answered.

"Well, Mike," said John, "can you tell if he's lying?"

"Yes," said Mike as he releases Joe's hands, "and he has told us the whole complete truth."

"So, can we help him? Do we help him?" asked Sharon. "I know with your abilities we could, but you said that would be cheating."

"It's cheating if we make money for ourselves for money's sake," said Mike. "But to help someone else in a life-and-death situation would be completely a different circumstance. As long as we're not taking money away from someone who is betting, but rather taking a little money – and I do mean little – from the House which is ripping off people unnecessarily to begin with, and even ruins some people's lives to the point of suicide, well that would be a just reason for me to help. If you need $125,000 for the operation, I'm assuming you are going to either take care of your wife yourself, in which case you'll have to take off from work. How long would that be?"

"About a month, providing I'll still have a job after that," answered Joe.

"Which brings me to the second alternative, which would be to hire a nurse to take care of her. Either way, you'll need money. $25,000 should take care of all your bills. So we have to get you $150,000 or close to it. Now that we know how much, the next question is how. Since we have to do it through the casinos, it would be best if we made the money through four of us and not just through me. $100,000 alone would bring too much attention from the House, not to mention $150,000. And, if we do it just as I say, we should have the money within two hours," explained Mike.

"That sounds like too much money for just two hours," said John. "Why don't you have all seven of us working on it?"

"That sounds even better, except it will have to be six," said Mike. "I can't and shouldn't ask Joy to help in this way. She's already stretching her guidelines way too far. So, Joy's out."

"Thank you, Mike," said Joy. "It's true. I couldn't go so far as to bet, but that doesn't stop me from rooting the rest of you on."

"That's okay Joy," said Billy. "I think we all understand. So, how do we go about doing this?"

"John, is there a place where we can bet on the horses simulcast throughout the country? I thought I saw one up there," asked Mike.

"You're right," said John. "There's a big one called 'Just a Furlong More'. They have twenty-five windows. Ten for smaller bets, eight for fifty dollars or more, and seven for $200 or more. And, that's just the main betting area. The clubhouse upstairs has just as many windows."

"Great!" said Mike. "When we get there, I'll get six racing forms. We should each have one so it looks normal. I'm going to mark off the winners as well as the winning trifecta's in four races. Bet everything on the winner of each race, except for $12. You use that to bet a two $2 Trifecta box. By boxing, it makes it look to the teller that you're not sure how they're coming in. We'll each have different racetracks to bet on, and we'll also have different windows to bet at. I believe we can each start off with $3,000. As for Joe, I'll give him $3,000. Each of us will stay 'til we make $30,000, whether it's all four races or even just one. The extra money will cover our initial bets with our own money. Anything over that will go to Joe. Joe, do you and does everyone else understand? If not, then I'll explain it in more detail while driving there."

Everyone kind of responds affirmatively…

"When we get there, we'll rent a room. So, when you make the money, come back to the room and stay there. Joy, is it okay with you if you stay in the room the whole time?"

"Sure," replies Joy.

"Fine. Once we're all back in the room, we'll get our own money back, give Joe the rest, and say our good-byes while Joe puts the money in a regular suitcase and leaves. Then, the rest of us can go get some rest at Braxton's house in Idaho Springs… I guess we should leave now. The sooner we get this over with, I think the better we'll all feel. There also might be some snow in the mountains, more than we got here in town the other day."

The seven of them head up to Central City in the SUV. They rent a suite and go over final plans.

"After giving it some thought, I hate to do it, but I have to readjust our betting strategies," said Mike.

"Oh no, Mike. Do you *have* to?" asked Joy.

"I'm afraid so," said Mike. "You see, when I calculated the figures, I forgot to factor in the IRS withholdings."

"You mean, they will tax our winnings?" asked Sharon.

"Yes! Anything over $5,000 they take out 25% of your gross," explained Mike. "So, that means instead of stopping at $30,000, we have to stop at $45,000. That would give us around $240,000. After 25% is taken out, we'll be left with approximately $180,000. Even still, if you bet the way I wrote down for all of you, you'll still have it after the second or third race. Remember, don't flash the money and come right back here after you reach the goal. We should all be back here by 5-5:30. This is it, guys. Good luck to each of you. See you in a couple of hours."

So, they all descend to the betting lines with confidence.

"$3,000 to win on number Five in the sixth race at Laurel," announced Billy to the teller. "Also, a $12 Trifecta box at the same on Three, Five and Eight."

Everyone else places their bets within fifteen minutes of Billy, at the other tellers. The bell sounds and Billy's race is off. A quarter way around the track, the Five horse is in seventh place in a field of ten horses. Halfway, he's in fourth place, and then second around the far turn. He has a slight lead coming down the stretch and then wins the race by two lengths with the Eight and Three horses in second and third, topping off the Trifecta. Each person has Mike's perfected finishes, as well. They collect the money and pay the IRS their due. By 5:15, everyone is back in the room. The monies add up to $187,000. Each person gets his or her initial money outlay. They're left with $166,000 which Joe puts into a plain looking suitcase. After locking the case, Joe turns to all the others.

"I have no words to thank all of you, especially you, Mike," said Joe with tears running down his cheeks. "You saved Gloria's life and mine, which is also rescued. If there's anything we can do to show our appreciation, just name it. Anything!"

"Well, as a matter of fact, there is something the two of you can do," said Mike.

"Great!" said Joe. "We're at your disposal. Please tell us what we can do, now or anytime in the near or upcoming future."

"Sometime within a year from now, you'll be approached by a man, woman or both concerning religion, and you both will be invited to a supper the following night. We would be grateful to the two of you if you would accept the invitation. Not only will it be pleasant and safe, but totally legal as well, just to put your mind at ease. If you do this, you'll be rewarded beyond your best dreams. I wish I could tell you more, but that's about all I can inform you of it at this point in time," explained Mike.

"Thank you, and believe me, for what you all did for us, I can promise you that we'll follow your requests to the best of our abilities. And now, I will bid you all farewell until sometime in the future, perhaps. God Bless all of you."

Joe hugs each of them, but especially Mike. He gets his two suitcases and departs; one with his personal items and the other with the $166,000.

"I guess it's time the rest of us get our things and head to the SUV," said Joy. "Haven't you realized, Mike, that since coming here to Denver on Sunday, things have really been going quickly and packed with incidences, especially for you?"

"Well that's an understatement at the very least," said Mike. "And the $10 million promised each of us based upon Sunday's decisions would be very real and tangible if Braxton and Silver represent the kind of organization we suspect them to be involved with. I just don't feel right about you only getting $3 million to our ten. You're just as involved."

"It doesn't bother me," said Joy, "so it shouldn't bother any of you. Besides, just because they have or at least are involved with people who have a great deal of money, it doesn't mean we're going to get $53 million. As we know, until we find out much more about them, getting that money could mean nothing. I suggest that when we meet, tomorrow at noon, we insist upon some answers. Otherwise, we won't continue with this game of theirs."

"Answers is right," said Mike. "How much do they know about any or everything that has happened to us since Sunday? And, they should have a good explanation about the detailed information they have on each of us."

"If it's all the same to you guys," said Doreen, "I just prefer to put all this aside until tomorrow. Right now, how about we all get some relaxation at the Idaho Springs house. I think we can use some rest."

"That sounds good to me, too," said John.

So, they all load up in the SUV and drive to the Springs. Once there, the directions send them into a wooded area. They follow a long, winding road that leads to a long driveway, which in turn leads to a high house built sometime around the turn of the century, the 21st century. They pull up to the front door.

"This place looks like it's about 50 years old!" added John.

"It also looks like it has a dozen or so rooms," said Sharon. "How about we go inside?

They do, and investigate the first and second floors. The house has 14 rooms with 10 bathrooms. Definitely a room for each of them, with plenty more to spare. On the first floor, down a huge hallway, they find a big metal door with a large bolt on the outside. When opened, there is some kind of large basement. They opt to go down in an hour or so after they have some rest and something to eat.

"How about that," says Sharon. "This door not only has a bolt on the outside, but one on the inside, too."

"Almost as if not just to keep something downstairs, but to keep something up here from getting down there while one is in the basement," said Billy.

"Don't let your imaginations run wild now," warns Joy.

"I agree," said Mike. "The kitchen seems fully equipped with everything, including food and snacks."

"And drinks of all kinds," adds John, "including pop, juices and energy drinks."

"We're all big boys and girls, so I think you can choose your own drinks," said Mike. "As for me, I'm going to have an ice-cold cola and some of that delicious looking spinach pie. Some of that Greek Salad looks good, too."

"And look, here's pasta of all kinds," observed Doreen. "Also, Chinese food and Thai. Wow, it looks like there are foods of many different nationalities, here."

"Well, let's grab some and eat," said Billy.

They all get food and drinks and go to the Dining Room. They fully enjoy all the delicacies. After an hour or so, when they finished, everyone goes into the Living Room and finds a comfortable seat.

"That was a good meal," adds Billy. "Anybody have the time?"

"Yes, it's 9:55," reports Joy. "You know, I would like to check out that cellar."

Just then, Mike has a familiar drop to the floor, but this time he's able to speak a few words before he blacks out.

"Mike! What's the matter? Can we help you?" asks Joy.

"No. I'm having another death experience. I'll only be gone from all of you for just minutes, but for me I have no idea how long. I just want…"

Mike then blacks out, and after the usual trip through the clouds, he finds himself on top of a beautiful mountain with Genia.

"Welcome back, Mike!" announces Genia. "It's good to see you."

"You know, I never had the chance to thank you for helping me with that bomb. If it weren't for you, there would have been many deaths and a lot of destruction. So, thank you very much," said Mike.

"You're welcome. You and your friends were more help in that incident than you think. But, we'll discuss that in more depth later on."

"It's always 'later on' with you as well as with Braxton and Silver. By the way, we really would appreciate it if you can shed some light on the two of them. Who are they really, and what do they want from us? Also, why is it every time we meet, it's in a more secluded area; I mean why can't we be around people or something?"

"First off, we're always in a secluded area so we can talk without distractions and where it's peaceful," Genia explained. "As I said before, some answers will have to wait until a future time; until you've grown spiritually and mentally. As for answers to Mr. Braxton and Mr. Silver, you and your friends have the responsibility to find out who and where they're from on your own. Otherwise, none of you will pass the test."

"TEST!" exclaimed Mike. "What test?... I'll bet I know. I'll have to wait to find out 'til later on. Am I right?"

"You see, you're finally catching on... Now, before we visit other levels and areas of the spirit world, I want to tell you about angels and the angelic world. This will be of great interest to your friend John Ralph. First let me tell you that most of his theories on that subject are incorrect."

"I'll have a hard time telling him that."

"Nonetheless, in order for him to grow, he'll have to accept it before Sunday comes, when you all choose or do whatever will be asked of you," said Genia.

"That's the second time you made reference to our seven days with Braxton and company. What does our seven-day time limit have to do with my time limit of coming here to experience the spirit world and get information from you? Is there a connection between the two?"

"First, there's no guarantee that Sunday will be our last visit. It depends upon other circumstances. Secondly, after the seven days are up on earth, you will not see Mr. Braxton or Silver again, so the connection ends there. But again, everything will be based upon what you and your friends do in conjunction with what you all learn from here."

"So, in short, what you're telling me is, 'Anything can mean anything.'"

"If that's how you wish to accept it, then let it be so, for *now*."

"Okay, okay, Genia. You win. So, where does our next lesson begin?"

"First, we must understand that God created angels to be his servants. The angels would have a deeper, richer ability to receive and give love to God and to His children. The three main angels in order of, well let's say rank, are Lucifer, or as you know him now, Satan; Michael and Gabriel. Satan rules evil, while Michael and Gabriel fight fervently to stop him."

"I got it! Braxton is Michael and Silver is Gabriel. Right?"

"Sorry Mike. They're not who you think they are. Please let me continue."

"Now *I'm* sorry, Genia. Please go on."

"So, angels relate to God as servants and messengers and do tasks for him. One problem is that humans often feel that they get their value through doing or mastering a task or by making something. This isn't true. We are to have a heartistic relationship to God that should be perfected love, but this is an alien concept to us. Angels, on the other hand, never reached heartistic perfection at all because humans never reached it and therefore couldn't model it for them. This is all because they're servants while humans are children of God. Lordship is reserved only for humans and not for angels. Even many people think that we are just one piece of creation or just another creature, instead of Lords. Angels are not responsible in the same way humans were supposed to be. So, fallen man doesn't see his true responsibility, either. We think we are servants at best, and all responsibilities are God's... Getting away from heavy info, let's go to a lighter topic. Angles do have wings, but very rarely exhibit them while on earth. And in case you're wondering, angels do not have physical bodies. It's true they can manifest themselves on earth as if they have a physical body and you can even touch and feel them. There are many examples in the Bible that lead you to believe they have physical bodies, but only humans have a physical *and* a spiritual body. Just as you mentioned to Jack Perro, animals don't have spirits, while angels are without a physical body. Only humans have both. And, speaking of Jack, I should let you know that as of 4:08 this afternoon on earth, he passed away. Since each of you cared so much for one another, after our time here you will be allowed to visit him in Heaven. Right now, he's going through transition before he meets his wife."

"Genia, I would like to ask a question; I mean a really serious one, at least to me. If the gates to the Kingdom of Heaven have been opened for some time now and I've been allowed to be there for only a short time, does that mean I'm not qualified to live in Heaven when I die, or am I? I mean, I always meet you in Paradise."

"Well, Mike, I'm going to give you a complete and honest answer; and that is, because of some serious mistakes in your life, no, you're not qualified for Heaven, just Paradise. But don't fret. If you continue on the path you're on for another year or two, then you would be qualified to go to the Kingdom of Heaven when you die. I mean for good; not just when you temporarily die."

"Then I guess I have the potential, but what do I have to do to be ready?" asked Mike.

"Just follow what makes you feel good and your righteous mind. You can never go wrong with that advice. Your original mind will tell you what is good and righteous, and what isn't."

"Let's get on with it, then. I'm anxious to see Jack with his wife. It'll be good to see him happy and in good health again."

"Very well," said Genia. "Let's continue. Second, our identity as males and females is unclear. People have come to feel a unisex culture would be better because we are all the same. This is the same with angels who are male only. Women often have difficulty finding their place, value, or identity in the world of men. So, we have many kinds of sex crises. Remember, much of this is merely believed by mankind and isn't necessarily true. But, that's the problem. Our warped sense of belief is what is causing so many difficulties. If we correct these misunderstandings, then we can have a deeper relationship with God... Mortal marriages have the belief that it's 'til death do we part," but in God's realm of existence, we will be together throughout eternity. Otherwise, we would live like angels in Heaven, only happy like servants without a parent-child relationship; just single beings without a spouse. Some people, even *married* people, don't want to become parents. We're weak when there's an issue of parental heart and instincts. Angels don't know the experience of being parents for two reasons. One is because there are only males. Two, even when there will be female angels, they still won't know because they're only spiritual beings and spirits cannot have children. Remember, only humans are God's children, not angels."

"But how about people or couples who haven't had any children on earth and want some, or even couples that have had children and want more? Their hearts are aching, especially those completely without children. What will be done for them?"

"There's a simple solution to that. In the spirit world, there are millions of parentless children for one reason or another. The couples can adopt as many and any sex or nationality they want;

black, white, red, yellow or brown. And, there won't be a long, drawn-out process to adopt. It only depends on the true desire of their hearts. That is what decides their qualifications. So, you see, no one will be without in the spirit world."

"That's wonderful! Truly Heaven... How about single people? Will there be someone for each of them?"

"Heaven is a place where families dwell. Eventually, everyone will find a spouse just right for them. Then, with children, they will live in peace and harmony for eternity. It also goes to say that whatever you wish for, as long as it's righteous, will be granted. One will never be wanting. This will all one day be for everyone, once they have been restored back to God. God has Willed it, and it will come to pass."

"That's a beautiful concept. Then, that means that one day even the people in hell and the lower realms will be restored."

"That's right. Just imagine one dies and goes to Heaven, but a family member – maybe a child – goes to hell or some gloomy place. Could one be truly happy knowing this? No, they wouldn't be happy until that family member or whoever it might be, will be with them in Heaven. If you truly love someone, you would want them to be with you in Heaven."

"I've asked you this before, but could not get an answer. Maybe now you can tell me *how* everyone, even those in hell, will be restored. I know you said that many spirits will have to work with someone on earth with faults similar to their own and help them overcome them, and then they grow, but what about so many of the spirits that are trapped in lower realms? How do they grow?... I can tell from the expression on your face that you're not going to tell me now either, are you?"

You're right, Mike, but the time is getting closer when all will be revealed to you… How about for now we go visit Jack reuniting with his family; at least a few of them. He has recently met his spirit guide, who explained things to him, and is ready in a few minutes to meet some family members. Be prepared, though, for the first earthly person he will meet is *you*, Mike."

Genia and Mike then disappear into the bluish cloud he has become so familiar with. Shortly thereafter, they transform into a place Mike has seen to be as beautiful as when he was in Heaven, because they *are* in Heaven. Everything is alive with glorious reality. The smell of lilacs in the air is evident. Mike sees Jack, young again as if in his twenties, but yet he recognizes him by his very spirit. He's with a charming fellow who goes over to talk to Genia. This must be Jack's spirit guide. Jack then spots Mike as he walks toward him.

"Mike! It's good to see you again. I was told you would be visiting me, even though you're not here permanently yet. You have a very important mission here."

"Everyone seems to know what I'm supposed to be doing except me!" says Mike. "I bet you can't tell me anything about it, either?"

"No, my good friend," replies Jack. "That will be up to your spirit guide, Genia. But, please let us speak."

The two men talk heartedly for about half an hour, then Genia calls Mike over as Jack's spirit guide goes back over to him and tells him that someone dear and special to him is coming. And, in a minute, his wife Anne appears.

"Anne! Anne, my darling," says Jack with tears streaming down his face. "I've been waiting to see you again for years. My beloved, how are you? Is anyone else with you?"

"The rest of our family waits to greet you. Shall we go?"

"Oh Anne. Anything you say, sweetheart."

He turns to Mike... "Mike, I will be seeing you in the near future when you come to stay here for good. Until then, may God be with you my friend." Then, turning back to Anne... "I'm ready to go now, dearest."

"Not quite yet," Anne interrupts. "There's still somebody here to greet you. I made it possible for your reunion. Look!"

Pointing behind then, Jack turns around and sees a small figure running towards him; his closest friend, his dog Rocky. As he jumps up into Jack's outstretched arms, tears roll down heavier now. "Rocky! Rocky! My boy! I just knew it would be possible to see you again," as he pets and strokes him as his friend licks his face. "Come, Rocky. Let the three of us go together to meet everyone else." Then, the three of them disappear while Mike is holding back tears of his own.

"That scene meant more to me than any ad I ever put together," he said.

"I knew you would be touched and happy for Jack. That's why we kept you here to see it. You see, God has made it so that every dream we want does come true... So, let us now go back to the mountain in Paradise."

They do, and Genia talks to Mike for about another two hours. "It's about time for you to go back to your friends. This time, forty-five minutes have passed on earth."

"If I'm not mistaken, it should be about 10:40 there now. It seems like time is starting to catch up on earth to the elapsed time here."

"That's right. Eventually, time will have just about caught up to ours. Remember, stick together body and soul and you'll all be able to conquer any situation. The most important trials are yet to come. Remember, God's heart is waiting for His children to come back to Him. Be one of the first to accomplish this… Now go back! Go back to your earthly body. Go back! Go back!"

Mike returns to his body in the Living Room of George Braxton's house. He lackadaisically gets up. Everyone was sitting down in front of the TV, and they get up and go over to welcome Mike back.

"How are you doing, buddy?" asks John.

"Just a little out of it," replies Mike, "but I'll be okay in a minute or two."

"We didn't know if we should ignore you this long, but considering that other time that you were out for an hour and were still all right, we thought it would still be safe," said Sharon. "We really were concerned."

"I know you probably have a lot to tell us Mike, but before you do, we would just like to tell you that we were watching the 10 o'clock News," said Joy. "It had the attempted bombing of the Rocky Mountain Mall by the bomber Robert Lack. He was apprehended by the FBI after gaining information from Captain Haney and the two officers. Lack was a demolitions expert in the Army and had access to the parts to make the bomb. Sit down and we'll explain in more detail."

They inform Mike of all the details, and in turn he tells them everything that happened on the other side.

"This news will make me think a little more intently about angels," said John. "I'm not quite sure what to believe."

"You have a responsibility to believe in the truth. And, the truth is what you have to decide it is from all the information given and the things that have occurred since we first met. Keep a completely open mind about everything and your decision to believe or not will become clear," explained Mike.

"Okay, Mike. I'll do as you say and hope to get an answer about all this soon," answered John, "and also that it be the complete truth."

"All right, John… I'm sure the rest of you also have some soul-searching to do as well. I say sleep on it and we'll come to some conclusions tomorrow," said Mike. "It's 11:45 and I know you're all probably very tired, but I would like to check out the basement. Do you think we all can manage that?"

"Well, we all *are* pretty tired," said Joy. "What's the big rush about checking out the cellar tonight?"

"I have the deep premonition that there's much more to that basement than any of us have imagined," said Mike, "and we should check it out tonight; not tomorrow."

"Then, I guess we'd better check it out tonight," said Sharon.

"It does give me the creeps," said Doreen, "as well as us, if you don't mind me saying so for all of us. I'd rather do it in the morning, but if we must, then we must tonight. I just say let's do it, then, and get it over with."

"It looks like it's settled," said Billy. "So why don't we head on downstairs and see if there's more to the basement than meets the eye."

"Fine!" said John. "Let's go before we change our minds."

The six of them go to the cellar stairs, turn on the lights and head down to the center of the basement. There, in the center is a big wood carved table. Around the walls are book shelves filled with all kinds of books. At one wall is another metal door.

"This looks more like a library than a basement," said Joy as she walks over and browses through many of the books. "All the books I've looked at seem to be dealing with history; the history of countries throughout the world, focusing on times from as far back as the Book of Genesis in the Bible and as recent as last year. Of course, I don't know if all the books relate to history, but I'm willing to bet they all do."

Everyone else starts flipping through the books and comes to the same conclusion.

"It appears you are right, Joy," says Sharon. "They all seem to deal with world history." She grabs a fancy wooden box that contains a big leather-bound book. "Look at this," as she puts it on the table. All of them gather around it. Then, opening it to reveal the book... "Look at the title: *Completed Testament*." What do you think that means? I know of the Old Testament and the New Testament, but what does *The Completed Testament* contain?"

"Open it up and let's find out," replies John.

"I can't!" exclaims Sharon. "As you can see, there's a lock on it, and there's no key."

"Just bust the lock open," said John. "It doesn't look too secure. Here, give it to me."

"I don't think we should," said Doreen. "It may not be a sturdy lock, but nonetheless it's on there for a purpose."

"Doreen's right," said Joy. "It's not our property and we should respect Braxton's wish to keep it closed. I'm just as curious as you are, John, but we shouldn't damage it in any way; no matter how curious we are."

"Mike, you're the one with some answers," said Billy. "Spiritually, you should be able to tell us what we should do with the book."

"I can," answered Mike. "We shouldn't break into it, but we should bring it with us tomorrow when we meet Braxton and Silver at noon. If we ask Braxton if he would let us read it, I guarantee you he will allow us to."

"I think you're absolutely correct, Mike," said Joy. "Let's do it the right way. How do the rest of you feel about that?" They all agree.

"Good!" said Mike. "Let's put this in a safe place until tomorrow."

Just then, the basement door slams shut.

"WHO SLAMMED THAT DOOR SHUT?" shouted Mike.

"My God, someone's locked us in!" said John as he runs up the stairs to check the door. "The door isn't locked. But how did it shut? There's no one here and there's no wind in the hallway."

As John looks down the hall, the lights start to dim as he sees shadows slowly gliding towards the door. Then, everyone hears moaning, screams and agonizing yells.

"Oh my heavens, it's happening here," said Sharon. "John, quickly, shut and bolt the door. Quickly! Quickly!" As he bolts the door, between the moans, screams and yelling, he hears something dragging across the floor, which then stops on the other side of the door.

"What's happening here, Sharon?" said Billy. "What is that?

Upstairs, John has his ear to the door. Then suddenly, there's a powerful crash against the door that sends John hurtling down the stairs. Everyone gathers around John to make sure he's okay.

"Good Lord! yells Joy. "Are you all right, John?"

"I, I think so. No broken bones or anything like that," reported John as he gets to his feet. He *has* sprained his wrist and ankle.

"You're lucky you didn't break your neck," said Joy. "Then the crashing at the door turns to horrendous pounding. It now sounds like it's going to break through the metal door and find its way to our six friends downstairs. As the screams and pounding at the door intensifies, the five of them turn to Sharon.

Yelling over the noise, they grill her: "Is this the kind of stuff that happens to you when you're alone?"

"Something like that," she replies, "but as I mentioned, it gets worse every time, and this time all five of you are here with me as it's happening. It's never happened before with witnesses."

All six of their hearts begin to pound faster and faster, almost as if they're going to pound and burst right through their chests. The only one that seems as scared almost as much as Sharon is Mike. For Mike, it's as if he's frightened by what he knows rather than by what he doesn't know, like everyone else.

"It sounds like it's about to cave that cellar door right in," yelled Billy. The lights in the basement now start to flicker as the six of them fear they will go out permanently. "Do you see this? It's so cold down here you can see your breath."

"Remember, as I told you," said Mike, "the farther one goes from God, the colder it gets. And, by the looks of things, the uninvited are from the depths of hell."

Now their senses turn to a foul odor in the air. "Do you smell that? Another sure sign that this thing or things are from the lowest part of hell," added Mike.

"It smells like rotting flesh," observed Joy. "We must get out of here. Let's see what's on the other side of *that* metal door over there."

They quickly run to the door and open it. It looks like a food storage room."

"Great!" says John. "At least we won't starve to death while waiting to be frightened to death. And look, there's a window!"

"Rather small, but I think it's big enough for all of us to get out of," commented Joy. "Hurry! Let's get inside and bolt *this* door shut."

They hurry inside and bolt the door. Then, they go to the window and open it up.

"Damn! There are bars on the outside," discovers Joy. "It looks like we're trapped in here. The bars are mounted in solid cement."

"Dog gone it, Mike!" said Billy. "Why did you have us come down here at this time of night? It really could have waited 'til the morning. Now what do we do? From behind the door they now hear something slithering down the basement stairs. "Good God! It's in the basement now. Maybe if we all be quiet it won't find us and go away."

Everyone stops making any sound and waits to see what happens next. It's all silent now as the only sound they hear is the dragging on the basement floor. It appears to be on the other side of the cellar. Now the dragging noise gets louder and louder as it gets closer and closer to the storage room. It now stops right outside the door. Then, with great force, there's pounding and scratching on the door with evil laughing and high-pitched screaming.

"It's right on the other side of the door," says Doreen in terror. "WHAT ARE WE GOING TO DO?"

"Look," says Joy. "In the corner of the room. There are several tool boxes. Maybe they might help. It's worth a try."

"I'LL TRY ANYTHING AT THIS POINT!" yells Mike. As the three men search frantically through the tool boxes, Mike shouts out, "Look! Here's a cordless drill set, and it has bits for concrete."

Mike puts concrete bits into the drill and starts drilling into the cement around the bars. Then, there's dead silence outside the room. Now everyone becomes horrified as they see the hinges on the door begin to loosen more and more. The lights now start flickering in the storage room as they did in the basement minutes before. "If these lights go out, we're screwed because without a moon tonight, it will be too dark for me to see the bars." Billy goes back to one of the tool boxes where he saw a flashlight, takes it out and tries it. The flashlight works fine. The lights then go out as Billy proudly brings the flashlight to the bars.

"Good job, Billy, said Mike. "Now we should have these bars removed in five minutes or so."

"That's if we have five minutes!" observed John. "Quick, Mike. Shine the flashlight on the door."

He does, and the hinges are getting looser with every minute. Then suddenly, the door begins to almost breathe in and out.

"Oh my God! What's out there?" yells Doreen.

"Hurry, Mike. Get those bars free," cries Joy.

The door stops breathing and the hinges begin to loosen again. Just then, Sharon jumps, pounding and yelling on the door.

"WHAT DO YOU WANT FROM ME; FROM US? Leave us alone! Leave us alone! Do you hear?"

Joy then goes over and pulls Sharon away from the door, trying to console and calm her at the same time. Now everyone is sweating with fear. The only thing they can do now is wait for Mike to remove all four bars and lead them to freedom from this insanity. Mike is down to the last bar as he goes faster and faster.

"There. I got all of them," Mike reports. He then shines the flashlight one more time and is horrified to see the hinges just about separated from the door frame. "Quick! Clear that table off. Bring it over here and put that chair by it. Now Billy, you go out first so you can help the ladies out." Billy encounters no problems and waits for the women. "Sharon, you first, then Doreen and Joy, followed by John, then myself," said Mike. In several minutes, everyone but Mike is out. "Now it's my turn."

As Mike gets halfway through the window, he hears the door come crashing in. Then, all of a sudden, a cold chill runs down his spine. Something has grabbed his legs and is pulling him back in.

"HELP! IT'S GOT ME. IT HAS ME AND IT'S PULLING ME BACK IN!"

"Quick!" said Joy. "We have to help Mike!" All five of them run over to Mike, grab him and start trying to pull him out.

"Whatever has him has him pretty strong. I can't see what has him," said John. "It's too dark down there."

"FORGET ABOUT THAT!" said Joy. "JUST GET HIM OUT!"

"Let go of him, you bitch, or bastard, or whatever you are!" shouts Sharon.

As this happens, Mike wonders whether or not this will be the time when he will go back to the spirit world permanently. The icy cold hands of death, of hell itself, have him and won't let him go. But no. He can't give up. He has to try to free himself any way he can.

"Listen, guys!" says Mike. "This is my last chance. On the count of three, I'll jerk forward and all of you pull with everything you've got… ONE, TWO, THREE. NOW PULL!"

One great lurch and Mike becomes free of his hellish captor. They all run to the SUV and drive off the grounds back to the Hotel. Once there, they all gather in Mike's room and discuss what has happened.

"If that was a sample of what's been happening to you, Sharon, then I think you have all of our sympathy," said Doreen. "I don't know which one of you have it worse, you or Mike. Dying all the time, or dealing with those that are dead. By the way, which one of you grabbed the book? You know, *The Completed Testament*? I know I didn't."

After a silence, "Oh no. You mean we left it there on the table?" asked Mike. "We have to go back for it."

"Not until daylight," answered Joy. "I don't think any of us want to go back there during the evening hours. Besides, we need some rest. At least four our five hours. How about we go to our rooms, meet in the morning at 7:00, get some breakfast, and then head on back in the daylight?" All of them agree.

"Are you kidding?" said Billy. "I was going to ask Mike and John to share a room with *me*."

After a nervous laughter, everyone bids good night and goes to their rooms. All except for Mike.

"This whole trip is becoming too dangerous," said Joy. "From bombs to spirits attacking, to dying and high-stakes gambling, not to mention so many other things, and the most puzzling is Braxton and Silver. Three and a half days down with three and a half to go. Who knows what's going to happen next, if we dare to ask?"

"I can't help feeling all this is tied together somehow. Anyway (almost jokingly) how's your research going? I think you already have enough to write a book, if you really want to," said Mike.

"With what's coming up in the next several days, I think I could write a novel. The problem is, who would believe me?" Joy remarked.

"You can always write it in 'fiction'. Fiction readers will believe anything." Mike replied.

"Speaking of believing," said Joy, "I do believe that we should get some rest, too. I'm not trying to get rid or you, but good night!"

"Good night, Joy." And as they part, they give their pinky-bending ritual to one another. It's 4:05 a.m. and Mike is having his familiar nightmare, just with one twist this time...

"This is the 21st Century. That no longer works," says the demon to Mike. "Besides, this is the last dream you'll have of me. Next time, I'll be seeing you in waking hours for the second time, and then one last time when I take you with me forever."

Then, the demon's face draws closer and closer to Mike's face; so closely that it becomes a hideous blur as Mike wakes up screaming again; his body drenched in sweat.

"This has to stop!" declares Mike. "Once and for all, it has to stop."

Mike eventually falls back to sleep. He wakes up at 6:30 and at 7:05 meets everyone in the lobby. They all have breakfast, and then load up the SUV. They drive back to the house, but this time with a different outlook and enter it going to the basement door.

"Look at this!" said Billy. "The door is fine but it's still locked from the inside... I'll go in through the storage room window and unbolt the door." ...Looking to Sharon, "You sure these things don't come out in the daytime?" he asks.

"They never have to me. The daylight is safe," Sharon said.

"That's good enough for me. I'll see you guys in a few minutes," says Billy as he heads for the basement window. In less than five minutes, Billy is standing on the other side of the basement door, opening it up.

"Great!" John declares. "Thanks, Billy. Did you happen to notice the book on the table?"

"No! I didn't. Let's go down and get it."

But, to their amazement,..

"Gone!" said Mike. "No where in sight. That's incredible. Where did it go? Surely the spirit would have no use for it, but yet it's not here."

"Nothing since Sunday makes any sense whatsoever," said Joy. "This is like a bad 'B' movie."

"I don't care if it *is* daylight," said Doreen. "This place is giving me the creeps. Let's get out of here and head back to Denver."

"I agree," said Sharon. "Let's get the hell out of here."

They board up the storage room window, lock the house, and then head back to Denver. As usual, Mike is doing the driving.

"Do you think we should confront Braxton and Silver about what we found out about them, or just keep quiet?" asked John.

"I think we should keep it to ourselves until either we find out more or until Sunday morning," said Joy. "We don't want to tip our hands too early."

"Mike. Stop the van. Right here!" said Doreen. "Now, please, a little girl is in trouble."

Mike pulls to the side of the road and stops. "I have to get out. John, will you come with me? Please, John?"

"Sure, but where are we going?" asks John.

133

"About a half mile in the woods over there. Quickly, she's in desperate need of our help."

"Please be careful," said Joy as Doreen and John head north into the woods.

"I was wondering if she would have any kind of premonition or such after her second visit to the spirit world," said Mike.

"Well, whatever it was, it was definitely real enough for her. I wonder if they'll actually find a little girl in trouble," pondered Billy.

They find a little girl by the edge of the Rocky Mountains.

"Little girl! What happened to you?" asked Doreen. "What's your name and what are you doing out here all alone?"

"My name is Anita Clayton. I was walking in the woods when I got lost. I think I'm a long way from mommy and daddy. I went too far and fell off the rocks; you know, these big ones."

"I believe she's talking about these boulders. How do you feel, Anita?" asked Doreen.

"My left leg hurts really, really bad; and my right arm and also my head."

"She probably has some broken bones as well as a possible concussion," said John. "If we don't know where her parents are, we can't take time trying to find them. *Her* precious time, that is. We have to get her to the SUV. You go with them to the hospital. I'll stay back here and see if I can find her parents."

Doreen walks away from Anita so she can't hear them. "You've come a long way from several days ago while we were in the same general area and Joy asked if you would go with Mike as he searched for his phantom. And you said something like, "I don't want a close encounter of any kind." What happened?"

"Joy was right," replied John. "I was ashamed of myself, and after everything we've been through these past two or three days, I guess I just found my courage."

"I'm sorry that Sharon and I insinuated that you had no guts, but I'll make sure everyone knows your change of heart. Right now, I think we should get back to Anita. She's frightened and hurting, too. We need to get her help in any way, now." But, when they go back to her, they receive a shock.

"She's gone!" exclaimed John. "Where did she go?"

"That's impossible," said Doreen. "I could tell her leg was broken, and she had numerous other serious injuries. Besides, we were just five or six feet from her. We would've seen her get up and limp away, even if that was possible. I assume you didn't see or hear anything, either. Did you?"

"Of course not. I would have said something. Besides, we only talked a minute. That's not enough time for a young girl in her condition to go anywhere without making a sound... Look!" as John points to the leaves where they found her lying. "There's no indentation where she was lying."

They both yell out Anita's name and search the general area where she was found, but no luck. "I don't know what's going on, but I have a very eerie feeling about this," added John.

"I'm inclined to trust your feelings. Let's get the heck back to the SUV. There's something not right about this whole thing. And damn it, it's just not natural for these things to happen in broad daylight. Also, being in these woods doesn't make things any easier to accept," said Doreen.

"Come on, let's get out of here before we disappear, too," said John.

All of a sudden, a heavy fog rolls in. "Where did that come from?" asked John. "I can barely see you anymore."

"Here, take my hand so we don't lose one another," said Doreen.

Then they hear Anita crying out. "Doreen, John, please don't leave me. I'm frightened. Please come find me."

"John, we have to go find her. The poor girl; she's all alone."

"Listen, Doreen, I don't know who or what that is calling, but it can't be Anita."

"Why?" asks Doreen.

"Because whoever or whatever that girl was, she couldn't have disappeared so quickly and silently, even if she wasn't injured. But, she *was* injured severely. And, even more strange was, she knew our names and neither of us told her, did we?"

"You're right, John. Let's get the hell out of here, NOW!"

The fog has become so thick now, neither of them can see one foot in front of themselves.

"Grab my hand again, John, and let's find our way out!"

They walk and walk without saying a word, just desperate to get out of the fog. They walk for what seems like miles, but know it was only half a mile to the road and SUV.

"I know you're afraid, John, but so am I. Wait! I see a clearing. I think I see Mike, Joy and the others."

John suddenly falls in the leaves and Doreen loses hold of him.

"I'll be right back for you, John. Just give me a couple of minutes."

The fog lightens and just about dissipates as Doreen gets to the others by the SUV. I'm so happy to have found you, but we must go back into the woods because John fell and might have hurt himself."

John then comes running over from the SUV.

"Doreen, are you all right?" says John.

"Sure I am. I was worried about you, falling down some fifty feet from here."

"What are you talking about, Doreen. The last I heard from you was when you said to me 'Grab my hand again John and let's get out of here.' After that, I totally lost you. I found my way back here in twenty minutes. Then you showed up some forty minutes after me. We were just about to go looking for you."

A chill runs up Doreen's spine. "Oh my God! Who was I dragging all the way back from there? What or whose, in the name of God, hand was I holding on to for almost an hour?"

"The fog bank just came off the stream down the hill there. As it passed us and went into the woods, it became thicker and thicker. John came running over to us saying that you were lost in there. So, we were waiting for the fog to lift some before going to look for you. Otherwise, there would be six people lost instead of one. Just as it started to clear, we saw you coming out of the fog in our direction," explained Joy.

"You must have gone in the wrong direction 'til we finally found you," said Mike. "John told us what happened when we decided to wait for the fog to lift."

"This whole trip has been eerie and creepy," said Doreen. "I just want to leave, and I mean NOW!"

So, all six of them gather in the SUV and drive back to the Hotel Stanwick. Once there, everyone refreshes themselves and then they meet in Joy's room.

"Am I the only one to notice all these things happening to us in a limitless time," asked Billy.

"You mean, 'time limit', not limitless time," said John.

"Who cares whether or not my English is correct?" barked Billy. "Everything is happening too close to one another for my taste."

"Billy's right," said Mike. "We go from one thing to another to another, and if I'm right, it's going to continue even more so, from now."

4. The Rules Don't Match

"It's 11:40, twenty minutes until we meet Braxton and Silver. Why are you watching the Sports Channel?" asks Sharon.

"I'm finished," answered Mike. "I needed some relaxation, so I was watching the Baseball Play-offs. My team, the L.A. Dodgers, are in the World Series. They're tied two games apiece with the Alaskan Pipe Builders. Oh! Not much time left," as he glances at his watch.

"So! Are we really not going to say anything to Braxton or Silver?" asks John.

"I think not," says Joy. "If they don't show their hands by Sunday, then we'll have no choice. But for now, as Mike says, let's continue to play cards with them."

"I guess we should go down now," says Doreen. "You know how they feel about tardiness."

"Considering they're always on-time to the minute, I guess we should be on-time ourselves," says Billy.

All six of them go downstairs and into Conference Room 3. As they talk, the grandfather clock strikes noon and, sure enough, our two guests greet them.

"Good afternoon," says George. "I trust all of you had a good, prosperous two days or so."

"Are you kidding? We had…" Mike interrupts Billy.

"A wonderful time. Thank you," continues Mike.

"You're all very welcome," says Grea.

"This is one of those rare times when Silver actually talks," whispers Doreen to Joy. "Shhh, Doreen," says Joy. Even if you are correct, shhh…"

"Even though you're all halfway through, you still have a long way to go," begins George. "You've all passed with flying colors right now. But, stay together and help one another. That is most important to get to the next phase. This is where the $10 million will come into effect by your decisions. Of course, for you Miss Bender, you'll receive $3 million no matter what you decide. The money is yours to keep regardless of your decision on Sunday. If you make your mind to stay, you'll be used as an advisor. Or, if you don't, there is no further commitment needed from you. We will replace anyone who decides to leave. There will be a one-week trial period to decide on the replacement. That also goes for everyone. The second person will commit or not to the qualifications. Each person after that will have to decide either to stay or go on with their own lives. This is a decision that each will ultimately have to make. They'll be given the same time as you were. If one fails, someone else will be given the equal amount of time until one person gratefully accepts and finally all six are ready to go. More will be explained in a future meeting. Provided, of course, they have fulfilled theirs. More will be explained next time, whereas everyone will know what the other has chosen. We'll meet again tomorrow at 6:00 in the evening. Good bye and good luck. Oh, and remember, if any of you fail or decide not to take our offer, then you will, in turn, be replaced."

"As one of you once said, 'his words are short, but to the point' or something like that," said John after everyone went into the lobby.

"Well, did you check? Where they gone again?" asked Billy.

"No!" said Mike.

"Why not? It would be nice to know," said Billy.

"What difference does it make? If they're there, it means nothing. If not, we still won't know how they get out or if they're even hiding somewhere in there," answered Mike.

"You might like to know that they weren't in there," said Joy, "nor were they hiding unless they have a secret passageway."

"And the mystery continues…" said Billy.

"The only mystery I want answered right now is what shall I have for brunch." After brunch, Mike goes up to his room and finds a small note under his door. It reads: "You and your five friends might find it stimulating to visit this Holy Ground Church. It can change your whole life. But beware, there are some wolves there dressed in sheep's clothing. They are poison. Here is the address."

"Guess I should go find the others," Mike says to himself. Then, he falls to the floor as he has another life-after-death experience, not realizing his front door was not all the way closed. He drifts into the bluish cloud until it vanishes. This time, though, as he is greeted by Genia, he realizes he is now in a garden-like area with grass, flowers, trees, streams, and many other beautiful sights populated with people and animals.

"Why the change of scenery, Genia?" asked Mike. "I'm not complaining; believe me, I'm not. This is a fantastic place." People are flying, making beautiful art, all kinds of animals around and even people bathing in the springs, nude, for there are no sexual hang-ups or self-consciousness. The enjoyment of God's love is abounding. Animals of all kinds run freely as they have no fear of man. Mike can see tens, and even hundreds, and even thousands of miles as far as the eye can see. "Wow! Is this Heaven, too?"

"No, Mike. This is just the top of Paradise, level 32. With as beautiful and wonderful as Paradise is, it still doesn't compare to Heaven. I brought you back so soon because there are several points I must go over with you before going on. I thought it might be lighter and more pleasant to do that in this are of level 32. Relax, and let's begin. There are only six points left to go over. 1) Radical individualism. We think of ourselves as islands unto ourselves. Even in marriages, we tenaciously hold on to our individualism and independence. Individual salvation; individual destiny, and individual eternal life... We have to stop this way of thinking, especially in our relationship with our spouse, and then parents with their children, and most importantly our family's relationships with God. Until recently, with the advent of old movies like 'The Davinci Code' and others, we never imagined Jesus taking a bride and thus having a family. Jesus, being a perfected human being, expresses even more of a reason why he should be wed and have children. This is the perfect example of the Four-Position Foundation: Jesus and his bride, numbers one and two; their children, number three; and completing the Four would be God, with His love binding them all together. Homosexuality is a subject that should be dealt with only when you have an open mind about it and learn much more here in the spirit world and on earth. Imperfect, fallen people often have a weak sense of marital commitment, such as with wife-swapping, divorce, the idea of 'what's in it for me?', not living for the sake of your spouse and vise versa... Also, some people think relating to their parents on a first-name basis is better, not vertically. We need to have respect for our parents as they are the parents in the subject position, while we are the children in the object position. And finally, many fallen people are 'truth-centered' rather than 'heart-centered'. Truth is good and wise until heartistic love takes over. Following one's heart is the most important attribute there is. Heart first, then comes truth and logic. There is a fine line between truth, logic and heart. Love.

Things I've discussed with you may seem a little unclear right now, but time and actualization, plus study, will make everything become clear. Also, have faith, and the knowledge will come to you… Now, I've gone over 25 points with you. These were just some of the sections of what I wanted to discuss with you. Besides those 25 points, I have gone over dozens of other items which you should know. Even after talking with you about numerous more points, there will be hundreds, even thousands of other things left to learn. Again, time and investigation will help you to know the whole truth. But, don't worry, Mike. Some of the answers to the questions you asked when I promised you answers, you will receive as I promised. There is one level and area I would like you to visit with me. You will find it interesting as well as irritating. But, you must learn to deal with and understand it, as well as others. It's a level area where people are unusually ridiculous."

"Is this some low level?"

"No! By no means. It's in the higher levels of the Growth Stage. The people there are good and harmless; just confused. Would you like to go there with me now?"

"Certainly," answered Mike. "Let's go! At least I think, I mean, let's go! I'm skeptical about what I'll find out."

So, Genia and Mike disappear and then reappear in a quite pleasant area of a city. Everything is clean and orderly. Mike and

Genia watch several people go by until Mike asks what they're waiting for.

"This is a level where people are obsessed with time. I'm waiting to pick up two or more people that will have a dispute about time… There, I see two such men ready to progress in one such episode. Come, let's watch."

"Excuse me! My watch has stopped. Do you have the time. I have a 1:00 appointment and I don't want to miss it," said one of the men to the other.

"Yes! It's 10:30. I hope I've helped you," said the other man.

"That's strange. My watch stopped at 11:20. It's got to be later than *that*!"

"Well, if you don't want the time, then why bother to ask me?" said the second man.

"Because I was looking for the correct time," said the first man.

"You didn't ask me for the correct time, you just asked me for the time. Next time you want the correct time, ask me for it and I'll tell you I have an incorrect time," the second man replied.

"That's ridiculous. I said my watch has stopped which means it obviously has the wrong time. So, why would I want the wrong time from you, too? It's evident that I want the correct time, you idiot."

"Then, next time ask for the correct time. Then, I'll inform you that I have an incorrect time, which means then that you should ask someone else for the correct time… Here, take my watch. Now you have two incorrect times, and that is better than having one correct time. Don't worry about me. I'll find another watch with the incorrect time," said the second man.

"Why would you want another watch that has the incorrect time?"

"Because, if I have the incorrect time, I can always start up a conversation with somebody asking me for the time," said the second man.

"You're crazy! Let me outa here," said the first man.

"He's not the only one, Genia," said Mike. "Let me outa here too, before I lose my mind."

They both appear in the same area they were just in a few minutes before. "Whew! I'm sure glad to be back here again. Tell me, is everyone is that area of that level all like that, or is there some normality there?" asked Mike.

"Good heavens, no and yes to your second question," said Genia. "That was one of the most extreme cases you'll find there."

"Then why did you show me that?" asked Mike

"Because if you could handle that, then you could handle anything in that area. Admittedly, you did struggle, but you would have come around. Believe me when I say this: I have come to know you better than you know yourself. And that's not meant to be something bad, but rather something very good. You see, I can see all your wonderful and heavenly potential; qualities you never knew existed within yourself," explained Genia.

"You're not trying to tell me I'm in the position of the returning Christ, are you?" asked Mike.

"No, Mike, I'm not. With all your endearing qualities, you're far from that title. Above and beyond all your good qualities would be a perfected individual as well as a sinless man, and I'm sorry but you have neither of those qualifications, as well as many others."

"Oh, you don't have to apologize to me, Genia. I wouldn't want that kind of responsibility to God, mankind, and even spirit-kind, if you want to go that far."

"Then, I don't know if what I'm going to tell you is good or bad news for you," said Genia. "And that is, you still have a big responsibility to mankind."

"Everyone keeps telling me something like this, but yet I still don't have a clue. Do you think you might clue me in to some of this now?"

"Mike. I'll tell you this much, and that is from your next visit here I will begin to give you answers to all your questions. I believe you're ready for many answers, now."

"Well, at least some of my questions are going to be answered next time."

"And each time after that more and more of your questions will be revealed."

"So, I guess it's time for me to go back, now."

"Yes," said Genia, "and when you return, things will also begin to fall into place. Let it begin with you and your five friends visiting The Holy Ground Church. They will have an idea of what's going on because when you passed out, you left the door to your room open. So, out of concern, they came in, found you and the note, and then stayed with you, waiting for you to regain consciousness. You blacked out at 12:55. In time, you were here an hour and ten minutes. By earth standards, you will find also seventy minutes have also passed. You'll notice this happen more and more often. The time there is 2:05. Go back! Go back to your body! Go back, Mike, back, back, back..."

"It looks like Mike is starting to come to," said Sharon. "I hate taking chances with his life when he's out so long. At least we had the mind to give him a pillow and blanket this time so he would be more comfortable."

"Yes, thanks for the little comforts," said Mike. "But you really didn't have to worry about me."

"It's easy for you to say," said Billy, "but this time you were out the longest time you ever were."

"Actually, excluding the time I went to see Genia about the bomb, this was definitely the shortest time I spent there... Well, excuse me; I forgot about the time difference from there to here. This time, our times coordinated exactly the same with each other's time. Seventy minutes there was the same as seventy minutes here. The time line is becoming identical. It does that so time becomes stable."

"Are you up to telling us what happened there this time, Mike?" asked Joy.

"Yes! Let me start..."

So, Mike tells everything as his photographic memory is working as usual; especially since there was so little to remember.

"And Genia didn't say what is supposed to begin with 'The Holy Ground Church'?" asked Joy.

"No, she didn't. You all read the note," said Mike. "John, is that address far from here?"

"Only about 25 minutes from here," he replied.

"Great! Let's freshen up and meet in the lobby at 5:15. Okay with everyone?" asked Mike. (Yes!) "Fine. See you in two to three hours."

Each of them goes to their room and freshens up. Once everyone is ready, they all meet in the lobby. From there they proceed to the SUV and drive to the Church located in an older, but quite quaint part, of Denver. Before going in, they all agree it best not to mention why they came there or even why they are all there in Denver, period. They park the SUV in a parking lot behind the Church which looks as if it was to be used by members of the Church.

"This Church looks more like a cloister," said Doreen. "And look at the carvings," as she goes to the front for a closer inspection.

"Look at this plaque on the wall by the door," said Joy. "It says 'Founded and built by Rev. Jonathan M. Stevens in 1956'. It's almost a century old. It's been kept up pretty well, though."

"This place is close to your age, Mike," observed John.

"Not quite. I'm only ninety-two," joked Mike. "Shall we see if anyone's at home? Mike pushes the doorbell which has a very pleasant chime.

"Can I help you?" asks a lady in her mid-fifties who answers the door and introduces herself as Alice Beamer.

"Yes!" said Mike. "We were driving by your Church and were very interested in checking it out, providing of course that we're not disturbing anyone or anything."

"No. Come on in," said Alice. "We're always open to the public for worship or just plain curiosity."

"It's a beautiful Church," said Joy. "Where does your Church's name come from?"

"Well, since it was built in 1956, we, the Church members, have blessed many areas in the United States as well as all around the world. We call these blessed areas 'Holy Grounds', thus giving us, or the Church, it's name."

"Do you have a specific purpose?" asked Joy.

"Yes. We're preparing the way for the return of Jesus Christ," said Alice. "You might know him better as "The Lord of the Second Advent" or "The Second Coming of the Messiah," she explained.

"Do you really believe in all that?" asked John.

"Most definitely," replied Alice. "And, we believe we're actually living in that time period now... You see all these pictures on the wall? They're of Church members years and decades before us. They start from the earliest and work their way up to the present."

"John, come over here," said Doreen. "Take a look at this picture. It says it was taken twelve years ago. Take a good look."

"So, what's the big deal about *this* picture?" asked John. After a closer inspection... "Oh my goodness! It's Anita Clayton with a man and a woman standing in front of a house."

"You're right!" exclaimed Alice. "That is Anita Clayton and her parents, standing in front of their house in Boulder, here in Colorado. But, how do the two of you know her?"

"It's incredible, but somehow she hasn't changed from this picture and when we..."

Doreen interrupts John's comments with, "When we last saw her several years ago..."

"I'm sorry, but you have to be mistaken. It's a sad story, but one year after this picture was taken, Anita and her parents were hiking in the mountains when all of a sudden a heavy fog came in. Her parents lost Anita and went looking for her. The fog was so heavy they didn't see a shallow ditch. They stumbled into it and her mother bashed her head on a rock, but was still conscious. Her father fell and broke his neck. He died instantly. Her mom could hear Anita crying for help, but was too badly hurt to help her. This went on for about an hour. Then, Anita's cries were finally silenced. After the fog lifted, about two hours later, the Police found Anita's parents. In tears, her mother explained what happened and shortly thereafter died from the concussion, never finding out what had happened to her daughter. Shortly after that, they found Anita's body. She evidently fell off the rocks, breaking several bones, and like her mother, she also had a concussion from which she, too, died. Strangely enough, not ten feet from her was the body of a child abductor. The Police had been searching for him the past two years. They had recently found out who he was. For him, it ended when he got his due as he was bitten by a poisonous snake and died. A crazy ending to a tragic story. So you see, you couldn't possibly have seen her unless it was more than eleven years ago," explained Alice.

"Well, in a little while we're going to tell you the strangest story," said Doreen. "I just hope you won't think us crazy or any such thing."

"We've heard some pretty wild stories here, most of them actually true, so believe me when I say just be honest and chances are we'll believe you," said Alice.

"I have a few questions if you don't mind," said Mike.

"Certainly, Mr. Wakings wasn't it?" asked Alice.

"Yes, but just call us by our first names. My first question is, what connection did the Clayton's have with your Church? And secondly, do you remember that child abductor's name?"

"Well, the second question first," replied Alice. "His name was Kyle Thompson. And the first question's answer is the Claytons were extremely high contributors, financially. Their family went all the way back to Denver in the 1800's. They came here from California after striking it rich with gold. After coming here, they bought quite a bit of land and prospered with it. Over the years, though, all the Claytons left Colorado for other prospects around the country. Some of them even went to Europe. Finally, in the early 21st century, there were just a handful of Claytons left. They were still quite wealthy and joined our movement, or Church if you prefer, in 2007. After the three of them died eleven years ago, the last few of them moved on to New York City. They still send us contributions, though. Anita's parents' names were Julia and Kenny. They served us the most and will forever be in our hearts."

"You have many pictures in this long, beautiful hallway," remarked Joy. "When you're quiet, you can almost hear a pin drop."

"It's almost 6:00," said Alice. "In a minute you'll hear our members singing what we call a Holy Song. The echo throughout the halls will be especially glorious to hear. Just listen to the first verse; then we can go to my office to talk more deeply. Listen! They're starting."

When I behold the Lord of all,
my old self dies away.
So dies the world of sinfulness
giving birth to good.
Soon a new self emerges,
clear and bright and pure;
come and behold the new life,
heaven and earth reborn.

"That's beautiful," said Joy. "Who wrote them?"

"Different members from the early years of our Church," said Alice. "Come, let's go to my office." They all file in and take a seat in her spacious office. "Begin wherever and whenever you like," said Alice.

So, Doreen begins with the moment she heard a little girl's cry up to the point where her five friends found her and drove back to the Hotel.

"That really was some story," said Alice. "But while you were walking through the fog, holding John's hand for an hour but not seeing him, didn't you even talk to him during that time, or at least didn't he talk to you?"

"Yes, we did talk, but who or whatever it was sounded just like John, and was familiar with our situation."

"Did you tell your friends this point?" asked Alice.

"Yes," said Doreen, "but they were just spooked and mystified, as I was."

"Look, I'll tell you, I'm excellent at being able to discern who's telling the truth and who's lying. My gut feeling, putting all logic aside, is that you *have* been telling me the whole, complete truth. Which means Anita's spirit is earthbound for some reason, and we must help her. I say 'we' because it's obvious she has some reason to connect to you and your friends. What it is, I don't know."

"I think I do," said Joy. "But, that would take a story even wilder than the one Doreen just told you. You can believe me on that."

"Oh! Now you really have my interest," said Alice. "Wouldn't you please try to tell me about it? It's 6:35 and everyone goes to bed at 10:00. You can talk to me up to that point, and if you're not finished, we can continue after we all have a closing prayer. I don't care if I have to stay up all night. I really need to know the whole story."

152

"Everyone looks to me for guidance, or to Mike. And, I think this would have to be your decision, Mike; not any of us," said Joy.

"Alice, can I hold both of your hands for a moment. It's very important," said Mike.

"If you say so, Mike… Did you find what you were looking for?" as Mike releases her hands.

"Yes!" says Mike as he now turns to the others. "Alice is telling the truth. She really does believe us. So, I guess we can tell her the complete story, but in a nutshell."

"How did you know this from holding my hands?" asks Alice.

"It's all part of the story, Alice," answers Mike. "Shall we begin?... It all started several months ago when I was having these nightmares…"

Mike explains the whole story while each of his friends add their stories, as well. They go on 'til 9:55. Alice takes a break to end the day for her people. At 10:20, Alice comes back and Mike and the others continue their stories. This goes on 'til 2:15 a.m., when Mike finishes.

"This may sound crazier than *your* story, but I believe everything all of you have told me," reported Alice.

"Alice, would you mind giving your hands to me once more?" asks Mike.

After holding her hands for a couple of moments, he is content with what he has picked up. "Once again, Alice was truthful with us. She *does* believe everything we told her," he reported.

"Actually, I believe *that* is more amazing than the stories themselves," said Sharon.

"Yes, that's true," said Mike. "But, it probably has something to do with the factor that she and the followers know something very deep and just as amazing as our stories. What it is happens to be unclear to me, and she is not ready to tell us what that is, yet."

"You're right, and the reason is because I must wait for all of you to learn a little more before I confide in you," said Alice. "Then I can be totally open and honest with you. You see, it's not a matter of whether or not you believe me, but it's because you won't know whether or not I'm just imagining it or not. Even with Mike's power, he won't be able to tell if I'm actually imagining it. So you see, I must wait for you to learn more before I can share the truth with all of you."

"I think we all understand," said Joy. "When would you like us to come back?"

"Well, this is now early Friday morning. How about you come back Saturday morning at about 9:00," said Alice. "Then after that, we can meet again tomorrow evening at 8:00. Is that okay with all of you?... You all will be ready to hear, understand and believe me by 8:00 tomorrow evening. Will all of you join me in a closing prayer?" With a little hesitation, they all say yes. "Would you please hold hands? Let me begin…"

Alice leads them in a prayer that lasts five minutes. She closes, and then bids everyone good night. The six of them load up in the SUV and start driving back. During the trip, they all converse about all that transpired that evening and early morning. When arriving back at the Hotel, tired and exhausted from the whole day, they say their good-nights to one another and agree to get a little extra rest since it is now 3:00 a.m. They plan to meet in the lobby again at 10:00 a.m. Everyone goes to their rooms except, as at other times, Joy and Mike. They meet outside her room, agreeing to talk for only five minutes, so they can get some decent rest. Joy then suggests they go into her room to talk more privately.

"It seems every day, without fail, you have journeyed to the other side," said Joy. "No reason to believe today, tomorrow or Sunday will be any kind of exception."

"I know," agreed Mike. "And, with so many unanswered questions from our lives here on earth and those concerning the spirit world, I expect things to be moving even faster than they already have… At least I won't have to worry about another nightmare tonight. I just have to deal with this demon in reality now. It just seems like all the rules just don't match up with reality in so many ways. If only I could make some sense out of everything that's going on."

"Don't worry, Mike. I believe in just about everything now, and that means that there's a solution coming to everything," said Joy.

"Amazing! You believe in everything now except for the fact that I went to Heaven, right?"

"I'm sorry, Mike," said Joy. "I can accept almost all that has happened, but that… I don't believe you saw Heaven."

"Why is it so hard for you to believe when you have no trouble with anything else?"

"Because it's my *deepest* spiritual belief that just can't be shaken."

"All right, Joy," said Mike. "I'll keep trying, though. For now, have yourself a good night or good morning or good whatever it is."

"You too, Mike"

They bend their pinkies at each other as Mike goes to his room for hopefully a good sleep this time... The next morning, after everyone's had a good breakfast, they all get together in the lobby at a little past 10:00. After morning greetings, John is the first to speak."

"You know, last night I had this dream. It was so real. So real that I can't deny it."

"That's strange," said Sharon. "So did I, and I couldn't wait to tell all of you about it."

And in turn, Billy, Doreen and even Joy reported having a dream so realistic that they all wanted to share it with the others; all, that is, except for Mike.

"That's peculiar," said Mike. "All I had was the best night's sleep in months. But, I'm contented with that. I just hope that I'm not going to pay for it with some extra weird stuff in my waking hours. But, I think it best you all share your dreams up in my room."

"Good idea, Mike. Let's go there right now," said Joy. And the six of them gather in Mike's room, share a refreshing drink, and then begin to tell of their dreams. John starts first...

"I was teaching at one of my seminars when all of the people in the audience started to turn into angels, one-by-one. There wasn't much of a physical change in them. Some had wings, others had features in their faces change in such a way that you just knew they were angels. Within a few minutes, they all had changed in one way or another. I knew, though, that they were all angels. Then, in turn, they all asked me questions about my life and what I thought it meant to be a man, or as some said, a child of God. I asked them what they wanted from me and they said that they wanted me to know the real truth about who they were

156

and what their purpose was. I told them I thought I knew. Then they said I was all wrong and that the truth was being give to me from the spirit world, Genia and Mike Wakings. Finally, they said not to throw away this special gift given me or I'll forever regret it. At that point, I woke up. It was as real as us talking here now. I now resolve myself to believe all that you have said, Mike. I can't go back to teaching the way I used to. This was the final straw that broke the back of my own reality. I trust and believe in you."

"Well John," responded Mike, "I don't know what to say accept welcome aboard. I'm happy and thrilled that you have accepted the truth... Who wants to go next?"

"I will," said Sharon. "I'm sure, after what we all said and especially John, that for each of us, this was as real as John explained... In my dream, I was trapped in the attic of a house I was unfamiliar with. The spirits, or whatever they were, were coming up the staircase to the attic. There was a clock on the wall and it was going backwards at a tremendous pace. As the time went in reverse, everything around me was changing. The, I was in a graveyard, all alone. I was so frightened, but it became unbearable when a hand came out of one of the graves. The, a face and torso, until the whole body of a young woman came out and walked up to me, face-to-face. She started to speak to me, but as she did, dirt and worms were coming out of her mouth. As words began to form, they said I must pay, and to look to Genia and Mike Wakings for the answer to all of our salvation. Then, I woke up... I've only known you a little over five days, but yet it seems like you've become a beacon of hope for all of us."

"It looks like a trend starting here," said Joy. "Why don't you go next, Billy. Unless, that is, if you have something to say, Mike."

"No. I think I will wait until everybody's spoken."

"Well," proceeded Billy, "for me it started out where I was wandering through a desert of trash. I was so depressed. All of a sudden, as I was walking, there came to be thousands of people crying for me to help them. I said I was sorry for I had nothing to give them, but they kept on asking me for help. As I continued walking, the desert turned into a road. All around, the trash turned into decent items, better than I ever had. I wanted to rest, but I had the enthusiasm to continue on. As I kept on walking down the road, it turned into solid gold. Everything around me became beautiful and priceless items. I was so happy I decided to stay there. Also, there were foods and drinks that would make your mouth water. Then, a bright glowing sign said, 'continue this way'. So, begrudgingly, I continued on. Finally, I came to the end of the road where I found a gorgeous city built of gold and diamonds. The, I saw Mike and a lady next to him whom he called Genia. They said, 'Follow us to the city and enjoy everlasting peace, love and prosperity'. Then, I woke up. I now feel I have no choice but to follow Mike."

"And the trend continues," commented Joy. "I trust you can all understand the basis of your dreams, and where they're leading. Doreen, why don't you go next."

"It looks like besides Mike, I was the only one who saw Genia in actual life," she began. "And, that's where my dream begins. I was with her in Paradise, enjoying myself. Then, quite quickly, Genia started to show me each of the lower levels. It went from happiness and joy to despair and loss of hope, then finally to the tormented souls in hell. I was so depressed, I begged her to let me go back to Paradise. She told me that I had to spend twelve days at each level, which added up to 396 days altogether.

Next, I would have to spend four days in limbo for me to contemplate my whole life. I pleaded with her to let me go back to Heaven where I spent the last twelve days of my 396, making a total of 400 days. Next, she pointed to a figure in the distance and said to follow him. And, you guessed it. As the figure came closer, I recognized it to be Mike. Then, I woke up... Okay, Joy. It's your turn, and I can't wait to hear this one, as I'm sure everyone else feels the same."

"Well, mine is pretty short, but meaningful," explained Joy. "I was in my office at L.A. when in came someone who looked just like me. She sat across from me and started talking to me. She said I was an excellent therapist except for when it concerned Mike Wakings. Then, all of a sudden, her head started to enlarge bigger and bigger. Next, she became a reflection of myself in a large mirror. I took a hand object and smashed the mirror into dozens of pieces. But, before I knew it, my own head started to enlarge as well. It got so big and heavy, I couldn't keep it up any longer and I fell to the floor. Finally, in came Mike and who I assumed was Genia. She said to listen to what Mike tells me and my head would become normal size again. So, Mike came over and started preaching to me. As he did, my head grew smaller and smaller until it was normal size again. Then, he stretched out his hand and said 'Come with me now, and I'll bring you into the light. So, I took his hand and walked with him into a brilliant white light. It was so warm and peaceful inside, I wanted to see where it led to, but then I woke up."

"Wow! That was wonderful," said Sharon. "But your dream was no shorter than any of ours. As a matter of fact, it was a little longer."

"Well, there you have it ladies and gentlemen," said Joy. "We've all been lead in our dreams which we admit were as real as life to Mike, who seems to have all the answers. Even *I* can't deny the reality of what has happened to us all. And, you say that you didn't have any special dreams, Mike?"

"No, nothing out of the ordinary, except my dreams *were* ordinary and no nightmares," Mike said. "But, the biggest nightmare is going to be reality for me. I can't escape it… For your dreams I'm quite honored that you all had such a high esteem for me. I feel as if I know all the answers to your questions or situations. But, for some reason, I'm still not qualified to help all of you, yet."

"That's okay, Mike," said Billy. "We all still have faith and trust in your abilities even if we have to wait a little longer for them to surface. I mean, you've done so much already, we just don't want to push you."

"That's right," said John. "As long as we have answers by late Sunday afternoon."

"John, please have consideration, even though I think you've received many answers already about the spirit world and especially about angels," said Joy.

"You're right, Joy. I shouldn't be so antagonistic toward you, Mike. Forgive me," said John.

"It's all right, John. I need…"

Then Mike drops to the floor as so often before.

"Speaking of answers, it looks like he's gone to get some more as we speak," said Doreen.

"Let's make him comfortable," said Joy. "We have no idea if we'll be here a minute or hours.

Now Mike travels back to a stream-laced garden where he meets Genia.

"Hi there, Genia. I was just…"

"No time for pleasantries, Mike. I'm here to tell you that several facts or comments I told you while you were here are false."

"Why would you tell me lies?" asked Mike.

"Don't bother me with that now. I'm sending you back to your body on earth, and tell your friends back there that I'm finished with you and them. They, as well as yourself, can forget anything about the Kingdom of Heaven. None of you will reach it."

"But what did we, what did I do to deserve all this. My friends were really just starting to accept everything. Now you tell me for us to forget all that's transpired."

"I have no more time to waste with you. Go back to your earthly body and leave here," said Genia.

"Will I ever see you again, Genia?" he asks with almost a tear running down his face.

"Go back I say! Go back!

Then Mike feels a rush as he awakens back in his room.

"He's coming to," said Billy. "Must have been a time difference again. He was only gone a few minutes… "Hi Mike. How are things on the other side?"

"Sit down, everyone," said Mike. "I have something to tell you I don't think any of you will like. Personally, I don't like it one bit."

After Mike tells of his meeting with Genia, everyone is in shock.

"Well, what do we do now?" asks Doreen.

161

"I'll tell you what I'm going to do and suggest you all do the same, provided of course you feel the same way as I do," said Mike. "I'm going to do everything as planned. And, that includes going out of my way to help others. If Genia thinks she has made a miser out of me, let her, but so far I've given a lot and received even more. We still have earthly mysteries to deal with like Braxton and Silver, and other things. Are all of you in this with me?"

"You bet, Mike," said John. "We all have given and received a lot, and damn if I'm going to quit now."

"That's fabulous, John. How about the rest of you?" Everyone agrees with John.

"It just won't be the same without Genia," says Sharon.

"We're adults. And more fuller adults than when we first got here," said Mike. "Besides Braxton and Silver, we have the Holy Ground Church to deal with. And, I tell you where my mind is at right now. And that's back in the mountains where you (pointing at John) and Doreen first met Anita. I believe she needs our help and even though I'm cut off from Genia, I still have my gifts or powers as you may see it and am still spiritually open. I also feel there's a connection between Anita and that child snatcher, Kyle Thompson. I say we start there. How about you guys?"

"You bet, Mike," they all say. "What do you think, Joy?"

"I'm proud of all of you. It's back to the mountains."

They all gather in the SUV and head back to the area where they first heard Anita's cries. It's 12:15 p.m.

"This is where we left the two of you, Doreen," announces Mike. "Why don't you and John bring us to the place where you found Anita."

They make it to the exact spot where John and Doreen first saw Anita lying on the ground in pain and agony. But, little do they know that someone else is watching their every move.

"Anita! If you can hear me," says Doreen, "I'm here with my friends who want to help you as much if not more than myself. Please, Anita, come to us so that we may help you. For some reason you can't cross over to the other side, but we're here to help you do so, so you can be with your mommy and daddy who are still waiting for you to go to them."

Faintly at first, but then becoming stronger and stronger until full volume is heard... "I can't leave; he won't let me. He has all of us here. Please, help us, please! He's a strong and powerful bad man."

"Anita," says Mike, "are you talking about Kyle Thompson?" (Yes!) "Joy! Did you get that information I asked you to find out on your laptop?" (Yes!) "What was it?"

"According to the Police reports, Thompson had kidnapped eleven boys and girls. Their bodies were found scattered all over this area."

"Maybe Anita was the twelfth... Anita, did Kyle hurt you in any way?"

"Yes! He hit my head on a big rock. It hurt so bad. Then, I found myself with eleven other boys and girls around my age. We were all trapped in these woods by that man, Kyle. He is strong. He won't let any of us go back with our families. *Please* help us go home."

"Just as I thought," said Mike. "It wasn't the fall that killed Anita, but Thompson himself. He killed them all in this area of the woods. Now he has control over their spirits because they were too young to fight back. They date back to 22 years, when he went on a killing spree."

"Good Lord!" said Sharon. "What can we do to save these poor imprisoned souls?"

"We have to send that creep right to hell. And, since she's a little bit more spiritually open than the rest of you, it's now up to Doreen and myself. But, we need all of your support. Can you do it, Doreen?"

"Anything to free these children. I'm ready."

"Then let's start!... Anita, can you show yourself to Doreen and myself? If you can, then do it now. Now, Anita! Now! Show yourself now!"

A white mist starts to materialize into a little girl's shape. In a minute, it takes complete form. The spirit of Anita has now completely appeared.

"Good girl. Can you ask the other eleven children to appear, as well?"

"I'm trying really hard," said Anita, "but the spirit of Mr. Thompson is not allowing them to come, too."

"Kyle Thompson, I command you in the name of Jesus Christ and God Himself to appear before us this instant..." Mike and Doreen wait a minute, but nothing happens. "Thompson, if you do not appear right now, then we will take the souls of all twelve children away from you," declared Mike.

"I feel a strong evil approaching," said Doreen.

"We can also feel it too, you guys," said Joy. Another mist appears, but this time it's dark and faded. This too now takes the form of a person. A man about six feet tall, 200 pounds, with a darkness all his own. The wind starts blowing and the withering orange and brown leaves of Autumn whirl around him. He has the look and smell of death all around him. The man becomes solid. The features of his face are distorted by a huge sinister smirk. His eyes are cold and deep as if his sockets go all the way to the back of his head. He stares a few moments, then begins to speak in a rusty, deep-toned voice.

"Really, you didn't have to evoke the name of Christ for me to appear. Just the threat of taking my twelve children away from me was enough to rile my spirit up before you. And six of you all here just for me. You do me more honor than I deserve. But, putting all humor aside, six of you could never take my children away from me. You'll soon find that out."

Mike and Doreen can clearly see the form of Kyle Thompson's body, while the other four can only see a mist masquerading as a human soul. But, they do feel and sense the evil that is transmitted from it.

"Stop calling them your children," objected Doreen. "They each have their own families which you bar them from ever seeing or being with."

"Be kind, Doreen," said Mike. "Thompson suffers from the delusion that he is actually their parent. Sick and twisted for sure, but real enough for his warped mind."

"Warped, you say. Then how come they stay with me and don't leave to go elsewhere?"

"Because from the first child, you made a deal with evil demons that once killed by your hands and your hands only, that their spirits are bound here in these woods until the day comes when even your soul will be freed from bondage. Until that deal is broken they remain in your possession. Oh, but we do intend on breaking this hold you have on them *and* sending you to hell, level one, rock bottom, where you belong until the day of cleansing comes which happens to be a long time for you. Many of the other souls in hell's bottom will be saved before you. Crimes against children are among some of the lowest offenses in hell. And, I've done my homework to reveal all the other murders you've committed over the years. Shame on you," pronounced Mike.

"What do you mean, Mike, by 'other murders'?" asked Joy.

"It seems as though killing the children wasn't enough for Thompson. Over the past twenty-two years, he also murdered the grieving parents that didn't die by some other means. As a total, between children and parents, he's murdered some thirty-one people," said Mike.

"So? Do you really think, as I said before, that six of you can stop me and free the children?" said Kyle. "I've dealt with far more power than six of you can muster!"

"Let's see. Everyone, surround him," says Mike.

"I'm afraid to stay here alone," said Anita.

"Don't worry, Anita," said Mike. "Soon you'll be with the spirits of the other eleven boys and girls. Trust me. Don't be afraid. You're not alone. Go over and be with Doreen."

"If you do, Anita, I'll punish you later when they're all gone," threatened Kyle.

"Don't listen to him, Anita. His power is soon going to become useless against you and the other children," said Mike.

The six of them form a circle around Kyle and the soul of Anita goes to Doreen.

"Everyone, I am going to summon the spirits of the other eleven children," said Mike. "I will be responsible for five, you Doreen will take on two others besides Anita, and the other four of you will be responsible for one soul each… I now call, with the love and power of Jesus Christ and God Himself, the eleven tormented souls of Kyle Thompson. I call you with the power granted to me from the spirit world itself. I now behold the authority from all 33 levels of all stages of the spirit world."

"My power is greater than yours, little man. I'll kill all six of you like I did all the children and their parents. Even the five parents that didn't die by my hands are tormented as well… I summon the demons and spirits of hell to appear and fight by my side."

Then Mike and the others, as well as the children themselves, can feel an even stronger evilness descend upon them. The forms of three demons and six evil spirits appear, making a stronger circle around Kyle.

"Our power will crush the six of you like bugs," declared Kyle. "Then, I'll take the children back with me and punish them for disobeying me. And punish the twelve of you, I will. You think you were in fear and torment all these years. You've felt nothing until I have you back in my strength after I dispose of these insignificant fools."

"Please Doreen, Mike and all of you," pleads Anita. "Please don't let him take us back."

All the other children cry their pleas as desperately as they can. Tears fall from their cheeks. The wind whirls up around the spirits and demons. "We all want to go home to be with our mommies and daddies."

"There is a reason why you picked parents with just one child, isn't there, Thompson?" asked Mike.

"If there's anything you can say or do, Mike, now's the time," Doreen anxiously said.

"Mike has a plan, uh, don't you Mike?" asked John.

"Of course he does," said Joy. "Don't even question him."

"We're all behind you, Mike. Show him our strength. Show them all," added Billy.

"I've dealt with spirits like all of you before," chimed in Sharon.

"And you cowered at them as well," said Kyle. "Why? Because you know you're not as powerful."

"Not anymore!" retorted Sharon. "I shan't run from them or you anymore. Go ahead, Mike. Why does he just deal with families of only three?"

"Because, as I once mentioned, God created man to exist in a Four-Position Foundation. That's God, man, woman and children. To deal with more than one child would weaken him and his demons and spirits severely. But, one of us for every two families offset the balance."

"So I can't disagree with you about that," said Kyle, "but you're missing one big ingredient."

"And what's that, you arrogant son of a bitch?" asked Mike.

"The parents. They're the missing link between the strength all of you would have since you don't have enough power with all six of you combined. And forget the children. They have no strength among all of them. And one more piece of information; the parents can't help because this is MY domain and they can't enter it without my permission… Now children, come with me and serve your punishment. No more sniffling, no more tears, no more mommies and daddies. It's time now to come with me, for these weak men and women have no more power."

"What do we do, Mike?" asked Joy. "And why the circles?"

"Because, Kyle, I was counting on you doing just what you did. You see, your demons and spirits created a circle around us

168

which made *our* circle around *you* even stronger. But, you're right; we still don't have enough power to defeat you and your spirits by ourselves until we all grow a little bit more, spiritually. So, that's why I'm going to summon the spirits of the children's parents, NOW. Now, Kyle Thompson, we're going to riiiiiip your soul from these children!"

"But you can't bring the parents," objected Kyle. "Not without my permission!"

"That's where you made your biggest mistake," said Mike. "By bringing the demons and spirits here first, you opened the door for goodness to work. If God's side is struck first, then God can give permission for the good to strike back. And, by bringing your spirits here you opened the door, or in other words gave us the opportunity, to bring down or give permission for us to call the spirits of these children's parents down here to help… The six of us, Joy, Billy, Doreen, John, Sharon and myself now call upon the parents of their tormented children to come down to this soiled ground and bring this tormentor of yourselves as well, back down to the bottom of hell. The gates are now open, and the walls have tumbled down. Come! We call on you with the grace of God."

Then, the sky becomes brighter and a warmth encircles everyone in the group. Twenty-four bright souls descend upon everyone below, so as to attack the demons and spirits guarding Kyle. With a horrifying screech piercing the woods, the demons and spirits now begin to fade away into oblivion.

"NO! COME BACK! COME BACK!" shouts Kyle.

"It's over now, Thompson," declares Mike. "Go back to the hell you came from willingly and save yourself the effort of battle. Go now! Go!"

ou're crazy if you think I'm defeated," retorted Kyle.

the spirits of the parents are busy pulling the nine evil
back down to hell, then I will now destroy the six of you,
after I restored these woods to my world, the children will be
e once again. Now DIE all of you, DIE NOW AND
OREVER LEAVE US!"

Kyle then raises his arms high as lightning bolts shoot out, striking each of the six men and women, causing them all to fall to their knees. Another bolt of lightning comes out again, this time striking the six flat on their backs and stomachs.

"You fools! You dare to battle my strength and power. Finally, this third bolt will kill all of you. Then I shall have my dominion over these children. PREPARE TO DIE!"

Then, with seconds left, the skies open up again and shine with bright white lights. The souls of the twenty-four parents come down and all grab hold of Kyle Thompson.

"Leave me alone! I'm not going anywhere with you," cries Kyle. "Especially not hell."

But Thompson's cries go unnoticed as the twenty-four spirits grab him and drag him down into the dirt.

"LEAVE ME! Leave me! leave me! Leave me! Leave me! Leave me! Leave me! Leave me!"

Kyle now disappears into the ground as his cries fade away.

"I believe it's all over," announces Mike. "Thompson was dragged back down to the rock bottom of hell."

The spirits of the twelve children are weeping, but this time all are weeping out of joy, happiness and relief. Do they dare ask if it is all over finally? But, Anita does ask as Mike responds back to her... "Yes, children, it *is* all over now."

"Will we be with our mommies and daddies again?" asks one child. "Will we? Can we?

Even before the questions are asked, the skies become bright again and a warmth encompasses everyone, even in this cold October weather. The spirits of the twenty-four parents appear as two-by-two go to each of the children until all twelve have their parents back with them. Tears of joy stream down their faces as the decades of torment come to an end. It's time to forget now and begin brand new, wonderful memories… Anita's dad speaks on behalf of all the spirits, children and adults…

"We can't thank the six of you enough for all you've done for us. We'll never forget. We'll be with all of you in spirit until the day each of you join us here on this side. You'll never be alone. We promise you this. So, with our love, we bid you farewell. We leave you in peace."

"Thank you!" said Anita. "I love you. Especially you, Doreen; and you, Mike. Good bye, good bye, good bye…"

Then, all 36 spirits disappear. The bright light is gone, along with the warmth of the air. It's now October cold again.

"What just happened here?" asks John.

"You can figure that out during our trip back to the Stanwick Hotel," replied Joy.

"I'm not in the mood to go back there after all this," said Sharon. "How about we go somewhere else. It's only 1:35 and our next meeting with Braxton and Silver isn't until 6:00 tonight."

"Okay. We won't have much time there, but I suggest we go to Vail for one or two hours and see if there is anyone we can help out there," suggested Mike. "If not, I say we all just enjoy the beauty and comfort there. We can leave around 4:00 p.m. to go back to the Stanwick. But even for the brief time we're there, I say we get a room."

They all agree and off they go. They arrive there at 2:10 and gather in their room.

"You know, I met Genia and I really miss her, even now," said Doreen.

"Well, I didn't meet her, but yet I miss her as well," said Billy.

"I think that goes for all of us, Billy," said Joy. "Mike has told us so much about her that she has become a dear friend to all of us. I think especially for Mike."

"That's right, Joy," agreed Mike. "I can't believe she's gone. The biggest thing to swallow is: What did we do wrong? I have an idea, though, and I need you, John, to help me with it."

"Sure! Anything I can do to help... What are you writing down, Mike?" he asks.

"You once said that you know enough people of all walks of life that you can get almost anything. Can you get these items?" asked Mike, handing John a list that he wrote up.

"I know the right people for this, but what in blue blazes do *you* want with this stuff?" asked John. "Also, I would have to go back to Denver to get to the right people in the first place. Even then, I can't be sure of getting this before we see Braxton and Silver tonight. I'll try my best, but who knows..."

"It looks like our trip here was for nothing, as well as paying for this suite," said Sharon.

"Look, I'll go down and settle our bill. I don't know why, but I feel I should take care of this. See you guys in about ten minutes," says John.

Some forty-five minutes pass and John still hasn't returned. Everybody's curiosity goes from questioning what Mike wanted, to where John has disappeared to.

"It's a few minutes past three and John's still gone," observed Joy. "I'm worried for him. Maybe we should go look for him."

At that moment, John comes through the door.

"John! Where have you been?" Joy asks. "You gave us all a big scare. And what do you have in that small, carry-on bag?"

"Sorry for the scare," John replies, "but it was freaky. Right before I paid our bill, I ran into a friend of mine; one that I would have looked up in Denver to see about getting the items on Mike's list. But, he was *here*, of all places; right down in the lobby. He was checking in as we were checking out. So, since our suite was already paid for, I told him he could have it by 4:15. So, we went to his friend's room and discussed what I needed. As a miracle, he did have the items on Mike's list, as well as other things. After telling him I had no need for anything else, he gave me my stuff in exchange for the suite. We talked a few, then I told him I had to leave. I came right back to our room and here we are."

"Another coincidence or what?" pondered Joy. "And what is in that bag you wanted, Mike?"

"I know what it is and I hope you're not planning to do what I'm thinking you're planning to do with it," said John.

"For Pete's sake already. What do you have in that bag!" said Sharon. "We can't wait any longer."

"Twenty 10mg Valium pills; 200 mg total. Plus, a syringe full of pure adrenalin to be injected directly into the heart, approximately 30 minutes after taking all 20 Valiums," explained Mike.

"My God, Mike," exclaimed Joy. "What are you planning to do, and why?"

"We need Genia's input into everything, and if she won't bring my spirit to her, then I'll have to send it to her. Because of my nerves in the past, I was prescribed 5mg of Valium to take one every four hours, not to exceed four pills, or 20mg every 24 hours. If I take all 20mg in one dose, that should stop my heart altogether. If things work out, then I should see her long enough to express to her the urgency of our meeting before my heart quits for good. That's where the adrenalin comes in. A shot directly into my heart should get it going again before it's too late. In theory, it should all work out before I permanently die."

"If's, should's, in theory... there's too many maybe's," said Joy. "You've been going on the basis of Genia stopping your heart and Genia sending your spirit back to your body. We have no idea what will happen if you try this on your own. You may not even see Genia and go straight to hell. You can't kill yourself and expect everybody to remain the same as all the times before. We were all pretty nervous enough with your dying before, but in this situation, I don't know if any of us could or even should try to handle it."

"Going to the other side myself, I have to agree with Joy," said Doreen. "If anyone else feels differently about all this, then please speak up now, while you still have a chance."

Everyone remains quiet... "I guess that shows how the rest of us feel," concluded Doreen.

"And besides, Mike," said Joy, "I think it's unfair of you to ask any or all of us to take such a risky chance with your life."

"After giving this deeper consideration," said Mike, "the fair and right thing to do is to forget about this whole crazy idea."

"That's the Mike Wakings I've known for all these years," said Joy. "I, as well as everyone else, feel a lot more comfortable and calmer with your decision."

"Now I'm going to throw this whole bag down the incinerator where it belongs," announced John.

"I don't even know what I was thinking," said Mike. "If Genia doesn't want to see me again, doing this insanity wouldn't have changed her mind."

John goes to the incinerator, dumps the instruments of death, and then comes back in.

"I don't know about the rest of you," continued Mike, "but I'm in the mood for a drink. Anyone else?"

As the hands all raise… "It looks like everyone's in the mood for one," announced Joy. "I think by now, Mike, you know the round for everyone."

"Right away," replies Mike. "I think if we…"

Mike drops the bottle and glass as he himself falls to the carpet. Joy immediately goes over the check his vital signs…

"Is he?" asks Sharon.

"Dead?" answers Joy. "Yes, just as all the other times."

"But I thought this wasn't going to happen again," said Sharon. "Or is… is this time permanent?"

"I don't know," answered Joy. "I don't know if we should wait an hour or so, or get some help immediately."

"What a decision," said Billy. "Wait to see if he gains consciousness, or take the opportunity to get him help right now, which could be right or wrong. Either way, we're taking a chance."

"This could be the wrong decision, and if so I would be willing to take responsibility, but I think we should let this take its course and hope it's the right thing to do," said Joy. "Now, let's get him a blanket and pillow."

Mike's spirit takes the usual travel through the bluish cloud and then appears on a beach with several people walking on it. The ocean is clear blue and fresh with white foam catching up to his feet. In a few moments, another cloud appears before him, turning into the form of Genia. Mike is so happy to see her, like a lost child finding their parents.

"Genia! I was so looking forward to seeing you again. I thought we would never meet again."

"Oh, my dear brother. I was always looking in anticipation of seeing you again," said Genia.

"But I thought from last we met that you were disappointed with all six of us, and our faith was a dismal one indeed. You had also told me that you had told several lies to me, but gave no reason," recapped Mike.

"Dear Mike. I had to pretend I was totally upset with all of you for one of many challenges. You see, before I could open up to you and your friends completely, you had to go through many challenges, especially you, Mike. The things I have to reveal, to you in particular, and to your five friends are meant for certain ears only at this point in time. Do you really think that everything that has been happening to all of you was pure coincidence?"

"You mean you made all these things happen to us on purpose?" asked Mike.

"Of course not. We wouldn't have made people suffer physically *and* spiritually as well as many people's possible deaths occur," said Genia. "These things were going to happen regardless of what we did. We just made it possible to use you and your friends to help solve these occurrences. But, your challenges were to accept the task of solving each incident accordingly. Without your intervention, goodness would be prolonged to a future date."

"How about the spiritual stuff that happened in Braxton's house concerning Sharon?" asked Mike.

That was to unite all of you in preparation for a more difficult occurrence in the upcoming future. It also prepared you for the happening in the woods with the children. Several things that happened here in the spirit world were challenges, too. The biggest, of course, was denying you from coming back here and letting you think that even hell was in your future. You and your friends' hearts had to overcome these things with love in your hearts. You proved yourselves worthy when all of you thought about helping Anita and the others. You overcame your own desires. You saved many spirit men and women, as well as sending several back to the lowest point in hell until the time of cleansing. There were many times you overcame yourselves for others. Time and again, all of you proved your rightful place in Heaven."

"How about the lies you told me here in the spirit world? What and why were they?"

"One was when I told you if you could guess right who the three vacant thrones were for in the Kingdom of Heaven, Jesus being the first of course, then you could earn a spot in Heaven. You were shocked that I even said that, and that was because if you said you would take that deal, then you would have become ineligible for the position that was intended for you," said Genia.

"You still haven't told me what my position to be is."

"Don't worry this time, Mike. Before you go back to your earthly body, you will know. I promise you."

Well Hallelujah. I'll finally know!"

"Mike, in order to explain to you answers to other questions you asked, then I must go back to the beginning of mankind... When God created Adam and Eve, they were given the Commandment. By following the Commandment, they would fulfill the Three Great Blessings which I told you were 1) to Be Fruitful or grow to perfection of heart, 2) to Multiply or have children, and finally 3) to Have Dominion or be Lords over all creation. But, as the Bible records, Adam and Eve disobeyed God's Commandment and they were banished from the Garden of Eden. Thus Adam, being the first Adam, fell from God's grace, never realizing any of the Blessings. God wanted to bring the Messiah, or Second Adam, in order to restore what the first Adam failed to do. Due to the fall of Adam and Eve, Satan claimed them. So, God had to use two people who were not claimed by Satan. This was Cain and Abel. Since Cain and Abel were still innocent, if the two of them could unite in love as brother-and-brother, then God could have sent the Messiah or Second Adam straight to Cain or Abel's direct family. It then would have been simple for the Messiah to restore a tiny population on the earth. But, Cain killed Abel, crushing God's hope for sending the Messiah. Ever since then, God was trying to create a condition where he could send his son. It was failure-after-failure until Abraham, Isaac and Jacob. The foundation was finally laid for the Messiah to come. The only problem was, God could only send his son to one single family, but now Satan had whole nations. It took God 2,000 years to develop a nation, which was the Israelites in Israel. The condition was now created to send the Messiah or Second Adam, Jesus Christ. Jesus grew to perfection of heart, fulfilling the First Blessing. But, because of the faithlessness of the people, he was crucified on the cross, never able to fulfill the Second Blessing or the Third. Thus, Jesus was only able to gain salvation for mankind spiritually. And, since Jesus was only able to reach the top of the Completion Stage, or Paradise, the gates of Heaven remained closed. They could only be opened when the Lord of the Second Advent, or now the Third Adam, can come and fulfill all three Blessings. It took God approximately 2,000 years of preparation to bring Jesus, the Second Adam, from Abraham and his family to the Roman Empire. After Jesus was crucified, it would take God 2,000 more years of preparation to bring the Messiah again. The Lord of the Second Advent, or the Third Adam. Many times throughout history it took God three attempts to accomplish His Will to gain the victory that was needed. This has been the course for Adam, Jesus and the Lord of the Second Advent, or Third Adam. God *will* finally succeed with the Third Adam. This is it. The final attempt to defeat Satan, and defeat him He will. Jesus said he would return, but he didn't mean literally. He meant that his spirit would come down to earth and help the Lord of the Second Advent to complete his mission. The Book of Revelation discusses many occurrences in the Last Days, but just like so many other things in the Bible, it's so clouded by symbols. The Lord of the Second Advent was born of a woman, just like Jesus Christ. His mission will be the same as Jesus', except for the fact that he will fulfill all three Blessings. Once that happens, then the gates to the Kingdom of Heaven will be opened; and in fact, this has already occurred. That's why Jesus is now in Heaven and no longer in Paradise."

"Wait a minute," objected Mike. "You use a lot of things in past-tense. According to what you say the Lord of the Second Advent has already come and completed his mission."

"That's right, Mike, I am. He has come, completed his mission on earth, and now must restore the spirit world," said Genia.

"Whoa! What are we talking about here? If this is true, then why is the physical world still in turmoil?" asked Mike. "Also, why hasn't anybody on earth been restored?"

"The Lord has come and has begun to turn humanity in the right direction. But, unlike Jesus, the Second Advent now has the whole world's problems and not just those of a small nation, to deal with. In other words, Satan has control of the entire world, not just one nation. In approximately 1,000 years, the whole world will be restored, meaning the Kingdom of Heaven on earth will have been realized; and not only on earth, but also in the spirit world as well. Thus, the Kingdom of Heaven will be effectively realized in the entire cosmos. The Second Advent was born, lived and died on earth. Again, that's why the Kingdom of Heaven is now open to anyone who has earned the qualifications to be there. In answer to your second question, many people on earth have been restored. One such group of people is the Holy Ground Church."

"You must be kidding me," said Mike. "Then who was the Lord of the Second Advent? What year was he born and died? Does he have writings?"

"For who he was, you'll find out soon enough, but not this very moment. As to when, let's just say he was born in the early-twentieth century and died about a decade ago. As for writings, he wrote a lengthy book explaining many of the things we have discussed, plus a huge amount of information we haven't even touched upon. He also has literally thousands of speeches in print, given during his lifetime. His speeches are gathered all over the world, but a huge number of them are located in the Holy Ground Church. As for his book, there are many copies, but only one original under lock and key, called *The Completed Testament*."

"Wait! I know that book!" exclaimed Mike. "The six of us held it right in our hands in the cellar of Braxton's house back in Idaho Springs. But, it just disappeared. Where to, I don't know."

"Of course, I *do* know. Take my word for it. It will be back in your hands very soon. This is the book I mentioned to you once, and you said, I quote: 'What is that something else? I only know of the Bible. What else is there?' Also, in answer to your questions about what could be done to stop evil spirits from gaining vitality from lower ones, or how can spirit grow to higher levels even though so many are so far gone in lower levels, even hell. That's one of the tasks of the Lord of the Second Advent. Between him and Jesus Christ, they'll be able to open doors and gates to go down to these places and help restore the lowest spirits as well as put an end to spirits stealing vitality from others spirits. In short, they can clean up the horrible mess in the spirit world. Together, they'll be unstoppable. That's their job – to bring the Kingdom of Heaven in the spirit world and then on the physical earth. Eventually, there won't be one soul suffering on earth or in the spirit world. There will be no more suffering, or crying or sorrow, for as the Bible says, 'for the former things have passed away.'"

"And I, with my five friends, can be part of it… Wait a minute. You once said something like there will be a happy match or spouse for everyone, right? (Yes!) Then even Jesus Christ, as well as the Lord of the Second Advent, will have an actual bride, am I right again? (Yes!) I got it! The four Thrones are for Jesus Christ, the Lord of the Second Advent, and their brides. Tell me

I'm correct! Please tell me I'm correct! There is no other possibility!"

"Yes, Mike! Congratulations. You are right," said Genia.

"But why was only Jesus on a throne?"

"Jesus was on the throne specifically for your benefit, Mike. By tomorrow night or Sunday morning, all four thrones will be occupied, again for your benefit. Even though, those thrones are not normally occupied because Jesus and the Second Advent will be hard at work restoring the spirit world while their brides support them. Everyone is hard at work until the spiritual and physical worlds have been totally restored to the Kingdom of Heaven."

"Then that's when I'll find out who the Lord of the Second Advent is, when I see all four of them."

"Yes, and since your position is so important, that is why this is all for your benefit once again," explained Genia.

"I imagine I will have to wait until I choose yes or no providing, of course, that this whole thing has something to do with either Braxton and Silver or The Holy Ground Church, or both."

"Maybe," answered Genia. "Either way you don't have much longer to wait… But, to change the subject, about one other lie I told you about, and that was when I told you angels have wings, when in fact they don't. I told you a falsehood for John's benefit. You see, he was struggling enough about what I said concerning angels as it was. To tell him they didn't or never did have wings would have been a little bit too much. And, in order for you to feel that you weren't lying to him, I told you that they did have wings to make it easier for both of your sakes. But, knowing that he would be strong enough to take the truth now, I felt it was a good time to tell you."

"Tell me," asked Mike, "The Holy Ground Church, how much do they really know? And should we tell them all about what happened in the woods with the children, parents and all the others?"

"The Church knows about much, but not everything. Through your own emotional feeling, you should be able to tell what they know and what they don't, let your emotions guide you. Also, the same as to whether you should tell them what has happened to all of you since your last meeting."

"I'm starting to feel like a fortune teller, except that I'm not getting any kind of fortune for what I'm telling."

"Ah, but you are, Mike," said Genia. "You're gaining the fortune of knowing you're enriching other people's lives with what you tell them. That is a most rewarding feeling, is it not?"

"Yes, you're right. There's something I gain by helping other people that no feeling in the world can replace. And, who would want to?"

"You're very special, Mike. You receive many times what little you give out... It's time now for you to go back. About fifty minutes have passed both here and on earth. It's almost 4:00 there now."

"Just enough time with a little to spare," answered Mike, "to meet Braxton and Silver at 6:00."

"Yes, my dear brother Mike. Go back and tell everyone the good news we've shared. Go back! Go back! Back! Back! Back!..."

Mike now begins to awaken in their room. Billy is the first to notice...

"Look! He's coming to. Thank God."

"Thank God is right," echoed Joy. "We obviously made the right decision," as everyone gathers around. "How are you, Mike? We were really, and I mean really, worried about you this time. We weren't sure if you were going to come back to us or not, but you made it."

"Back is right! And do I have something to tell all of you this time. No time to tell you right now. I'll tell all of you while we drive back to Denver. John, do you mind driving back while I talk?"

"No, not at all. I *can* listen while I'm driving. Let's go then."

They all pile back in the SUV and head back to the Stanwick Hotel. Along the way, Mike explains everything that Genia told him. With great joy and excitement over finding out Genia still loves them all so much, they gain a new enthusiasm.

"That's great. I just knew in my heart that she wouldn't abandon us," said Sharon. "I was right. Even though she's not an angel, I feel we *have* an angel on our side."

"She's better than an angel. Remember, angels are supposed to serve man. Genia is more of a subjective spirit to us and she is human, with human feelings and emotions to love us with," said Mike.

"I'm curious," began Doreen, "Did she say anything about our dreams? I know you think or take for granted that we all know what our dreams mean, but the fact is, we don't. But, I'm sure we would all want to find out."

"I know. And, I'm sorry I took that for granted," apologized Mike. "Genia didn't have anything to say, but if you're willing to listen to me now, I can give each of you a short meaning to your dreams. I picked it up spiritually just recently and was waiting for a good time to tell you. I guess now is as good a time as any. Understand, though, that even though much might be hard to accept, you must believe me. This is very important for us all."

"Go ahead, Mike," said Joy. "If we can't believe in you now, we shouldn't be here."

"All right! Let's start with the order in which you each talked, which means we start with you, John... Everyone in the audience changed into angels to tell you this is what your life is totally obsessed with. Then, they all started asking you questions, putting you in an object position which you shouldn't be to angels. When you did ask them a question about what they wanted from you, they told you they wanted you to know the truth about them because your belief was all wrong. They're telling you to change your belief about them before it's too late. The real truth is what Genia has told you, as well as everyone else... Next is Sharon. You were in an attic of a house you were unfamiliar with when the spirits were coming up for you. The clock on the wall was quickly going backwards and everything changed because time itself went back to another era. You were then in a graveyard as a woman came out of her grave to talk to you. You had to pay indemnity for something one of your ancestors did to her. These are the spirits that are hounding you. There will be a final confrontation between you and them, and if I'm not wrong, all of us will be involved with it... Now it's Billy's turn. As you walked through the desert of trash, this was a symbol of the depression you had in your life up to the point of coming here. Everything was like trash to you. All the people asking or even begging you for help are most of your ancestors. They cry because they're in a low place in the spirit world and need your help to get them out of there to a higher realm. When the desert

185

turned into a road, it meant you found a path to get out of your situation. It came true as everything around you became nice, useful items. You then had the drive to continue on as everything now became priceless items on the road of gold. This means in the near future, you would become very well off. You then saw a glowing bright sign pointing which way for you to go. You followed it, even though you wanted to stay where you were. It led you to a beautiful city where you met Genia and me. This signifies that you went on and finally reached Heaven. Once there, you would have met your wife and eventually, your son... Next is Doreen. Being with Genia in Paradise you, in a small way, resembled my course. You had to go to all the lower levels in order to understand how to help these people. You experienced their feelings and emotions. You then had to spend four days in limbo totally ending up being four hundred days. This was to understand your own life as it affected everyone in all the other levels. Then, you were told to follow me as in everyone else's dreams. My position is to guide each of you to Heaven for eternity. I imagine this is the reason why, in reality, I have to visit all the levels and then meet Jesus Christ as well as the Lord of the Second Advent. I guess I'm answering my own question. I'm supposed to help everyone in the world, or at least some people, to follow the Lord of the Second Advent, or something like that. It also makes me think of Billy's dream. He went from rags to good stuff, and finally riches. In real life, he went from nothing to good things as in this week, and finally riches which could be the $10 million from Braxton and Silver."

"Wait a minute," said John. "Are you saying that we should trust in them because of a dream? We don't even know who they are or where the heck they come from."

"It would certainly make sense since even I agree, these are more than mere dreams," said Joy.

"Hold it, Joy," added John. "Let's first hear what Mike has to say about interpreting *your* dream."

"Well, the person who came in looking just like you *was* a reflection of yourself, entirely," said Mike. "She said you were an excellent therapist because you *are* one. Concerning me, though, it became tough to evaluate me properly because of all the spiritualism involved in my case. The head of your reflection grew larger and larger because, well, I hate to have to say this, but because you think there's nothing you can't solve. Because of your record with patients, you're thinking higher and higher of yourself. You couldn't bear to watch this, so you smashed the mirror, hoping to stop what was happening. Once you did, though, your reflection became your actual self. When your head became so big and heavy and you fell to the floor, it took myself to help you get back to normal. After talking to you, I brought you back to yourself with the truth and you listening to me. Then I took your hands and started guiding you to Heaven. I know this may sound hard for any of you to swallow, especially for you Joy, but I'm in a position that I'm not too happy about with all the responsibility. Genia said, though, it's not just because of things I've done in my life, but more importantly it's due to my ancestral merit that I'm in the position I'm in. If one of you want to take the responsibility I have, just say so and I'll relinquish it to you… Then I assume I must continue. I'm only a flawed human being. I can only try to do my best and hope it's good enough."

"Well, Joy," said John, "what do you have to say about everything Mike had interpreted from your dream?"

187

"All I can say is I, as well as all of you, we can't argue with results. And, the dream was mine, not Mike's. To be humble, maybe for the first time in my life, I have to agree with Mike's interpretation of my dream."

John now pulls into the garage of the Stanwick Hotel.

"It's 5:30. Just enough time for us to freshen up and get down to the conference room to meet with our distinguished guests," said Sharon.

Everyone disappears to their respective rooms. While Mike is in his restroom washing, he hears a noise coming from the living room. As he looks in the mirror, he swears he saw a figure go into his closet. He dries his face, then goes into the living room. He stares at the closet door. His heart starts to race faster and faster. It's so quiet now he can hear the ticking of the clock on the wall.

"I know I heard and saw something," said Mike to himself. And, that something went into my closet. I know I did. It's not my imagination. "WHO'S IN THERE? COME OUT OR I'M CALLING SECURITY," he shouts. "I said COME OUT!... All right now," as Mike picks up the phone to call hotel security, the line is dead. "Oh no. Not now," Mike says to himself. "Maybe I should just go downstairs and get security myself. But, if I do so, then surely who or whatever is in here will leave; then security won't know what to think. No, I've got to go into the closet myself." As Mike walks slowly to the closet, he notices the lights in the room becoming dinner and dimmer. "What is happening? I can hardly see where I'm going." But, Mike does see well enough to make his way to the closet. He sticks out his hand, puts it on the door knob and starts turning it. As he has the knob turned all the way in the open position, he gets ready to open the door. Then, all of a sudden, he feels the door knob quickly force its way

188

back to the closed position. Someone or something on the other side doesn't want him to open the closet door. "Good Lord. The hell with this. I'm getting out of here." He races to the front door and tries to open it. The door knob turns but the door won't open. He runs to the bedroom, but those doors won't open either. He thinks fast. Ah, there's a window in the bathroom, big enough for a man to crawl out of. He once again races to the bathroom, but as he does, the door slams shut. He tries to open it, but to no avail. He's trapped in the living room with the closet door facing him. The lights in the room just cast a dark shadow now. Mike regains all of his strength and confidence from everything he has been through. The fear is gone now as he thinks about Genia and all the spiritual levels he's been through. Putting everything behind him, he confidently calls out, "Okay, the game's over. Come out or I'll bust the door down." After a moment of silence, the closet door slowly creeks open. There's a figure in the darkness. It, too, slowly comes out. It's in full sight now as Mike gasps.

5. Preparing for the worst

It's 5:50 according to the wall clock in the conference room. All five people are there except Mike. Finally, Joy speaks out…

"It's ten to six and Mike still isn't here. He's always a little early. Someone should go to look for him."

"You sure that's wise?" asked Doreen. "You know how Braxton and Silver feel about tardiness. Maybe we should give him 'til 6:00."

"Okay, but if he's not here by then, then you go looking for him, John," said Joy. "I'll take care of Braxton and Silver. At least I hope I will."

"Alright, but I've got a bad feeling about this," replied John.

Back in Mike's room… "So it's you, demon; right out of my dreams again. I've had it with you and your games. I know what's real and what's not," said Mike.

"Do you, Mikey? Let's see how much reality you can find out of this."

In moments, Mike finds himself in a straight jacket inside a white padded room. There's a small table in the middle of the room as he sits on a chair on one side, with a doctor on the other. The doctor seems annoyed with Mike.

"Where am I?" demands Mike. "What is this place? Who are you, and why am I in here in a straight jacket?… Don't just stare at me; give me an answer! NOW!"

"You still think you're on a mission to help save thousands of lives?" the doctor asked. "Remember, your name is Frank Barow. You killed a man claiming he was a demon from your dreams. Your wife left you with the kids and all you had left were your five closest friends. They tried to talk sense into you, but to no avail. The court found you insane and you wound up here. You've been here for two and a half years. I've gotten nowhere with you and the last drastic action will be a lobotomy. This meeting was your last chance at gaining reality back. They'll be coming for you in a minute for surgery. It looks like you're going to leave us murmuring the name Mike Wakings on your breathe, saying how you visited the afterworld many times. That woman, Genia, you talk of. If she were real, surely she would save you now. But, it's all in your mind which will be altered in a few minutes."

The door opens and four men in white uniforms come to take Mike to the operating room.

"NO! Let go of me! I'm not insane. The demon; he's doing all of this. I swear," yelled Mike.

"It will go a lot easier for you if you don't resist."

The four men drag Mike down the hall to a room. In it is an operating table with straps. There are all sorts of tools nearby. Mike struggles, but it's no use. He's now strapped down to the table as his cries go unheard. The doctor takes a bone cutter to Mike's head and turns it on.

"Now, this won't hurt a bit," declares the doctor.

"Please, put me out! This is inhuman," cries Mike.

"Now this will be over in just a minute," the doctor reassures him.

"NO DON'T! NOOOOOOO."

In the hallway outside Mike's room, his five friends hear his cry.

"Mike! Can you hear us?" yells Joy. "Are you all right?"

"We have to bust the door down," says John.

"We can't," said Joy. "It's solid oak… Billy, go get the manager with a pass key. HURRY UP! We may already be too late."

"I'll be back in a flash!" said Billy.

Back in the operating room… "Keep his head still. It'll get messy if I miss."

Then, a bright light begins shining in the room. It's the spirit of Genia.

"Leave this man alone!" demands Genia. "for he is protected by both Lords and myself."

"GENIA!" Mike exclaims. "Thank you. I knew you were real. This is the hallucination. Please, get me out of here!"

"I will, Mike, but this place is no hallucination. It's a certain part of level two, just one above rock bottom. Your demon put you here."

"No. It's not fair," objected the doctor. "Demon Andrea gave him to us. When we finish with him, you can have him back."

"You have no right to him," declared Genia. "Andrea was not supposed to do that, and I say now that he will be punished for his actions, as you will be as well for yours unless you give him back to me now."

"Fine! Now take him and leave all of us alone here," replied the doctor. "We don't want trouble with you or the Lords. Demon Andrea went beyond his boundaries. We want no part of it."

"Wise decision," announced Genia. "Now, let him loose."

The four men unstrap Mike. Once freed, he quickly goes over to Genia.

"Get me the hell, and I do mean the hell, out of here. Now I know the difference between what's real and what isn't, as well as what is the spirit world and what is the physical world."

"A hard lesson for you to learn, but you have grown from it... I have to send you back to your room in the Hotel as you face off against demon Andrea."

"That's fine. And Genia, Thank you so very much!" says Mike as they part.

"You're welcome. I'll see you tomorrow."

Mike disappears and reappears back in his body, standing, looking at the demon. "You're a piece of garbage," declares Mike. "Get out of my room, and my sight. And I mean *NOW*!"

"Certainly. But remember, I'll be coming back for you and your friends when I see you for the last time here on earth," declared the demon. And let me warn you, I won't be as easy to get rid of as you did this time. Be warned, the time is coming. You won't have Genia there to help any of you the last time we meet."

"All right. You had your say," said Mike. "Now GET OUT!"

The demon vanishes as the front door to his room bursts open.

"Mike! Are you okay?" asks Joy. "We've been pounding on your door for twenty minutes with no answer. Then, we heard you scream out. Also, we heard someone else in the room with you. Is there somebody else here with you?"

"There was, but no longer," answered Mike. "I'll tell you all after the meeting with Braxton and Silver. Oh my gosh, the meeting!"

"Don't worry," comforted Doreen. "Joy got them to excuse us for a while due to the fact that something had happened to you up here."

"You mean, even with their strict adherence to time, they were still willing to let all of you go?" Mike looks at his watch. "It's 6:35 now. We'd better get back down there before they change their minds."

"Right!" said John. "As long as you tell us afterwards what went on in here all this time."

"I will. Let's go!"

So, the six of them go down to the Conference Room where they find Braxton and Silver patiently waiting.

"Is everything all right with you, Mr. Wakings?" George asks.

"It is now," answered Mike, "but I had the damnedest time in my room for about 45 minutes."

"Is there anything we can do for you, Mr. Wakings?" asked George. "Especially after what you've been through. I figure there's something we can do for you if you let us."

"What do you mean?" answered Mike. "How do the two of you know what I've been through for the last 45 minutes? What is it with you guys, anyway? You've known way too much, far more than two normal guys could know. Rich or not. Come on, you two. Time has just about expired. You promised us answers."

"And you'll get most of them tomorrow afternoon at 3:00 when we meet for the most revealing talk in our entire week. The few questions not answered will be dealt with Sunday morning. You'll have the answers to all your questions by the time your departures are ready, that's if you still want to leave by then."

"For mystery men, it sounds like there won't be much of a mystery by Sunday morning," said Billy.

"That's right," said George. "Even to the questions of where we disappear to after each meeting, and who are we really, and where are we from."

"You mean you know the questions we have? Then, why let us go on?" asked Joy.

"We even knew why you threw us that surprise to get our fingerprints," said George.

"So, that's why neither of you were surprised or upset with us that morning," said Mike. "You already knew everything we had planned. But why did you give us the impression you were wiped out by 10:00 in the morning?"

"Because we were up all night making plans for the next several days in advance," answered Grea.

"Then what's the real truth behind you guys?" asked Doreen.

"I'm afraid you'll have to wait for those answers as well as everything else. Tomorrow, 3:00 p.m. will be the beginning of all your questions being answered, including how we know as much as we do. This is just the beginning," said George.

"Between the two of you, The Holy Ground Church and the spirit world, this is going to be one hell of a conclusion," replied Mike.

"Not to mention what's going on in each of our lives," said Sharon. "We're each in a soap opera. This whole thing is getting to be too complicated. Oh, I wish it was Sunday afternoon. Can you at least tell us what organization it is you are with?"

"I'd like to know, too," said Joy, "because it's one of the most powerful ones on this planet."

"Be patient just a little bit longer," answered George.

"All right! But answers had better come by 3:00 tomorrow, and Sunday morning," Mike demanded. "Let's go. I'm sure they want to do their disappearing act as usual. That is, if you're finished with us now."

"We only had these few, but important words to tell you. Do remember that your sticking together and helping one another will be most important tonight and tomorrow, as well as Sunday. And, this time we're going to walk through the front door," said George.

"Well, wonders never cease," commented Mike. "Come on everyone; we're going to witness a monumental moment..." as they all witness Braxton and Silver leave through the doorway.

"Let's go to your room, Mike," suggests Joy, "so you can tell us what happened to you in there."

"If you don't mind, I'd feel more comfortable going to someone else's room."

"How about mine?" suggests Billy... they all go up to Billy's room where Mike explains everything that happened to him previously in *his* room.

"That must have been terrifying," commented Doreen.

"It was!" agreed Mike. "Up to the point where Genia came and explained to me that demon Andrea is pushing the bounds of his limits. He didn't have the right to send me to hell. So, that gave Genia the right to intervene and help me. He's getting desperate and is taking chances. He's making mistakes."

"And he says his final appearance will be dealing with all of us? asked Sharon. "Did he mention how?"

"No. But I do believe that it will be our biggest challenge of all. Maybe combined with other spiritual challenges; possibly with your spirits, Sharon," answered Mike. "And somehow, we have to find a way to defeat him and possibly your spirits. We'll have to be stronger than them without Genia's help."

"And how do we accomplish that?" asked John.

"By working with and trusting one another," said Mike. "Also, by following Genia's words, and I don't mean to sound arrogant, but by trusting in what I have to say because it comes straight from the spirit world. We're at a point where we have to believe and follow, or disbelieve and die."

"I think we're all at a point where it's almost easier to believe than not," said Joy. "And, I say at this juncture of time, that we all take the rest of tonight and make the final decision as to whether or not we really do believe in everything as a sign for us to follow, or on Sunday take the plane back to the lives we had before all this happened. I also suggest we meet by 6:00 a.m. and discuss our decisions. Those who will go on can go to the Holy Ground Church for our 9:00 meeting. For anyone who has decided to go back home, we give our best wishes as we say good-bye. This is also the same choice I have to make, as well. Do you all agree? (Yes!) Then, let's say good night and meet at 6:00 tomorrow morning."

"But wait," says Sharon. "How about Mike? He can't go back to his room."

"Yes I can," he replied. "I'm all calmed down now and feel up to any challenge."

"Okay. We can all go back to our rooms now," said Joy. "I'll see Mike to his room."

They all proceed to their rooms as Joy and Mike go into his room. "It seems like everything is starting to come to a head," says Joy. "Doesn't it to you?"

"You're right about it just starting," said Mike. "I feel we still have a long way to go."

"For all our sakes, I hope you're wrong about that." said Joy. "Do you really feel comfortable staying here in your room after everything that happened tonight?"

"I'm pretty sure I have nothing else to worry about tonight, except for the rest of you," replied Mike.

"What's your worry about the rest of us all about? Is it just a feeling, or what?" asks Joy.

"It's more than a feeling. It's like a premonition or something like that," answered Mike. "Listen Joy, be careful. I wish I would have warned everyone else... Look, I'm going to stay up until 3:00. I'll be praying most of the time."

"You! Praying! What's come over you, Mike?"

"Let's just say I'm earning my stripes. I have things to say and I'm going to say it. Forget the old Mike Wakings. I've come to a new life and direction. Actually, I think every one of us have. We're growing, and we can't be stopped. Whatever challenge is coming to each of us tonight, I'm sure we'll be able to overcome them. So remember, Joy, we have a special mission and we're up for anything, good or bad... Well, my dear therapist, it's time for you to go back to your room and for me to start praying."

"Thank you, Mike, for becoming the man I always knew you could be," said Joy. "A leader with a very special mission. Good night and God bless."

Joy and Mike give their famous pinky bending sign to each other, and Joy leaves and goes back to her room. It's 10:00 p.m. Billy is in his room. The phone rings. It's his wife, Cindy, on the other end.

"Cindy, I didn't expect to hear from you tonight!" said Billy. "Is anything wrong?"

"Yes! Calley and I need you to come back right away. It's a matter of life and death. Come back while you can."

"This doesn't sound like you. What's this matter of life and death you're talking about?... (No answer.) Cindy, do you hear me? I asked you a question. What's happening?"

"You bastard, we need you to come back right now or we'll die, and it's all your fault," the voice said.

"This is crazy. You're talking irrationally. As a matter of fact, you don't even sound like my wife at all. Tell me, Cindy, when did we get married? (Silence) I'm waiting! Surely you know our anniversary; you know, the day you're always questioning me on?" said Billy.

"How dare you ask me these questions!" the voice answered.

"Because you don't know, and you don't know because you're not my wife! You're just someone trying very hard to make me leave here before Sunday. Well, it won't work. I'm on to your games now."

"Are you sure you won't change your mind?" the voice asked. As they talk, Billy doesn't notice the phone line connected to the wall jack is unplugged and starts to quickly wrap itself around his throat and begins to tighten.

"Wha... what's going on! It's getting harder to breathe. It's getting tiiiggghhhtttteeerrr. Billy pulls and yanks at it. "Itttt'sss nnnooo uuussseee. Heeelllppp! Pllleeeaaassseee heeelllppp meee!" On the other end of the line, you can hear a voice yelling "DIE BILLY PACE! DIE!" Then, an unlocked front door bolts open and Mike and Joy rush in to help Billy try to loosen the cord.

199

"It's useless, Mike," says Joy. "It won't loosen up." Mike quickly runs over to the phone jack on the wall and starts smashing it to bits. When it's totally demolished, the cord loosens around Billy's neck as the line dies. Billy starts hacking as he grabs his throat.

"Are you all right now Billy?" asks Joy. "That was a close call."

Tha… thank you guys, but how did you know I was in trouble?" asked Billy.

"I saw it in a vision," explained Mike. "I quickly got Joy to help for I've discovered it takes at least three people to break the hold the spirit world has on us. The number three represents the three main levels of the spirit world, Formation, Growth and Completion."

"Do you think the others have something to fear?" asked Billy. "It seems like something wants us to leave here before the seven days are up on Sunday."

"The visions seem to align with all those that were given invitations by Braxton," said Mike. "Doreen's next, then John and Sharon. Even you're in danger, Joy. But, it looks like we can't help until the person is in actual trouble."

"But, how about if we all get together now and stay together?" suggested Joy.

"It's worth a try, but I'm afraid somehow that each person will fall into danger," said Mike.

"Shall we at least try?" said Joy.

"I guess so. Let's get everyone and gather in Doreen's room since she should be next."

All six of them gather in Doreen's room as Mike explains everything to them.

"So, what are we supposed to do? Just wait?" asked John.

"While praying, I received the information that we just have to make it 'til 3:00 this morning. Approximately one hour for each of us to go through. It's 10:55 now, almost time for the next person. At least, I feel it's right around the hour that something happens. For Billy, it was 10:00."

"If you're calculating right, then why was it 5:30 for you, Mike? An exception to the rule?" asked Sharon.

"It seems like I'm the exception for everything that goes on. I don't know. Maybe I'm wrong about the time. Maybe I'm wrong about everything. That's the problem about being psychic. You're never quite sure about your predictions."

"Well, you have a pretty good track record in my book," said Billy.

"That's right, Mike," said Joy. "Without your guidance, we would be pretty lost by now."

"I think it happened to me at 5:30 because it was designed to get me to give up and tell Braxton and Silver that I've had it. Their hope was for me to also discourage all the rest of you about staying... What time is it? asked Mike.

"11:01. Shouldn't something be happening by now?" asked Sharon.

Just then, Doreen gets violently ill and drops to the floor.

"Say, isn't that a page out of your book, Mike?" comments Sharon. "Seriously though, how is she?"

"Let me see," says Joy... "She's dead; just like Mike and the one other time it happened to her."

"Let me take a look," said Mike. He grabbed her hands and was horrified. "She's not temporarily dead, but *dead* for good. She's not in a good place, either."

"What! What can we do?" asked John. "Wait a minute… I've got an idea. I have to run to my room for a quick minute, but I'll be right back."

John then leaves while the others focus on Doreen, who seems to find herself in a very low level of the spirit world. It's dark, and devilish creatures wander around her. One such creature who seems to be in charge comes over to her.

"Who are you and where am I?" asks Doreen… "Where's Genia? I don't like it here!"

"This is the place, Doreen Perry, where you will come back to and remain eternally unless you go back and give up this foolish quest of yours and your friends. By earth's time, it's October 20th, 11:10 p.m. If you don't end this effort of yours and go back home on Sunday, then *this* will be your eternal resting place," said the spirit.

Doreen looks around and sees other spirits suffering in torment. Their moaning, their pleas for help, their agony wishing they even had just one more day on earth. The stench is too much for her to bear. Is this really her fate if she doesn't quit the path she's treading? No! She knows that what she's doing is right. She won't abandon it. But, how does she leave this hell and return back to her friends on earth?

"Leave me," said Doreen. "I want to go back and continue the path I'm traveling on. LET ME GO BACK!"

"Then you will remain here forever," replies the spirit. "Come! Let me show you your area that you shall remain in for eternity. Let's go; it's too late now."

Doreen screams and screams, but to no avail. Back in her room on earth, everyone is in bedlam. They try all they can to revive her, but it's no use. John comes running back into the room.

"Here you go, Mike," announces John. "This should help, I hope."

"The syringe with the adrenalin that I gave you to use on me! I thought you threw all this stuff down the incinerator."

"Most of it, but I thought this might come in handy in the future. Was I right?" said John.

"You bet! Joy, would you unbutton Doreen's blouse, please?" asked Mike. "I must get this with one big thrust into her heart or it won't work." Mike nervously prepares... his palms are all sweaty; his hands shaking. He says to himself, "Come on, Mike. You must relax! You're only going to get one shot at this. Doreen's counting on you, and so is everyone else." Mike lifts the syringe above Doreen's chest, aims it at her heart, and with all his might plunges it right into her heart. With one big gasp, Doreen jerks her upper body straight up and regains her composure.

"You did it, Mike," cries Joy. "You did it! You saved Doreen's life. How do you feel?"

"Grateful that John kept that syringe," replied Mike.

"And I'm so grateful to all of you for bringing me back from that hell," said Doreen.

"You're more than welcome, Doreen," said Mike. "But, I must say that it would be helpful if you told us everything that happened to you while you were on the other side."

"Of course," replied Doreen. "Let me explain..." She explains clearly, especially since the severity of the situation threatens the welfare of all six of them.

"Now what do we do?" asks Billy.

"Just let faith take its course," answered Mike. "Next is John, 15 minutes from now, and then Sharon. It's anybody's guess as to whether or not you have to go through a similar episode as the rest of us, Joy."

"I guess I'll just have to wait until 2:00 a.m."

"It seems like being all together won't stop the inevitable, as things will happen nonetheless. It's just reassuring having your friends around to help you out of your dilemma. And. I don't mind saying I feel extra assured with the five of you by my side," said John.

"It's good to know one is in such a trusted position; especially when one's turn will be at 1:00, shortly over an hour from now," said Sharon.

"If you guys don't mind, I'm going over to the couch and close my eyes for a few minutes," said John. "I'm really bushed."

"We don't mind," said Joy. "You go catch forty winks. Maybe, with a little luck, you can sleep through 'til 1:00. And, we'll check on you to make sure you're still alive, seriously."

John falls asleep pretty quickly. The time is now 12:10. John wakes up and is startled to see everyone as if they're almost transparent. But, in the center of the room are three men; men whom John senses to be angels. Cautiously, he walks toward them.

"What's happening here?" John asks. "And I know you three are angels, so don't try to deny it."

"Deny it? We wouldn't dream of it," they said. "It's very important that you know who we are. First, and the foremost important lesson you must learn is, everything you have been told about us angels in incorrect. Don't throw the beliefs you had of us asunder. If you do, then you'll be lost forever. Assure us that you'll deny this whole trip here and go back home on Sunday, and we'll let you go back to your body."

"Go back to my body?" says John as he turns and sees his body sleeping on the couch. "Am I dead?"

"No, you're not," answers one of the angels. "Your spirit has left your body and is in the midst of both worlds. You are neither dead, nor whole. That's why your friends seem transparent to you. But, time goes on as usual here. So, consider yourself in the midway position. Regardless of what your friends have said about this past week, you're all in error; even up to the part where it says angels don't have wings. For example, observe..." Then the three angels produce wings twice their own size. Back in the firm world, Joy decides to try and wake John out of a fear she has sensed.

"Everyone! I can't wake John," exclaims Joy. "He's not dead, but he just won't wake up."

Mike goes over to him and grabs both hands.

"You're right," said Mike. He's not dead, but his spirit *has* left his body and he's in Limbo. We can only dream of what's going on with him and where he is. We must get his spirit back to his body and bring him out of this."

They try everything they can, but nothing works. Meanwhile, back in Limbo...

"Foolish man! You balk at our offer," said one of the angels. "Then you will never leave this spirit land."

"I'm not listening to you anymore," said John. "I'm going back to my body and wake up. But, as John turns to go to his body, it has become vague and unclear. He can't locate where his body is anymore. Then, the three angels start flapping their wings

205

together, which creates an absorption of the air. It becomes thinner and thinner as John begins to suffocate.

"Look!" cries Doreen. "He's acting as if he can't breathe."

"What can we do, Mike?" yells Joy.

"Joy! Quick!" says Mike. "Take hold of his hand. The rest of us, hold hands leading to the other side of the room. We must build a spiritual line which he can follow back to his body. Once he takes a single breath, then everyone focus all of your energy onto him and then we yank with all our might."

"But he's breathing all the time," said Billy.

"He's gasping, not breathing," corrected Mike. "I said once he breathes, then yank, after forcing all of your energy into his body."

They create a link from John's body to across the room with Mike at the end of the link. An agonizing John in Limbo is desperately trying to get a breath of air, where it is dwindling now to nothing.

"DIE NOW JOHN RALPH!" yells one of the angels. "See where your attitude has brought you. DIE! DIE! DIE!"

Instantly the human chain appears now in the Limbo state.

"John! John! See us. Hear us. Take my hand. Follow us back to your body! NOW JOHN! TAKE MY HAND and let our hands guide you back before it's too late!" shouted Mike.

"My God! I see all of you, but I can hardly breathe. Must rush! Must get back!"

John then grabs ahold of Mike's hand and follows the other four to his body where he immediately jumps back into it.

"He's starting to breathe again!" says Mike. "Now focus your energy on him, QUICK!... Now everyone, yank as hard as you can! YANK! YANK! On the count of three… ONE, TWO, THREEEEEE."

All at once they all jerk on John's hand. He bursts awake as they all exhausted themselves and all drop to the floor. After a minute, they all begin to regain their composure.

"Thank you," declares John as he is still gasping for air. "For a minute, I really thought it was the end for me. Thanks to all of you, it wasn't."

"I don't know how much more of this I can take," said Billy. "I'm just glad we did it."

"I think I'll stay awake when my turn comes. It's now 12:55. It looks like no matter how careful we are or what we do, they find a way to get to us," said Sharon.

"I suggest we all prepare for anything, for we have no idea what's going to happen," advised Joy. "I can say one thing… it seems like they pick our weakness and then play on it, which means, Sharon, that unfortunately they'll use your spiritual problem somehow against you. But, at least you know we are all right by your side for whatever it is they have planned for you."

"Besides being a little frightened, I'm prepared for anything they can throw at me, or at least I think I am," replied Sharon. "Good Lord! I mustn't lose my nerve, not now at least. What time does anybody have?"

"It's 12:57," reported Joy. "I still have no idea of whether or not I have a turn coming up at 2:00."

"It's strange coming from me," said Sharon, "but why don't we all sit down and try to relax."

"Good idea, Sharon," said Joy.

As everyone gets comfortable, the time ticks away. 12:00, 12:05, 12:10, 12:15. A deep sleep befalls all our friends, even

Sharon. She starts to dream, but as once before, this dream is as real as waking hours. Sharon finds herself on a beautiful beach during sunrise. At first, she's the only one there as sweet gentle music plays in the cool fresh air. Suddenly a lounge chair appears as she is in a one-piece bathing suit. Next to the lounge chair is a glass stand with several delicious snacks and her favorite drink beside them, a Bahama Mama. She lays in the chair and takes a sip of the cool refreshing beverage while nibbling on the delicacies. Laying there for half an hour as the sun makes its way through the darkness to lighten up the sky, she sighs a sigh of relief and joy and peace and tranquility. This is not what she expected at all. Where are the demons, spirits and horrors that she has become so familiar with? Now a gorgeous woman in a beautiful dress comes over to her and sits down in a chair which appears just to the right of Sharon's.

"Are you enjoying yourself?" says the woman. "Are you at peace in your own mind and heart?"

"Oh, very much so," answers Sharon. "But why? Why all this and not the terrors I'm used to?"

"We just want to show you that we are not all bad," said the woman. "We can produce beauty, joy and happiness, too. This can all be yours in your awake time as well. We can and will leave you alone and your life can resemble this part of your consciousness if only you go back home Sunday and put all this foolishness aside while you still can. To gain all this peace and joy, just say 'I turn my back on this week and all it stands for. Ignore the final two days and then go back home Sunday while disregarding any more of this foolishness. Will you do it and have everlasting peace, or will you invite all of the harshness the spirit world has to offer?"

"This really is too much to deny, so I…"

Just then, each of the other five appear in Sharon's reality, or dream if you would call it that.

"Sharon! Don't listen to them," shouts Mike. "Please!"

"Mike, Joy, and Billy, Doreen, John! What are you doing here?" cries Sharon in surprise.

"We're all connected now. What happens to you must go through all of us."

"Don't you see, Sharon," says Joy, "They're giving you bliss provided you give up everything we fought and are fighting for. You'd be giving up your very soul for a little peace and quiet."

"Once they get what they want from you," said Mike, "it won't be long before everything reverts back to the way it was. Don't give in!"

"We're all family now, sweetheart. Fight it!" said Doreen.

"Our lives are now intertwined," said John. "We all feel your misery and heart. Don't surrender!"

"I can't go on knowing you'll all be suffering again soon. Stick with us," cried Billy.

"They're not going to keep their promise," said Mike. "If you give in now, you'll be at their mercy later. You know we love you and won't let you down. You're listening to evil talking. God, through us, is offering you eternal peace, happiness and salvation. Come back and fight with us. Now, listen to your logic and your heart. Whatever they tell you to do, then don't do it. Please, you know we're right. Your only real hope is by following what we do."

All five of them say in unison: "We love you. Follow us, not them. Come! Let's go back together. NOW! NOW! NOW!

"You're right," says Sharon with tears streaming down her cheeks. "You're right. Yes! What they tell me is all an illusion. Let's go back together."

"NO! DON'T BE A FOOL!" yells the woman. "If you go back with them, we'll never give you any break from our attacks."

"Come! They now speak desperate words," said Mike. "Take my hand and let's go back before it's too late."

"Yes!" says Sharon as she takes Mike's hand. "Let's go back now."

"NO! NOOOOOOO" The woman changes into a horrid figure as the six of them disappear and then all awake together in Doreen's room.

"Is everyone okay?" asks Joy. "Yes!" they chorus, as everyone gives a sigh of relief. "They knew scaring you again wouldn't necessarily work. So, they tried reverse psychology, and it almost worked. They're so desperate. They'll try any means possible, even turning peace, love and beauty into a tactical weapon... It's 1:45. I'm next. This might not be the best decision, but I'm going to go back to my own room to face this trial by myself."

"You know there is power and strength in numbers," reminded Mike. "We need to all be together. Otherwise, you can't be assured of total protection. Surely you can see that, Joy."

"I believe my protection is in my seclusion," Joy said. "At least for a short period of time."

"What do you mean by that?" asked John.

"If I'm with the five of you, then he won't be comfortable talking to me. Once I've given him some time, say fifteen minutes or so, *then* I'll need the five of you to come separate me from him. He'll then have no choice but to leave me and go back to his world."

"Who is '*he*' you keep talking about?" asked Doreen.

"He is Mike's demon. He started with you, Mike, and he'll end with me," explained Joy. "I know this by pure intuition, same as you know through your gift. Come on, Mike. You tell me. Am I right or wrong?"

"No, Joy is right," replied Mike as he turned to face everyone. "I should have sensed it before. It looks like for fifteen or twenty minutes you'll be totally on your own."

"Since Joy knows what the demon is up to, are you sure you need us?" asked Billy.

"I don't know exactly what he has planned for me," said Joy. "It must be a doozy; something even I'm not ready for. Here, Mike. Here's the extra key to my room. At 2:20 and only 2:20 come in. No matter what you may hear before that, don't come in 'til 2:20. I hope and pray I'm making the right decision about this... I'm going to leave all of you now. I love you all very much."

"Remember, hold on for twenty or so minutes," says Mike. "Then, we're coming in like gangbusters. Take care, and we'll see you shortly."

Everyone tenderly says good-bye as Joy goes down into her room. She locks her door, but only to avoid the accident of someone entering by mistake, for this isn't a time for mistakes. It's 2:02 and suddenly Joy sees a fog-shrouded figure emerge from a corner of her living room. A disfigured eerie soul of the demon steps toward her. He has a scent of hatred and evilness about him. His sunken eyes glare at Joy. Then, he speaks...

"Besides Wakings, you have been a most troublesome soul, Miss Bender."

"Do you expect me to cower at the very sight of you or just stand here and scream?"

"I expect nothing from you," said the demon. "But, I want a lot. If anyone could convince Mike Wakings to give up this silly quest, it would be you. For once he gives up, then it's only a matter of time for everyone else to do so, also. He and all the others have too much to lose by continuing this endeavor. If you all follow him, he'll lead you to total destruction."

"And how is that, demon?"

"Those two hosts of yours, George Braxton and Grea Silver, they're bent on destruction and deceit over the six of you and thousands more," said the demon. "Wakings will ultimately fall prey to their scandalous intentions. Protect Wakings from the direction he and eventually all of you will fall into before it's too late!"

"And you expect me to believe that you have all of our welfares at interest to save us as well as thousands of others?" asked Joy. "Why would *you* want that? What's in it for you? And don't tell me it's because you had a change of heart."

"By all means, no! I'm willing to save all of your necks so that I alone will have Wakings in my domain. So what I'm saying is I'm willing to give up the five of you as well as thousands of others for the right to have Mike Wakings come with me. I'm offering you a trade. The lives of the five of you and thousands of others for just one soul, his."

"Even if I believed in what you say, which I don't, I couldn't in all good conscience give you his life no matter what the cost. I don't have the right to make such a deal, especially with the likes of someone like you."

"I warn you," said the demon. "My patience is growing thin. If you don't help me, I'll have him in the end, anyway. You would just save me time and energy. GIVE ME WHAT I WANT! MAKE HIM QUIT! NOW!"

"The answer is NO! Go back to hell!"

"You've earned my wrath. Now see the horrors that await all of you."

Joy falls to her knees and begins to see all kinds of hellish sights, too much for her to bear. She starts screaming. Outside her door are her five friends who hear her screams of agony.

"Mike! Use the key," says Sharon. "Joy's in trouble!"

"It's 2:19. We must wait. One more minute," says Mike. "You heard what Joy said. No matter what, we hear, and wait 'til 2:20."

"You won't make me change my mind," Joy cries between screams. "It's 2:20 now. Quick! Come in. PLEASE COME IN!"

At Joy's call, everyone comes in time to see the demon disappear. After affirming Joy is all right, she proceeds with telling everyone what transpired in her room. Stunned, the five of them are in wonder of the demon's intentions.

"What I'm wondering," said Billy, "is why was it so important for us not to come in 'til 2:20?"

"Because I knew the exact time the demon would be finished with me, and I wanted to get the full impact of just what he had intended for me," explained Joy.

"Another intuition?" asked Mike.

"You could say that," said Joy with a smile.

"All I know is next time a woman tells me she has an intuition, somebody remind me to listen to her if I'm not already," said John.

"The demon did remind me, Mike, that the next time he sees you will be the last," said Joy. "He's then going to take you with him. But, don't worry. He's going to have to get past the five of us as well. Just remember, you're not alone!"

"I'm not worried *much*, any longer," said Mike. "We've all grown to a newer level. We're all formidable foes now."

Tell me, Mike," began Doreen, "didn't you say his name was Demon Andrea, because that sounds more like a female name as opposed to a male name. Why is that?"

"I'll tell you," began Mike. "I'll tell all of you. Through spiritual searching, I found out that his whole name is Demon Andreascopal Cornilioscatora. So, he uses Andrea as a short version. And, I know one other thing. It dates back to the Roman Empire days; maybe as far back as Jesus Christ himself."

"That's one heck of a name. Do you know the translation of it in modern days?" asked Doreen.

"No! It's probably not important," answered Mike. "But, nonetheless, I'll find out eventually, anyway."

"Well, guys, it's a little past 3:00 and I think we should get some rest before we go to The Holy Ground Church at 9:00 for our meeting," suggested Joy.

Just then, Mike has a familiar experience of falling to the floor, dead.

"Oh my!" exclaimed Joy. "What a time for Mike to have a spiritual travel. And, after checking, he *is* dead as usual. Let's get him a pillow and blanket. We have no idea how long or short this is going to be, so we might as well get comfortable ourselves.

214

"To change the subject," said Sharon, "I know Mike has given us a description of Genia, but I still wish I could see her in real life. I suppose Mike is with her this very moment." And, he is!

"Genia, it's a pleasure to see you, as always," said Mike.

"The same for me," said Genia. "Sadly, after today, I shall see you only one more time. That is, tomorrow, Sunday. So we must clear up as much as possible today and finish it all tomorrow… You've traveled extensively through the levels of the spirit world except for level one, the rock bottom of hell, and also Heaven. We will spend a little more time in both realms while you are here now. And, if you have any more questions, now would be the time to ask them. Like the song, 'It's now or never'."

"All right! Maybe now you can tell me what exactly my position is in all this? Also, what are my friends' positions in this whole thing, as well?"

"Yes, I can finally tell you now."

"FINALLY!" exclaims Mike. "My ship has come in, so to speak!"

"First," began Genia, "I would like to say that as you may have noticed, the churches today are failing to do their job. They are getting fewer and fewer people attending anymore. Their words and deeds are becoming further and further apart. That's why so many cults are attracting people, as well. But, you can tell the true one by what they teach. Is it principled or not? Also, do the core members practice what they teach? Do they teach love and unity instead of hate and separation? Some churches even say a man can have as many wives as he can afford, or some people are allowed to come in while other races are excluded. This is all

215

against God's Principles. There are many signs as to which religion is a true one, and which are false ones. You are one such person who can tell the difference. Just open your mind and heart, then no false truths can invade you. This is why you and your friends found The Holy Ground Church. You don't have to go through all the phases as other people do. We must speed things up, so your heart will tell you if this is THE Church, so follow it and lead the others to it for the word and the truth. If you and the other five make it through the challenges successfully, and accept the truth, then the real challenge begins. All of you, with you as the central figure for them, will have the task of spreading the word of Jesus and most importantly, The Lord of the Second Advent, and creating your own kind of Church that is free and open to all who come to learn more about the Second Advent and to follow him and the other Churches made with his teachings; the ones that each of the six of you have made. Then, your followers will spread the word, themselves, to all the countries of the world. You will build on the cornerstone the Messiah has laid, which is a giant rock in upstate New York called the Holy Rock, located on Holy Ground. Once everything has been laid, it will build and build from year-to-year, decade-to-decade, century-to-century, changing the fallen world until a thousand years have passed. Then, the Kingdom of Heaven will finally be created on the earth. Each of the six of you will go to whatever area in the fifty States you desire to begin your ministry; whether it be your home town or one unfamiliar to you. If you all succeed in your final challenges and you commit yourselves to this lifestyle, then and only then will *all* the answers come to you. At times in your life of faith, even the spirit of Jesus and the Lord of the Second Advent will come to your aide. Live a righteous life and all six of you will live past the 100-year mark. So, you see, much awaits you."

"Tell me," began Mike, "where does all this fit into the plans of George Braxton and Grea Silver? Are they even good, or are they evil?"

"You'll have to wait 'til 3:00 this afternoon in your time to find the answers to these and many more questions," answered Genia. "This will be a very special challenge for all of you. By Sunday tomorrow, everything will be clear and decided; not just on earth, but here as well. You may not be able to trust Braxton and Silver, but you know you can trust me. So now, put your mind at rest as we travel to the lowest and highest realms of the spirit world. Are you ready for this journey?"

"I guess, as much as I'll ever be," answers Mike. "So, let's go. Oh, by the way, I really enjoy this new scene of being by a fishing pond while what looks like families sharing time together fishing. A very relaxing atmosphere. I can feel the warmth and love."

So, they disappear and reappear in a cold, dark and dank place with the odor of rotting flesh in the air, sickening to Mike, but one that has become familiar to Genia. Mike realizes this could only be it, the rock bottom of hell.

"I've been here only for moments before, but I suppose I'll be spending a little more time here now."

As Mike walks around, he stops at an area where it seems like there are tens-of-thousands of men and women, young and old, naked and chained down to the ground. He goes over to one man and talks to him…

"Who are you people and what have you done to deserve a fate such as this?" asks Mike.

"Our names are inconsequential. We're here because we either committed suicide, murder, or practiced adultery," said the man. "We are the lowest of the low. Please, won't you help me? Please?"

"What can I do for you?" asked Mike.

"Tell my family to pray for me."

Then, one-by-one, the other souls start pleading with Mike, "Me too! Me too! Me too! Me as well. Please! Don't forget about me!" Tens, hundreds, thousands of prisoners all cry out at the same time. Mike can hardly stand listening to all the cries, echoing through the air, as stale as it may be.

"Genia, let's leave," begs Mike. "Please. I can hardly bear it any longer. It's not that I don't want to hear their cries; it's that I don't know how to help all of them and it's frustrating me because I want to help those poor souls."

"Fulfill your mission and ultimately you *will* help these and many more people," said Genia. "But for now, I want to bring you to another area of this level. I'm bringing you to a place where spirits have gained the power to go back to earth for the purpose of tormenting because they, themselves, were tormented and even killed while on the earth. It could have been a decade ago, hundreds of years or even thousands of years ago. The ones I'm going to introduce you to are of great meaning to one of your friends. Listen closely if you want to be of help to the one and all of your friends."

Genia and Mike travel to an area where the very air is full of hatred and resentment. Then, they stop where one spirit along with several others show their feelings and emotions in the very outward appearances of themselves. Mike approaches one and begins asking questions.

"Who are you and what are you doing and why?"

"My name is Geraldine Thine," the woman said. "I was born in Delaware in 1783. I fell in love with a man named Jason Worley. Joan Grace was an ancestor of the woman you know of today named Sharon Grace. Jason and I planned to wed in September of 1816. Joan also fell in love with Jason and became resentful towards me because of her feelings. I tried to console her with understanding and love, but it did no good in changing her feelings toward Jason and hatred towards me. Her disastrous feelings toward Jason made our lives miserable. It only got worse as time pressed on to August 1816. I had just turned thirty-three when Joan said she wanted to work things out before Jason and I married. She invited me to her lovely house a few miles away. I eagerly went to see her. Once there, we sat in the sitting room of her home. Joan told me that she could never go on without Jason. She pulled a revolver out and directed me to a freshly dug grave. I regret having pleaded with her for my life, but to no avail. She fired the pistol and as I felt the burn enter my chest, I fell backwards into my doom, the grave. As she shoveled the dirt and covered my frail body, I became conscious and realized I was still alive, but buried. I tried screaming out, but as I did, dirt filled my mouth. I desperately tried to get up, but it was too late. The last trace of air was covered up, and as the life left my body, I swore I would make her descendants pay for what she did to me. When I entered the spirit world, I was in a pretty decent realm. But, my hatred and resentment dragged me lower and lower until finally I was in hell. I became furious as I was eaten alive with hatred toward everyone and everything. As time passed, I became a devious, hateful and tortured soul. Before I knew it, I was in the lowest point, the rock bottom of hell. I enlisted the help of several other tormented souls. I had gained the right to attack up to the eighth generation of Joan Grace, which is now your friend, Sharon Grace. That is why she is tortured and punished until we either drive her to insanity or death. She can only free herself when she pays the price needed so all of us can find everlasting peace. I long for freedom from my agony, but only she can give it to me. I lost my chance when I murdered her and continued to murder her with my hate, jealousy and resentment. My only hope is through her."

"And what must she say and do for this to happen?" asked Mike.

"You and she must figure this out on your own. I'm prohibited from telling you. It's simple, very simple, but still you and she must figure it out for yourselves."

"How did you know who I was?" asked Mike.

"I know all about the six of you," said Geraldine. "No one can hide anything from those in the spirit world if we want to know... So now you know why, but the two of you must figure out how. I have said my peace. Now go and leave me to my misery. Go! GO! GO!"

"Come, Mike," says Genia. "Let us leave here."

Genia and Mike disappear and reappear in the most beautiful high spirit place of all, Heaven.

"Wow! What a difference." exclaimed Mike. "But, even being here in Heaven, I know Sharon and I must figure this out for the sake of all involved."

Waiting a few minutes, Mike is on a road glittering like diamonds; a road that leads to the most fabulous city that he had remembered seeing once before. Coming down the road toward the city is a man whose spirit is bright and clear. He comes up to Mike and he stops to talk to him.

"You're Mike Wakings, aren't you?" he says.

"You know me?" Mike asks.

"Yes! You're becoming very popular to many of us here in the spirit world. Of course, you still have many important things to accomplish."

"Good Lord! I never realized just how important what I'm doing is… Are you headed to the city," Mike asked the man.

"Just to pass through," he replied.

"May I ask how you died?"

"I took my own life," the man said.

"What! You committed suicide and you're here in Heaven? Not hell? How could that be? Please explain it to me."

"Well, you see, even though I took my own life, I didn't commit suicide," the man explained. "I was a soldier in World War II. I had extremely important information on the location of our submarines. Then, I was captured by the Germans. I was tortured over and over again, until finally I knew I would break, thus causing the deaths of thousands of innocent people. I had a capsule of cyanide hidden in a false wisdom tooth, to take if we knew there was no other choice to prevent them from finding out the locations of the submarines. In deep despair, I took it, thus giving up my life for the lives of so many concerned. I've since been waiting in Paradise for the gates to the Kingdom of Heaven to open. A short time ago, they finally did. I waited with many of my family members, as well as my loving wife-to-be. Many of us made it to Heaven while others were not as lucky. So, that's why I'm here, and not in hell."

"Your death was one to save many other lives, and not your own. One of selflessness. I'll let you be on your way," said Mike.

"Good bye, Mike Wakings. You have your own journey to follow. May the Lords be with you," added the man as he left, and as Genia prepares Mike to do the same.

"Our time together has just about come to an end, Mike," said Genia. "I will bring you back here just one more time, tomorrow, Sunday. Then, the final climax to your visits here will be realized, providing, of course, you succeed in your final challenges. So, go now my precious soul. Go and inform your friends of all you have witnessed to while here on this side. Maybe even Joy will believe where you have been. Go back. Go back, Mike, to your earthly existence. Go back! Go back! Go back!"

"Look! He's coming to," said Doreen.

"Mike, dear friend. How are you doing?" asks Joy.

"Fine, Joy," Mike answers groggily. "What time is it?"

"It's 6:10. You've been out for about three hours. How long were you in the spirit world?" Joy asked.

"About the same amount of time. It looks like time there and here have become totally equal in length," explained Mike. "We only have around three hours before we're supposed to be at The Holy Ground Church. Let me quickly tell all of you what happened."

"How about ordering coffee?" said John. "I'm pretty bushed, as I'm sure everyone else is."

After a cup, they all relax and listen to what Mike has to tell them. He finishes at 8:15.

"Wow! Just one more meeting with Genia," says Billy. "The week is almost up. Tell us, Joy, Do you believe Mike was in Heaven now?"

"I don't know what to think at this point. I'm not going to say yes, but I also won't say no. I need a bit more convincing."

"You're a real hard safe to crack, Joy," said Mike. "I have two more days to convince you. For now, I say let's all wash up and meet downstairs in the SUV so we won't be late for the 9:00 appointment."

They do just that and make it to the Church at 8:55. After ringing the doorbell, Alice herself answers…

"Welcome back, everyone! Let's go directly to my office where we can discuss things in private." While walking down the hallway to her office, Alice brings something to their attention. "You're in luck again. Your just in time to hear our members singing at 9:00 a.m."

"Do you guys do much singing?" asks Doreen. "I can't wait to hear *this* song."

"Yes! Singing not just Holy Songs, but uplifting songs in general lifts all of our spirits," explained Alice. "When here, you'll hear us singing every three hours; 9:00 a.m. being the first of the day, noon, 3:00, 6:00, and 9:00 p.m. for the end of the day. Listen! They're starting now."

Oh, my little lambs, wandering on the lonely plain,
Someday you may fall, overcome by your despair.
Weak, wounded souls, no one will come to comfort you,
Alone, you have no one to love you,
No one to bring the truth.

The title to that one, if you haven't guessed already, is 'Oh My Little Lambs'. There are four verses altogether, just like that other song, 'When I Behold the Lord' that you heard the other day. Come, everybody have a seat in my office... So tell me, what has happened to all of you since we last met on Thursday?" asked Alice.

"Please, Mike, why don't you be the spokesman for us as you were last time," suggests Joy. "Is that okay with everyone, that Mike speaks for all of us? (Everyone agrees!) Fine, then why don't you go ahead, Mike."

So, Mike explains all that happened Friday and throughout the night, right up to their coming there.

"This is all so incredible, if it weren't for our own situation, I wouldn't be able to believe you guys, but I do and you know I do."

"Alice, do you mind me taking your hands just one more time so that we can be sure; I mean really sure?" asks Mike.

"No! Not at all. I understand completely," said Alice. So, Mike takes Alice's hands and concentrates for a minute.

"It's true, everyone. Alice truly believes," announces Mike.

"Well, I'm glad someone else does," said Sharon. "Now, if only they can help us clear up some of our mysteries, I would feel a whole lot better."

"We will, but I'm afraid that we won't be able to meet at 8:00 tonight as planned," announced Alice.

"Why, what has happened?" asked Mike.

"We'll have to meet whatever time you are finished!" said Alice

"Finished! Finished doing what?" asked Joy.

224

"What you are all destined for," Alice explained. "I'm afraid I can say no more except I, as well as everyone else here, will wait for you no matter how long it takes. So, don't worry about that."

"If you knew this, then why did you tell us 8:00 in the first place?" asked Mike.

"Because things didn't happen exactly as was planned," replied Alice. "You did things according to how other entities affected you. We thought things would be finished before 8:00. But contrary to popular belief, there is no predestination. Plans change according to man's actions. God doesn't know what will happen next. He only knows what will happen depending on what man does. For example, on our terms, God doesn't even know which team is going to win the Super Bowl. He only knows what will happen depending upon what actions man takes; but not what actions he will take. So, we planned on 8:00, but as fortunes change, so does the time we planned on... Now, I would like to discuss something of great pertinence. It's 11:45 now and I want all of you to be on your way by 2:00. So please, let me explain."

Alice takes 45 minutes to explain the situation. At 12:30, she turns to Mike and instructs him: "It's important that you go to our prayer room and pray for 45 minutes. We'll all wait for you here. Good luck, Mike. See you soon."

Mike walks down the corridor and towards the prayer room when he runs into a man and woman in their sixties who stop him and begin a conversation with him.

"Are you Mike Wakings?" asks the man; "one of six people here searching for answers?"

"Yes!" answered Mike. "I won't ask how you know of us, because I believe everyone here knows about us. So, what can I help you with?"

"Actually," the woman answered, "we're here to help *you*. We've been members of this Church for many years. We found out all about it. There are many things we have to warn all of you about. It will definitely change your mind about it."

"I guarantee if you give us an hour, your outlook will be completely changed," echoed the man. "Please give us the hour so we can help all of you before it's too late."

"Very well," answered Mike. "You have an hour, but make it count. Our minds won't be easy to change."

The man and woman take the hour which makes an impact on Mike. After speaking to them, Mike angrily heads back to Alice's office.

"How was your prayer, Mike?" Alice asked.

Mike grabs a gym bag and gets ready to talk to everybody.

"What's in the gym bag?" asks John.

"Just papers I need from Alice. Why, I don't know what use they'll be now."

"Why? What's up, Mike?" asks Joy.

"We're leaving this place and not coming back. I found out all I need to know," said Mike.

"What happened while you were gone?" demands Joy.

"Let's just say I saw the light, and it has nothing to do with this Church. Say good-bye. We're leaving for good."

6. The Worst Becomes Reality

It's 1:45 as Mike and his friends head back to the Stanwick Hotel. He tells them that he doesn't want to discuss anything until they get back to his room. Once back in his room, Mike gives a brief discussion of his talk with the two strangers. Mike realizes he has little time before meeting Braxton and Silver. He explains that the couple were in the Church for several years because they wanted to get as much information as possible to destroy the Church. He goes on to report what seems like destructive facts about the members of the Church. It's 2:20 now as Mike winds things up. For some strange reason, the five of them, after listening to Mike, don't seem to be too surprised.

"Mike, remember that letter you received just before going to the spirit world several days ago?" asks Joy. "It said watch out for people who would have negative information about the Church. Do you recall that?"

"Yes, I do, but everything they told me makes too much sense," answered Mike. "So, I at least am heeding their warnings. If you trust me, then take my word for it and stay away from that Church."

"All right, Mike," said Joy. I at least will listen to you because you haven't been wrong yet. How do the four of you feel about this?"

Everyone, one-by-one agree with Joy and Mike. They all agree to stay away from the Church. Again, almost too easily.

"Good!" says Mike. "Now that it's settled, let's get ready for Braxton and Silver."

"You bet!" says Billy. "We're finally going to get the answers to many mysteries. I, for one, am eager and excited about this meeting."

"I think we all feel that way, Billy," says Joy. "Just 35 more minutes."

Everybody agrees. Mike's phone rings.

"Who could that be?" Mike exclaims. "Nobody but us and Braxton and Silver know I'm here."

"Hello!"

"Please help us! We're in room 1628. Please, hurry. We have little time left," said the desperate voice. "I know who you people are, and what kind of help you can give us. Please, quickly!"

"Who was it, Mike?" asks Joy.

"Someone begging for our help in room 1628. They sounded pretty desperate. He said come quickly. I'm not sure what to do."

"What do you mean?" asked John. "We have to go help them!"

"I know, John, but something about it just doesn't seem right. Still, they say they really need our help. He also knew about the things we can do. And how did he know my room number? It just doesn't seem right."

"Look, he said come quickly," said Billy. "We're wasting time trying to figure this out. Don't you think we should go and if something is wrong, we just leave?"

"You're right. It's our responsibility to help people if they really need us," responded Mike. "As you said, if something is wrong, we can always leave. So let's go."

They leave quickly and get to room 1628. After knocking on the door and getting no response, the door must have been unlocked and ajar, for it slowly opens.

"Hello!" says Mike. "Is anybody home?" (no answer) "We're answering your cry for help."

They cautiously go inside, turning on the lights and closing the door.

"This is a one-room apartment. No place to hide," says Mike.

"I'll go check out the restroom," says Joy. "No one in there, either."

"I'm beginning to feel the same way you did, Mike. We should have listened to you. How about we get out of here and go back to Mike's room?"

They all agree as John goes to the door and starts fumbling around.

"What's going on, John?" Is there a problem?" asks Mike.

"You can say that!" said John. "This door seems to be stuck. It won't open up."

"Let me try it," says Billy. He tries and tries to open the door, but has no luck as well. "This door isn't stuck; it's downright locked, and there's no way of opening it."

"What do you mean?" asks Mike. "There's no way to open it? Even if somebody locked it in the minute we were here, we'd still be able to unlock it from the inside."

"I understand that, Mike, but nonetheless somehow it's locked and we can't open it. We're trapped in here," Billy reiterates.

"Mike! Something's trying to make us late in seeing Braxton and Silver," said Joy. "You know how they feel about tardiness. Even if they do wait for us, which I'm doubtful they will, they'll at least be very upset with us. It's just past 2:30. We don't have very much time left."

Mike goes over to the phone to dial the front desk, but the phone is dead.

"Let me guess," says Joy. "The phone is dead, right?"

"Yes!" confirms Mike. "Everybody that has a cell phone, call the front desk. NOW!" Everyone who has a cell phone with them finds that they are all dead, too. "This is too much! Let me check out the window to see if someone has their window open. If so, I'll call for help. Since we're facing an enclosed area and not facing the street, they'll be able to hear me better!"

As Mike looks out the window, he realizes everyone has their window closed because it's too cold outside. He comes back in and shuts the window.

"No luck. It looks like we're stuck in here until they decide to let us out," says Mike.

"We're not going to let 'them' whoever them is, beat us, are we?" says Joy.

"We've come too far to get beaten now," says Doreen. "Of course, it's spiritual, but which spirit?"

"Mike, we're not really giving up, are we?" asks John. "It's obvious they want us to mess up with Braxton and Silver. Why is it so important? Besides, we'll see them sooner or later, won't we?"

"You're all right," says Mike. "I had a moment of weakness. And, we *are* going to see Braxton and Silver, eventually. Delaying us serves no purpose, except to get us pissed off."

"What's that smell?" asks Joy.

"What smell?" asks Mike.

"From the vents. My God! THAT'S CYANIDE IN VAPOR FORM COMING OUT! WE'LL ALL BE DEAD IN MINUTES. QUICK, OPEN THE WINDOW. THAT WILL GIVE US A BIT MORE TIME!" cries Joy.

"Now we know why they didn't care about when we saw Braxton and Silver," says Billy.

"YES! Because they don't expect us to be alive later," says Mike.

"Start yelling for help!" says Doreen as Mike opens the window. "Someone will hear us and get us out of here."

"Even if someone did hear us, by the time we get help, we'll all be dead," says Mike.

"Then, what ARE we going to do?" asks John.

"We have one and only one choice left. The ledge along the side of the building is approximately two feet wide. Plenty enough room for us to walk to the next room. Even if the window is closed, it's very slim that it would be locked. This our only hope left," says Mike.

"But it's 16 stories to the bottom!" reminds Sharon.

"Everybody relax!" says Mike. "Calm down. This is the ONLY way out. It's this way or die."

"Mike's right. We have no choice. Besides, two feet is a lot of room," says Joy… to which they all agree.

"Okay, Joy. You go first, then myself," says Mike. "Then Sharon and Billy and Doreen. Then, finally, you John. I did it this way so that there's a man behind each lady to help her if she gets in trouble."

"Why should there be any trouble?" asks Billy. "Didn't you say we had plenty of room?"

"Yes, but the ledge has quite a bit of ice on it. So, be careful where you walk. Keep one eye on where you walk, while keeping the other eye on the lady in front of you. And, whatever you do, don't look down. That would be a big mistake. For everyone else, be careful where you walk. Now, before we drop dead in here, let's get going... Okay, Joy. You first. Be careful!"

"If I hear 'Be careful' one more time, I'll scream. All right, here we go."

All six of them make their way onto the ledge. As they do, a cold breeze blows in their faces, almost as if the bottom has hell has touched them. Slowly but surely they make it to the window of the next room. Joy then attempts to open it.

"It's locked!" she reports. "I thought most windows would be unlocked."

"Can you see, is it occupied or vacant?" asks Mike.

"It looks vacant. Just our luck!" says Joy. "Two vacant in a row if you include the one we were in. It looks like we'll have to go to the next room. It's going to be tricky. We have to go right at the end of this ledge to get to the other ledge."

"Be extra cautious, everybody," warns Mike. "It looks pretty icy at the corner of the turn."

All six take their time as they come to the turn. First comes Joy, then Mike, and then Sharon. When it comes to Billy, he makes the mistake of keeping both eyes totally on Sharon. He doesn't notice a piece of ice on the edge of the ledge. Billy slips on it and falls off the ledge, but before he plunges to his death, he grabs onto the edge of the ledge with all of his might, but begins to slip off.

"Good Lord!" cries Doreen. "Billy's about to fall off. Help, somebody, HELP!"

Doreen and Sharon both grab ahold of Billy but don't have the strength to hold on.

"Please! HELP US! WE CAN'T HOLD ON!"

Mike and John hunch up to the girls and both grab Billy. But, because of the angle and Billy's weight, they're having trouble lifting him back onto the ledge.

"DON'T LET GO GUYS! PLEASE! HANG ON. I DON'T WANT TO GO LIKE THIS!"

"He's slipping! He's slipping," cries John.

"Girls! You grab hold of Billy, too," directs Mike. "Now, on the count of three, all of us start pulling him up, back onto the ledge... Ready? ONE... TWO... THREE... NOW ALL PULL 'TIL YOUR ARMS COME OUT OF THEIR SOCKETS! PULL! PULL!"

In unison, they all pull until Billy is finally back on the ledge.

"You okay, Billy?" asks John.

"Yes, but that was too close for comfort. What do you say we all get off this ledge NOW. No hurry, but NOW!"

They all gather their composure and head to the window of the next room. Mike tries this one and is successful. The window opens up and all six scurry inside to safety.

"This one looks like someone is in it," observes Joy.

"It will be hard to explain what we're all doing here," says Mike. "Let's get out, FAST! Once we're safely out, we'll call management anonymously on our cell phone, which by the way I'm sure works now, and warn them about room 1628. Now, let's go, and believe it or not, we can still make the 3:00 with Braxton and Silver."

They leave the room, make the phone call, and then head down to Conference Room 3. They all get in about 2:57, and await their hosts. At precisely 3:00, in come Braxton and Silver. They head straight to the podium at the front of the room. Then, they get started.

"Good afternoon, all," says George. "I hope your experience in Room 1628 and the ledge weren't too exhausting for each of you."

"That does it!" says Mike. "Are you guys going to finally tell us who you really are, where you're from, and how you know so much about us? Not just our past lives but also everything that's going on while we have been here since Sunday?"

"Yes, Mr. Wakings," says George. "The time has come for the truth to be revealed. We know all of you have been extremely patient with us. And, all the mysteries surrounding us. Also, as you all can see, we have a large screen to use here as proof of everything we're going to tell you, for we're sure with what we say, as intelligent as all of you are, you will find it hard to believe us *without* proof. Let us start by telling you that every, and I mean every, incident that has happened to any and all of you were not random and unrelated happenings. Everything from meeting your chauffeurs at the airport to your trips to the spirit world, Mr. Wakings, has been for a reason. A reason so each of you could spiritually grow from as an individual to a family. You had to grow to prepare yourselves for the future, providing of course you can have success tonight and then decide to take our offer that we are going to present to all of you in a short while. You will all have the night and early tomorrow to make up your minds. But, more of that shortly. Now, to begin giving you explanations for everything... The reason, Miss Bender, that you could find no information on either of us anywhere is simply because we have no history in your world to be found. Not unless you can go back to before man's creation. You see, we're angels, and not just any angels, but the angels Michael and Gabriel, who were with God from eons ago."

"But that can't be!" objected Mike. "When I asked Genia about the two of you, she said I was wrong. That you weren't whom I thought you were."

"You *were* wrong, Mike," said George. "If we may now become familiar with all of you? You said I was Michael and Grea was Gabriel. But that isn't true. You see, I'm Gabriel, and Grea is Michael."

"Whaaaaaat? You mean...."

"I'll take over from here, Gabriel," said Grea. "To further throw all of you off, we gave you the impression, in case you came up with this answer, that we weren't who you thought we were. This was to make sure you were totally confused, which in your case, Mike, was totally successful because of your asking Genia about us. We couldn't be exposed until we were ready to tell you who we were, which is now... Being archangels will explain how we know so much about each of you. You see, we were informed about all of you since the first day of your birth to this very moment. In case we need to recheck something, we have a complete record of your entire lives. All we have to do to locate some point in the timeline is to focus on the when and where; then that point of your lives will be up on the screen such as this one."

"Hold on a second," objected Joy. "I know we've been through some pretty incredible and unbelievable incidents, but all this is still just a little bit over the top. I think I speak for everybody when I say, it's not because we don't believe *any* of this without some affirmation about it all."

"That's exactly why we have this little setup with the giant screen," explained Michael. "Since you, Joy, and you, Mike,... Oh Mike. It looks like we share the same name; pure coincidence though! Please excuse my own interruption. As I was saying, since the two of you are the spokesmen for the group, I'll use the two of you as representatives for both the male and female sexes."

Michael points to the screen as a video comes on.

"Good Gosh!" exclaims Joy. "That's me when I was just a teenager, around sixteen or seventeen. I'm in a car with my mother, right before..."

"Right before she tried to beat a yellow light. See what happens next!

Her mother's car didn't beat the yellow light because a motorist came from the right and hit the car going about 20 miles per hour. Hitting Joy's side, it broke her leg.

"I can still feel the agony in my leg," said Joy.

Next, the scene jumps to Joy on the day she graduated from college. She watches as her parents are there, brimming with pride and hope for their daughter. "I remember that day as if it were yesterday," remarks Joy. Then, it shows the day before she met Mike at the airport, getting ready for the trip to Denver.

"These are just three stops in your road of life," said Michael. "I could just as well have shown every moment of your entire life. But, I'm not looking to invade your privacy to all of your friends here."

"Thank you," replied Joy. "I appreciate and understand what you've done here."

Michael now points to the screen again.

"That's when I was eight years old!" says Mike. "We were moving from my first home. It was an apartment in New York City. I remember when I was heartbroken to leave all my friends and everything I knew. We went to live with my aunt and uncle in Queens. You see, we didn't have much money, so we went there 'til we saved up enough to move to another home." (The scene changes.) "That's me now when I was thirty-five. I got my first job in advertising. I went out celebrating with my friends. That was in Chicago." (The scene changes again.) "I was forty-one there as I moved to Oxnard, California to start my new job in advertising. I received a promotion and had to change locations from Chicago to there." (It changed one last time to show Mike on the plane with Joy coming to Denver. Then, the film stops.)

"We could show every scene of each of your lives, but I think you all believe us by now," said Michael.

"That's incredible," said John, "but you made your point."

"I think we all believe you are angels now," says Joy.

Since everyone agrees, Joy asks. "So, where do we go from here?

"As mentioned in your introductory letters," said Michael, "you've been chosen from some 10,000 possibilities. Your selection was based upon your lives, especially your relationship to spiritual phenomena, and how righteous each of you were in your waking hours. Individually, you each have been chosen to inform people, not just America, but eventually the world, of what you have all learned, and what you'll learn in the future. All this is leading up to informing people of The Lord of the Second Coming. his words and teachings right up to the day he left this world and went to Heaven. And, most important, his identity."

"But, we don't know who he is or was. Mike hasn't learned that." said Doreen.

"Not yet," replied Michael, "but he will. Trust us, he will!"

"Also, how do we find what he taught?" asked Sharon.

"All that is taught in *The Completed Testament*, which by the way was taken by us from our house in Idaho Springs the night you all left in a hurry."

"We were pressured to leave that night," says Mike. "I'm sure you both knew what was going on there that night we were there. But, why did the two of you take it?"

"For that answer," replied Michael, "I'm sorry but you'll all have to wait until tomorrow. But, we can say this… You'll be given the original copy if you decide to take our offer. Let us explain in a little more detail. If you decide to become part of our family, you'll each be given different states for you to witness. You will also be given a time limit that you can spend on each state. Your goal is to attain at least four hundred people in each state. Then, you will all go to other countries where you will attempt to gain at least forty people in each country you witness in. You will all be given plans and strategies to help you along. With the help of Jesus Christ, the Lord of the Second Advent, and your good friend Mike, you should be able to gain victory wherever you go. You'll be a shining beacon for everyone. Don't worry. Spiritually, you'll gain all the knowledge and security you'll need to help guide all the others. Nothing for any of you will be left to chance. And now, the finances. As promised earlier, if you devote the rest of your lives to this goal, then tomorrow each of you will be given a cashier's check for $10 million. Even *you*, Miss Bender. I know we said you would receive only $3 million, but since you'll be giving up just as much, if not more than everyone else, then you should receive the same amount. Also, because you didn't complain or hold resentment, you've earned this as much as anybody. You can also use part of it to build a business, if need be, or however you choose to use it. If you decide to go on, then much more detail will be revealed. Succeed tonight; then tomorrow you will choose between a selfish life or a selfless one; one centering on yourselves, or one centering on the cosmos."

"WOW! And I do mean wow!" said Mike.

"Yes, please, let's talk some more," said Doreen.

"All right, we'll talk to 6:00 tonight," said Michael. "Then all of you will have to go back to our house in Idaho Springs. You have a date with destiny."

Michael and Gabriel discuss so many things with our six friends. At the end, everyone is enlightened. They all feel that they have found a new giving and rewarding life. Even Joy feels anew.

"We must leave you now but our hearts are with you always," says Michael. "One last thing, since we are archangels, money is no object to us. For God's work, we have an unlimited resource. We have no want, except for God's plan to be realized."

"But, where does the money actually come from?" asked Mike. "I mean, it has to come from somewhere."

"It does," explained Gabriel. "You see we did tell you the truth about the stock market. We make a fortune because we know the market like we know the universe. It has no secret to us. We have an unlimited fortune."

"So, now you must go," reiterated Michael. "We will be here tomorrow at 10:00 a.m. We hopefully will meet you all tomorrow. Good bye and God Bless you, and may the Lords be with you."

They all leave now and head toward Idaho Springs in the SUV. It's 6:45 now.

"I feel everything starting to wind down now," remarked Sharon.

"That's because it is, Sharon," said Joy. "We have less than a day left. And, whatever waits for us at the house, we must be prepared for. I really feel, myself, that all that has happened to us is leading us to this point. I just hope we have grown enough together as a family to make it through tonight. How do you feel about it, Mike? Can you tell us anything about tonight?"

"No, I'm at a loss. Just like the reason I couldn't pick up anything from Braxton and Silver, was because they were head angels with no recent earthly past, what's about to happen tonight is also hidden from me. But, I guess we'll find out soon enough... We're just passing by Black Hawk now. We'll be there in just a while."

Everyone grabs each other's hand. Even John, who's driving, extends his hand as they join in a prayer for the first time together. Mike leads in a heartwarming choice of uplifting words. Tears trickle down each of their faces. The prayer invites everyone to share some words of their own. By prayer's end, they find themselves pulling up in the driveway of the house. Everyone gets out and approaches the front door. Mike fumbles getting the key out and opens the door. They all go inside and relax in the living room.

"Well," says John, "it's 7:30 and dark outside. What do we do or where do we go from here?"

"Is anybody hungry or thirsty?" asks Doreen. "They have the kitchen full of food and drinks again. Just this time there's no alcohol."

"Just as well," remarked Billy. "We don't need it tonight."

"Why don't we all go in and get something. We might need the energy," suggested Joy.

Everybody goes in and gets something for themselves. By the time they finish, it's 8:25. There's a tenseness in the room. Whatever awaits them comes soon.

"Mike, you've been carrying that gym bag wherever you go," say Joy. "What's so important about it?"

"You'll find out, Joy," he replied. "You'll all find out sooner or later, that is... Hey, remember that history library of sorts down in the basement? What do you say we go check it out?"

"Yes! Let's do that," answered Doreen. "I found it most interesting. Provided, of course, our nerves can handle going back down there."

"I say 'let's go'," replied Billy.

Everyone agrees as they proceed down the stairs. They notice that the basement door is wide open. Hesitantly they proceed.

"Look!" exclaimed John. "The door to the storage room has been repaired. This whole thing looks creepy to me."

"Listen to this!" as Sharon reads from a passage of one of the books she picks up. "'Time has no beginning and time has no end, unlike man who has a beginning and whose end is still undecided. Will he live forever, or die a million deaths?' What do you think it means?"

"Man will either live forever in Heaven, or die over and over again in hell," answered Mike. "Speaking of hell, I got that feeling again, I got that feeling!"

Then, all of a sudden the basement door slams shut. The lights start flickering as they hear moaning, slushing and screaming coming from upstairs toward the door.

241

"Okay! It's happening right here, right now," says Mike. "Everyone into the storeroom."

They bolt into the storeroom, bar the door shut and wait as they hear the sounds come down the stairs and stop outside their door. There is banging on the door and the coldness begins.

"All right! We'll let this go on for a minute more, then it's our turn," says Mike."

As everyone waits in the cold and what should be a terror-filled experience, the door starts shaking so violently that the hinges start coming right off the wall. But no. This time it's not so much terror as it is frustration, and the desire to challenge the force that lies on the other side of the door. The six souls in there are just about ready to strike out at the unseen horror.

"All right, we had the suspicion that this might be the place of the attack, as well as when," acknowledged Mike. "We've been preparing for it, and the time has now come to fight back. Are you ready?"

"As ready as we'll ever be," replies Joy.

"Then prepare yourselves. I'm going to open the door *before* it has a chance to cave it in. Here goes!"

"This is it! cries Sharon. "More than any of you, I'm about to face my fate. Thank you all for standing with me!"

Mike unbolts the door, and then stands out of the way as the door opens with such force that it crashes against the wall. The wall crumbles into pieces. On the other side is a sight so frightening that you can barely look at it without screaming; a sight so horrible that the term 'hell freezes over' surely applies to it. A conglomeration of horrid, terrible souls; each stretching to reach our friends, trying to grab hold of someone who's tangible; someone they can squeeze the life out of so they can join them in their hell. Sharon comes up front and while shaking, speaks out to them...

"Why is your hatred of me so strong that you would punish not only me, but all those that come into your path?" she asks.

"I have waited hundreds of years in order to take out my revenge," said the spirit Geraldine. "We have no interest in harming anyone else, unless they interfere with our attacks upon you. My hatred of you is so strong that it has attracted many more spirits to join me. I will not, I cannot, rest until you die and find your own hell. We have prepared a place for you."

"Is there no other alternative?" asks Sharon as she finds it more and more difficult to look at them. "Can I not relieve your suffering in some other way?"

"There is, if you discover it," said Geraldine.

Then, all of the other spirits attack the five, who are picked up and tossed to the back of the storeroom. They get up with pain stabbing through their bodies. The very sight of the spirits is too much for them to bear; almost worse than the physical pain.

"Leave my friends alone!" demands Sharon. "NOW! Leave them! You said you wouldn't hurt anyone else."

"Unless they get in the way to protect you," said Geraldine. "And we see they were planning to come to your rescue. That is not permitted."

"We were just coming to talk to Sharon," retorted Mike. "Surely you have no objection to that."

"Then speak," said Geraldine. "Speak to her as you wish without any more interference from my cohorts. You have one minute. Now speak!"

The five of them gather around Sharon and use the time given constructively. When the time is up, they all back away from Sharon and hope they have given her the right advice.

"Being forced to kill you is most undesirable," said Geraldine. "We would want it to be your own decision, but since that is impossible…"

"But, it's not impossible," answered Sharon. "I offer myself to you so that your heart of injustice may be mended. My ancestor, Joan Grace, shot and buried you alive. For what she did, I repent. I'm sorry that you eventually became the spirit you are today. Those ancestors of mine who were female and unmarried always kept their maiden name, Grace. Since there are no males with the name Grace alive today, then once I am dead, that line will be erased forever. But, even knowing this, I sacrifice myself to you, Geraldine Thine." (Sharon falls to her knees.) "Please forgive us for what was done to you well over 200 years ago. It must have been torture for you to wait so long to get to the eighth generation, *me*, and hope to gain that eternal peace you longed for. Not only will my death free you, but free the other spirits with you, as well." Sharon cries. "My life is now yours to do with as you please. Take it, and go in peace. I must put an end to this suffering for you, and insanity this has created. I am yours to do with as you please. Take it, and let me wipe the slate clean, now and forever more."

"Are you really giving yourself to us?" asked Geraldine, in amazement. "Are you truly sorry?"

"I don't just ask you to forgive me and Joan; I beg you to. I have no resentment toward you for what you have done to me," said Sharon. "I deserve it. Truly, I beg forgiveness and understand why you're doing what you're doing."

With all her hatred, resentment and hurt from the depths of hell, a tear runs down Geraldine's cheek. "You have discovered my own weakness. Your unlimited sense of self-sacrifice, heart of purity and willingness to forgive even us, myself, for all we have done to you. My heart is melted. I no longer have resentment. We can go now and begin our growth, all of us. You, Sharon Grace, have released me from the chains that have kept me at the bottom of hell. All the spirits rejoice with me as the indignation is lifted from our shoulders. Just your sincere heart was enough. Go now in peace. Retribution has been offered and accepted. Good bye to you and your friends, for they truly are friends to adhere to."
Then, a cloud of white smoke appears where all the spirits were. The coldness is gone and so are the spirits.

"I'm free." declares Sharon, with tears running down her face. "I'm free at last, and so is Geraldine and her spirit friends." The other five come around Sharon and rejoice with her.

"We all knew that all she wanted for all these years was for you, the eighth generation, to take responsibility for what your ancestor did, apologize and offer yourself for retribution," explained Mike. "Then, she and the spirits with her could be free, along with yourself."

"It worked out for everyone with your humbleness," said Joy. "I'm proud of you. We're all proud of you... Now, let all of us go back in peace." Everyone heads towards the center of the room. "Come on, Mike. We're getting out of here and going back to you-know-where."

As the white cloud of smoke dissipates, Mike sees a figure coming out of it. After a moment or two, he realizes that it's demon Andrea.

"Stop!" said Joy. "Mike is in trouble."

"So, you've come back," observed Mike. "For the last time, as I recall. At least I hope so."

"You knew this time was coming," declared demon Andrea, as all the others back Mike up. "I'm here to take you back with me now. My thirst is hard to quench. So, as I mentioned, I'm taking the rest of you with me, as well. From your dreams to reality, Mikey, it's time to go!"

"I'm not going anywhere with you, demon Andreascopal Cornilioscatora."

"My gosh! What a name," remarks Doreen. "Where did that come from, do you know Mike?"

Now the demon throws a bolt at Mike which makes him fall on his back and cry out in agony, as if every bone in his body has broken.

"STOP!" screams Joy. "WHAT ARE YOU DOING TO HIM?"

"If he dares to challenge me, then he will suffer and be punished for it," declared Andrea.

"What are you? Some kind of school bully?" demanded John. "I say that because you're acting like a child. Punish him for standing up to you? Or is there a deeper reason for your punishing him, like to keep him quiet for some reason? STOP IT! STOP IT RIGHT NOW OR ELSE!"

"Or else what, little man?" answers Andrea.

The five of them start closing in on the demon. "You foolish little children. Now all of you will be punished for your actions." The demon then throws bolts at all of them as each falls to their backs in total agony. "Game time is over."

After a few minutes, all six of them recover and get back on their feet.

246

"No more of your foolishness, Mikey, or any of the rest of you. It's time to go!" declares Andrea. "There's six pills here. I want each of you to take one. They're cyanide pills. Each of you will be dead in less than a minute. I thought I had you all killed in room 1628 the other day. Yes, it was I who called you and asked you all for help. But, it didn't work. So now, take these pills. It's either that, or suffer the agony you just experienced for the remainder of your lives. But, if you take the pills, once you die, you'll then come back to the bottom of hell with me. You see, I have plans for all of you."

"And we have plans for you," said Mike. "Your reign here has come to an end. Now, let's get back to your name."

The demon throws another bolt at Mike, this time sending him to the wall. He feels as if he is being crushed by a wind that comes from nowhere which starts to force everyone to fall back towards the wall. They resist with all of their might, but slowly succumb to it as they all fall, pressed against part of the wall.

"If you persist with this nonsense, then I will crush all of you to death," Andrea declares.

"MIKE!" yells Joy, finding it hard to speak as the wind forcefully presses against their bodies. "WHAT ABOUT HIS NAME?"

"FIRST I MUST STOP THIS WIND! DEMON, I COMMAND YOU IN THE NAME OF JESUS CHRIST TO STOP THIS WIND!"

"Not that old trick again. I'm tired of it," barks Andrea.

"THEN I COMMAND YOU IN THE NAME OF THE LORD OF THE SECOND ADVENT TO STOP!"

All of a sudden, the wind stops and everybody gains their composure and gets back up on their feet.

"I hit a nerve, I see. Didn't expect that, did you?" asked Mike.

"It's only a moment's disturbance. I'll be fine in a minute, you fool!" responded Andrea.

"That's just the first of three surprises for you," declared Mike.

"Mike! Now tell us what is it with his name!" cries Joy.

"As the old saying goes, 'What's in a name?'. Well, in this case," said Mike, "quite a lot. His full name is Andreascopal Cornilioscantora. This was given to him by the spirit world. It has a special meaning to them and them only."

"SHUT UP! SHUT THE HELL UP! screamed Andrea.

"What does it mean, Mike?" asked Sharon.

"I tapped into the spirit world and found out," said Mike. "What that name stands for, and his real name is: Judas Iscariot!"

Thunder and lightning fill the basement.

"My God! You mean…." says Billy.

"That's right. It was bad enough that he betrayed Jesus for silver," explained Mike. "but he only compounded that by committing suicide. He was the very lowest soul in hell. He began gaining power and strength, little-by-little. By the end of the Eighteenth Century, he was the most powerful demon in existence. In case Satan could not destroy The Lord of the Second Advent, which he did not, then he had demon Andrea ready to destroy the followers of the Lord of the Second Advent, first by killing the six of us, and then by destroying *The Completed Testament*. Once these two things were done, then it would only be a matter of time before the followers became confused and demoralized, and then finally completely annihilated, thus causing

God's dispensation to be delayed for hundreds or even thousands of years to come."

"Isn't *The Completed Testament*, I mean the original, isn't it missing or destroyed?" asked Andrea.

"NO! You see," retorted Mike, "Michael and Gabriel took it from the basement here that night and brought it directly to The Holy Ground Church, where we got it from them this evening."

"But I thought you were disillusioned with them after…" said Andrea.

"You mean after I spoke to those two members in the hall? I knew it was you and another demon with you all the time," said Mike. "Alice's office was a sacred room. You should have realized that you could know everything going on around you except for anything in a sacred room. So, we made all our plans there. The six of us decided with Alice that once we left her office, we would act as if I became negative with the Church and never wanted to go back. Each of the six of us would talk and pretend with every word we spoke about my disillusionment and they not knowing what was in my gym bag. All pretense, until this moment."

"Then, what do you have in the gym bag?" asked Andrea.

"*The Completed Testament*, of course," shot back Mike. "This is surprise number three. With it, you'll be sent back to the bottom of hell where you'll be given the chance to grow and rise up to higher levels. You must understand that Jesus forgave you, even while he was on the cross. The time for shame and suffering is over. It's time for you to return to the love and bosom of Jesus and God once again. Even if you reject it now, you'll still be sent back for restoration."

"You invoked the name of The Lord of the Second Advent. Then you revealed my true identity. As for *The Completed Testament*, you don't know how to use it. I will destroy the six of you yet." insisted Andrea.

"Wrong again, demon, or should I call you Judas. Guys, get the book and that small table from the storage room out here too, so we can put *The Testament* on it," directed Mike… "Okay, as we discussed in Alice's office, so be it now." They all put their right hands on top of each other's and placed them all on *The Completed Testament*. Then, in unison, they speak out three times: 'In the name of Jesus Christ and the name of The Lord of the Second Advent, in the name of Jesus Christ and in the name of The Lord of the Second Advent, in the name of Jesus Christ and in the name of The Lord of the Second Advent, we request thy strength and powers so that we may send this soul, demon Andreascopal Cornilioscantora, or otherwise known as Judas Iscariot, back to hell where he may grow in faith and spirit until the day comes that he dwells in the Heavenly Kingdom."

"STOP! STOP THIS NOW! SIX INDIVIDUALS AREN'T STRONG ENOUGH TO DO THIS!"

Now with their left hands they hold each other and form a circle around the Testament.

"We are now 1) one heart, 2) one mind, and 3) one body. As one, we will fight evil and injustice wherever they be and bring those prepared back to Jesus, the Lord of the Second Advent and you, Heavenly Father."

Then, a bright white light glows around them all, bringing high spirits all around. As this happens, the features of the demon start changing until finally he returns back to the form of Judas

Iscariot. In the corner of the basement, an even brighter light appears, and out of it comes the Lord Jesus Christ.

"Jesus, my Lord," says Judas. "Is it true you have forgiven me from the cross?"

"Yes Judas, my brother. Now come, come back with me, for your Heavenly Father also misses you. Let us go together and let these Holy men and women tend to their heavenly mission. Come, it is now time for retribution."

Judas takes the outstretched hand of Jesus and walks into the light with him. The light around them dissipates as does the light around Mike, Joy, Billy, Doreen, John and Sharon.

"Did we just experience Jesus and Judas, as well as Jesus calling us Holy men and women?" asked John.

"Yes, John. We did, and he did," answered Mike.

"Don't you all feel something very different about us?" asked Joy. "Just like we're on a different plain of existence. We've come a long way in a week."

Not to sound arrogant or something, but I actually feel worthy to be called Holy men and woman," said Sharon. "And, my desire is to be just that. I'm ready to go back to The Holy Ground Church now."

"Well, it's 9:45 now and Alice said they would wait, no matter what time it be. So, I agree. Let's go meet Alice. How do the rest of you feel about that?" asks Mike.

They all agree and leave the house they now feel familiar with, and head back to Denver. By 10:40, their SUV pulls up to the Church parking lot. They all get out, go up to the door and ring the bell. Alice answers with great joy and anticipation. As they're all at the door, they hear the members singing another

Holy Song, even though it's way past 9:00 p.m., the time they would normally sing the last song of the day.

"Come on in, Reverends," welcomes Alice.

"Did you call us Reverends?" asks Billy.

"Yes, I did. From now on, each of you will hold that title before your names. You see, Silver and Braxton, or as you now know them, Michael and Gabriel, were just here and informed us of all that has happened in Idaho Springs."

"We didn't see them leave," said Billy.

"Of course not. Being angels, they could materialize and dematerialize whenever and wherever they wish," explained Alice.

"So, that's how they disappeared from the Conference Room Three after each meeting. We did, by the way, forget to ask them that when meeting with them this afternoon… Listen! The members are singing a verse of the Holy Song."

We're marching to the blessed land of Canaan with delight.
We're leaving all our heavy burdens here.
At last we are released and free from being slaves to sin.
We're coming to the blessed spring of life.
Coming to the spring where living waters flow.
In glory we'll be living evermore.
Going to the land where freely flows the spring.
In glory we'll be living evermore.

"Sometime we'll listen to a whole song, word-by-word… so tell us, what exactly is the purpose of the Church?" asked Mike.

"To support those that are following the teachings of The Lord of the Second Advent. Up until now, though, we have also been witnessing to people and encouraging them to join by *our* teaching them. But, our main purpose was just to take care of people that joined. That's where all of you come in, providing of course that you accept your rolls to go out and find people that you can teach and inform them about the Lord of the Second Advent. *You'll* be the witnessers and teachers. Then, once they're ready, bring or send them to us. We'll take care of them from there. Of course, you could all go back to the lives you had before this week started. It will still be better than it was before you came here."

"I don't think any of us could simply go back to our old lives now; not knowing what we know now," said Joy. "And, I believe everyone will agree with me." (Yes!)

"If that's really true," said Alice, "then I'll see all of you at least one more time. Tomorrow at 3:00. I'll have some final things to say. But, you can discuss that more with Michael and Gabriel tomorrow. For now, let's just talk some more."

They do talk for another hour, then at midnight, they leave to go back to the Hotel. Once there, they decide to meet at 8:00 a.m. They all go to their rooms for a much-needed rest except, as before, Mike joins Joy in her room for a few words.

"Well, I guess this will be the last night we meet like this," said Joy. "I also imagine you won't be needing my services anymore."

"That's true," agreed Mike. "But, in one sense we'll be seeing more of each other regarding our new professions. I mean you *are* planning to join us, right?"

"Definitely! I could never go back to my old job now, knowing what I know," said Joy.

"Tell me, do you still disbelieve I went to Heaven, or have you changed your mind?"

"I'm still not sure what I believe about that. I'm sorry, I guess that's one frame of mind I still have difficulty changing. But, don't give up hope," said Joy.

"At least that's a start. Well, I should be leaving. You have yourself a good night," said Mike.

"Good night, Mike," as they wink their pinkies at each other and Mike goes back to his room. The next morning, everyone gathers in Joy's room between 8:00 and 8:30.

"If I knew any better, I should still be tired and worn out after everything. But, I have a renewed energy and enthusiasm. I'm not tired at all," reports Billy.

The other five respond with 'That goes for me too!' and 'And me!' and so forth. They all agree to go down to the lobby and have a good breakfast. They finish at 9:35, then go to Conference Room 3 for what will be the last time. Everyone just chats for the remaining minutes until the clock strikes 10:00. Then, promptly, Michael and Gabriel come in as always before.

"Congratulations everyone!" greets Michael. "You've successfully completed the final two challenges. All of your challenges this past week have been of heart, faith and unity. We're proud to be here with the six of you. And now, the details. Why don't you tell them, Gabriel."

"Michael, I have a question for you before Gabriel begins talking," interrupts Mike.

"Yes, Reverend Wakings. What is it?"

"That's exactly what I want to ask you about. Is the term Reverend official or just a formality?"

"Oh, it's official all right," answered Michael. "Each of you have the paperwork and I.D.'s to prove it. And, that title will remain with you all of you, even if you decide not to take our offer. And, before you ask, we didn't just have them made up last night, but they were actually made before any of you came here. If you hadn't succeeded in all your challenges, then they simply would have been revoked, and then destroyed. But, you all accomplished every challenge you were faced with. Make no mistake, you *earned* this title more than most. So, let's move on."

"If you commit to your new way of life, then you'll be given a double-sized briefcase with all the details of what you should do," said Gabriel. "Four of you will be responsible for eight states, and one of you will also have Alaska, while the other one of you will be given Hawaii as a ninth state. All the paperwork you receive is Holy. Each of you will be given a copy of The Completed Testament. Any questions you may have will be addressed to Rev. Wakings, who shall have a multi-bit cell phone, on twenty-four hours a day, seven days a week. He'll have the full support of all the Holy Ground Churches around the country. They also have Churches throughout the world where you or even the rest of you can acquire assistance. Everything, and I mean *everything*, will be explained in detail in your briefcase. If you do commit, then you will receive a certified check for $10 million. There's also details in your information about starting up a lucrative business so you will always have money coming in constantly. Your airline tickets have been changed to leave early morning. You will have up to a month to close out details where you're now living and/or working... If you decide *not* to commit, then you will have the airline ticket, plus you will be given a check for $250,000, just to show our appreciation for all you have done and something to get you started in whatever endeavor you choose in life. That's all *I* have to say."

"Now. It's time we find out what decision each of you have made," said Michael.

"Excuse me, Michael," interjects Joy. "It's still hard to accept the fact that we're talking to two of the most famous angels of all time. Anyway, the group asked me to speak for each of them on their behalf."

"Yes, Reverend Bender," answered Michael. "I heartily approve of their picking you as their spokeswoman. Please go on."

"After deep discussion and decision, all six of us have determined to go forth all the way in great appreciation and humility. We no longer can go back to the lives we were leading, as well as for myself."

"Excellent!" said Michael with a sigh of relief. "We're thrilled with all of your decisions. May none of you regret the direction you are taking."

"Michael, Gabriel, tell us," began John, "Since you know everything we do, didn't you already know what our decisions would be?"

"You should all understand," explained Gabriel, "we have the ability to know everything you do, but that doesn't mean we continually watched you. Especially after your success last night, we stopped watching any of you altogether. So, you see, we had no idea what any of you decided."

"Well, it's good to know we had some privacy from the both of you," exclaimed John. "And I'm just joking, of course."

"That's okay! We know what you mean," said Michael with a chuckle. "I think this is a good time to give all of you your briefcases. In it is everything we discussed, plus the check for $10 million, as well as $10,000 cash, so that you can take care of immediate needs."

They all talk for another two hours, about almost everything. The time is 5:20 p.m.

"It seems like our time together has come to an end," declares Michael.

"Will we ever see either of you again?" asks Sharon.

"I'm sure you will," answered Gabriel. "If not here on earth, then later on in the spirit world, for certain."

"We'll never forget about the part you played, Gabriel. You certainly had us fooled," said Doreen.

"I valued our time together. Good bye and good luck. Who knows," said Gabriel, "maybe you'll need our assistance again here on earth."

Everybody says their good-byes to both Michael and Gabriel.

"Remember, if you ever find someone who seems to disappear in a room again, don't be surprised if it's an angel," said Michael jokingly as they all left and headed up to Joy's room.

"Well Joy, I guess you and Mike can go to see Alice for the rest of us," said Billy. "At least for myself, in another hour I'm off to the airport to wait for my plane."

Doreen, John and Sharon share the same sentiments. No one wanted any long good byes. It hurts too much.

"At least we can spend one more hour together," says Joy.

Mike falls to the floor. Joy goes over as usual to check on him.

"Dead! Just like all the other times," she reports.

"That's right!" reminded Doreen. "Genia told him he would visit her in the spirit world one more time, and that it would be today."

"Let's make him comfortable and wait," said John. "We have no idea how long he'll be this time."

"Yes! Let's do that," agreed Joy.

"I wonder what she'll have to say to him this time?" said Sharon. "Well, as least we may have the chance to spend an extra hour or two together. And, do you think I mind that? Not on your life."

"Or maybe we should say, 'Not on Mike's life,'" said John.

"Cute, John. I'm thrilled with the reason to stay longer, as well," said Doreen.

"Actually, I'm thrilled as well," added John.

"Me too! How about you, Joy?" asked Billy.

"I value the time together. It's our time. So, I jump at the chance."

As the five of them talk, Mike goes through the usual transfer from this world to the spirit world. As he materializes with Genia in front of him, he senses something different.

"Hello my brother. How are you?" asks Genia.

"Actually, *better* than excellent. With every breath I take, I'm breathing in love. I'm talking about God's love. Well, I'll be! I'm in Heaven, not Paradise. Even though Paradise is quite high, Heaven is more intense and powerful in love and relationships. Wow! How did I wind up here?"

"You've earned this right," said Genia. "If you were to die permanently right now, this is where you would come to."

"You mean in one short week I've grown that much?" asked Mike.

"Yes you have, Mike. Or should I say Reverend Wakings?"

"Just Mike is good enough, Genia. And yes, I'm just where I want to be. But, do I really deserve it?"

"Yes, you do. Shall we go on now?"

"Okay. I know I've really gone to a lot of places. How much more is there?"

"Oh, my goodness. You've barely scraped the surface," said Genia. "To experience all the places you can go to, well, let me put it this way: What you did experience is like one grain of sand on a beach, where each grain represents another place. Take all the grains of sand on all the beaches in the entire world, ten-fold, and you still will have more places to visit. Try to grasp that concept if you can."

"My God! I had no idea."

"You still have a lot to learn, Mike. Actually, you'll always have something to learn. If not, then one's existence would become boring, and the spirit world, especially Heaven, is anything but boring. I'm going to take you on a short, but far away journey. The time on earth will almost be frozen as it was when you first started coming here. Only a few minutes would have passed, but for ourselves, many hours will pass. Have you ever wondered what lies beyond other galaxies? Well, we're going to pass through one to get to "The Mind of Man" galaxy. Each planet has some aspect of man's creation, from the beginning of man's existence right up to the present moment, and even beyond to a preview of what man *will* create. Every planet has a creation of God as well. Between God and man, they're countless. But first, you're going to spend a few minutes in a galaxy nearby to that one. I want you to see the diversity of God, Himself. This is going to be a new experience in traveling. So, I

259

think you'd better hold my hand and *I'll* take you through these galaxies so you don't get confused. In time, you too will learn how to travel from one planet to another and from one galaxy to another. But, for now, my help is necessary."

"So, there won't be any problem checking these out since we're spirit and all the rest is physical?"

"No, not at all," explained Genia. "Take Michael and Gabriel. They're spirit, but yet interact with all the physical worlds around them. They can even eat for pleasure… Come. Let's visit the Eccon Galaxy for just a few minutes."

With the passing of her hand, Genia and Mike are transported to the Eccon Galaxy. They float in an array of colors, hundreds, maybe even thousands of different shades and colors; so intense that you can feel, and even smell a delightful fragrance from each shade and color. Every moment, they burst with new fragrance and colors. As they do, you can feel a tingling sensation throughout your entire body. This is truly a celebration of life itself, be it physical or spiritual. As they experience this gorgeous phenomena, Genia keeps them there for ten minutes, then transports them between galaxies. It's very dark and cold.

"Wow! I've always wondered what lays between galaxies."

"This is it, Mike. This is the black void that is talked about in the Bible before God created anything. It's not bad or evil. It just is."

"What a difference between Eccon Galaxy and this. Please, let's go to the next galaxy. The one called 'The Mind of Man'."

As they enter, they travel thousands of times the speed of light. This is the speed of thought. They pass several suns, then stop at a shiny planet. Appearing on the surface, Mike is amazed. The planet is celebrations of trillions of toys. Every kind ever conceived by man from the beginning to the present day. Most amazing is the fact that every toy has a beautiful glow to it. Mike thinks: That must be what causes the plant to be shiny. Every toy is pristine. No matter how long ago it was conceived, it's as if they were made hours ago. Looking and playing with them as if he were a child again. Mike is brought back to reality when Genia gets his attention.

"I know this is all fascinating to you and one day you'll be able to spend as long as you like here, but for now we can only spend a short time, as we have many more planets to visit. Of course, we can't go to every planet in every galaxy, or we would be up here for over a thousand years."

"I guess you're right, and I do want to see some of the other planets," agreed Mike.

"And remember, although this galaxy is called 'The Mind of Man', it's also representing God's creations, too. Not all, of course, but some. So, what do you say we go on now?"

"Sounds good to me. Let's go!"

Genia then brings Mike to several other planets; one where there are animals of every kind, even many not known of on earth. They visit a planet of sweets; anything known or conceived in the imagination. Then, a planet of all kinds of foods, and another of all different drinks. Also, a planet of pre-historic animals, all friendly to man. A planet that puts on light shows that are beyond imagination. Another planet where you could walk from one season to another. One that is totally water; water that you can walk on even as a physical body. Another that's totally clouds. And the final planet they visit is made of gold, silver and diamonds, for the beauty of it, not for the taking.

"Well, Mike, there's millions of other planets in this galaxy alone," explained Genia. "Then there are billions of galaxies with countless planets in them. But, our time has come to an end here in space. We must go back to Earthly Heaven which is pretty impressive all by itself. Are you ready?... (Yes!) Then let's return."

In a few minutes, they find themselves at the marble steps that lead up to the four thrones Mike was at once before. Each throne is brilliant with bright white light. As Mike watches, the first throne's light dissipates and he can see the figure of Jesus Christ.

"The Lord Jesus, as before," says Mike.

Then, the light dims from the second throne, revealing the bride of Jesus. "I don't recognize her," says Mike.

"She's a most high spirit, qualified for Lord Jesus Christ," says Genia.

The light dims once again for the forth throne, revealing the bride for The Lord of the Second Advent. Mike stares intensely as he comes to recognize the woman. He's amazed at her identity.

"I know her!" exclaims Mike. "She was a religious figure in her own right. A very popular figure."

The light at the third throne reveals his most anticipated figure of all… The Lord of the Second Advent.

"Good heavens! It's HIM. I knew he was a great religious figure, but I never dreamed he was the Lord of the Second Advent. My God! I'm standing before the two Sons of God," exclaims Mike as he falls to his knees. "I'm also in the presence of the two most important and influential women of all time. I'm really not worthy to be here in their presence, but I have the privilege of being here." As he looks on at the four of them, Mike says: "I give my pledge that I will follow whatever the four of you ask of me, right up until the day I go to the spirit world for good. I'll follow your words and directions to my death, if necessary. And, may the five people who have worked by my side be in your favor, as well. We all will live and die for God's dispensation."

"Reverend Wakings, our son. You and your friends have found favor in our eyes and that of Heavenly Father," said the Lord of the Second Advent to Mike. "Your missions are most valuable to us and God. Give of your best, and in three years all of you who are single will be matched to a special spouse and then blessed in a Holy Matrimony by myself, even from the spirit world. As for Reverend Pace, he will have a Holy unity with his wife, Cindy. Then, as couples, you will work together to succeed. More information will be given each of you in the briefcases now in your possession. From now on, everything any of you do will be for success and reward or failure and chastisement, for it is done to help bring The Kingdom of Heaven on earth as Jesus, myself and our wives will bring the Kingdom of Heaven here in the spirit world. All of you now have a direct line to us. Use it wisely. Now go, and remember, each of you are in a very strategic position, not just to the four of us, but most importantly to Heavenly Father, Himself. Peace and success be with you, now and always."

The Lord of the Second Advent sits back down as the light once again becomes extremely bright. Genia then transports Mike and herself back to the very spot where he first met her.

"I see we're back to where all this started a week ago," says Mike, still filled with awe. "By earth's time, it's been a heck of a lot longer here... So, I guess this is it. Will I ever see *you* again?"

263

"Most definitely! Remember, I *am* your spirit guide. When you come back for good, I'll be waiting for you... I valued our time together. I hope it has been extremely advantageous for you... Now, it's time to go back, Mike Wakings. Go back to your earthly body. Go back until we meet again. Go back! Go back! Go back!

Back in Joy's room, Mike starts to come to. Everyone gathers around him.

"He's coming back!" exclaims Joy.

"So soon? It's 6:15 and only been twenty minutes since he went under," remarks Sharon.

"Either it was a short visit, or there's been another time lapse between there and here," observed Billy.

"There was a time difference," says Mike as he slowly rises to his feet. "I spent about four to five hours there. Everyone, have a seat, and for the last time I'll explain everything."

All six of them eagerly listen as Mike explains all about his travels to other galaxies and then finally the revelation of the four thrones, especially the one seating The Lord of the Second Advent; who he was and what he said. Everybody was in shock. This was the most revealing of all his visits to the spirit world. They talk about everything for another hour, and at 8:30 say their heartfelt good-byes.

"Even though it will be good to see Cindy and Calley, I'm going to miss all you terribly," admits Billy.

"We've been through so much together," says Doreen. "How can you measure it by human standards?"

"I'll miss all your near-deaths, or should I say death experiences," said John. "So long, buddy, and you too, Joy."

"And I'll miss your tender caring, Joy," said Sharon.

Then, all six of them hug each other and say good-bye for the last time. They pick up their suitcases and bags, and exit out the door to their limos, giving one last look behind them. As they all leave, the door closes behind them, leaving Joy and Mike all alone.

"What are you going to do, Joy?"

"I'm going to take the plane back home and get all my businesses in order. Before I leave, how about you, Mike?"

"I'm going to delay my trip a couple of weeks as I get things in order at The Holy Ground Church. Then, for the final two weeks, prepare myself for my journey. I'm sure I'll be hearing from all of you often... Well, I guess we should go to the Church now."

Joy and Mike take their limos to The Holy Ground Church and meet Alice at the door. As they enter, it begins to snow heavily.

"I had a feeling it would be the two of you, coming to see me," said Alice.

"The others were too sensitive about coming here and saying good-bye. They asked us to apologize for them."

"I understand. What are the two of you going to do?"

"Well, Joy is staying an hour with you. Then, she's going to the airport to go back to L.A. As for me, I'm going to take a long walk outside to clear my mind. Then, I'll come back after Joy has left and have a long talk with you... Would you mind leaving the two of us alone for a few minutes?"

"Sure. I'll see you, Rev. Bender, in a few minutes and you, Rev. Wakings, in a couple of hours. By the way, you must try to remember to use your titles as Reverend."

"It'll take some getting used to," said Joy, "but I think we'll take to it."

"Okay, see you shortly," said Alice as she goes into her office. The members could be heard singing 'The Bells of St. Mary' as it echoes through the halls of the Church.

"I guess we'll see each other in L.A. a couple of weeks from now," says Joy.

"That's right, Rev. Bender," says Mike.

"I think among ourselves we can still use our first names," says Joy.

"You're right, Joy. Besides, I was just kidding."

"That's all right. I figured as much."

"Well, take care of yourself, Joy."

Mike turns and is about to walk away when Joy gets his attention.

"MIKE!" says Joy, very seriously.

"Yes?"

"You really *did* see Heaven, didn't you?"

"Just a glimpse, Joy. Just a glimpse."

Then, Joy and Mike raise their hands, and wink their pinkies at each other. Mike walks down the hallway to the door leading to the outside, turns and winks his pinky one more time as Joy reciprocates. Joy stares at Mike a few moments, then turns and goes back into Alice's office. Mike exits the door and walks out into the virgin snow. He pulls up his collar and proceeds down the street in the snow. As it falls on his head, he thinks to himself, I've changed the lives of many people for the better, with more to come. Yes! I've made a difference, and in exchange, a difference made him.

37567974R00163

Made in the USA
Middletown, DE
28 February 2019